# THE DISAPPEARANCE

Also by Susan Berliner

DUST

PEACHWOOD LAKE

# THE DISAPPEARANCE

by Susan Berliner

Published by SRB Books

ISBN: 978-0-9839401-2-8
ISBN: 978-0-9839401-3-5

Cover design by Book Graphics
Book layout by Dianne Paulet
Author's photo by Rachel Leib Photography

Published October, 2012

Printed in the United States of America

For everyone who loves time travel stories...
and for the third generation—
Samantha, Jimmy, and Joey—
with the hope you, and your contemporaries,
will still enjoy reading novels,
preferably on paper.

Thanks to my children, and to Lisanne Harrington,
for their insightful suggestions.
And, as always, a special thanks to my husband,
Larry, for his love, help, and support.

# CHAPTER 1

Jillian Keating walked into the apartment she shared with her boyfriend, totally unaware her life was about to careen out of control.

As she dropped two bags of groceries on the kitchen counter, Ryan greeted her with a shout. "Where the hell have you been?"

Jillian stared at him, dumbfounded, and nodded towards the plastic bags. "I told you I was going to the supermarket after work to pick up a few things. What's wrong?" She had never seen Ryan as angry as this. In fact, she couldn't remember ever seeing him angry.

"You didn't tell me," he said, stepping closer to Jillian and glaring at her. "I don't like your lies."

"But I told you this morning I was going shopping. I mentioned it right before I went to work and you even said 'okay.'" She shook her head. "This is a stupid fight over nothing. Is something else bothering you?"

"Where'd you really go?" he shouted again. "Out to meet some guy?"

That question left Jillian speechless. She had told Ryan everything about herself so he knew there was no other "guy."

She just looked at him and frowned.

"I knew it!" he yelled. "You sneaked off to meet someone else. The groceries are just a cover-up." Reaching into one of the plastic bags, he picked up an apple, and waved it at her. "You bought these so I wouldn't suspect where you've really been."

Jillian glanced at her watch. "Ryan, you're not making any sense. Think about it. I wouldn't have had the time to do what you said. It's not even six o'clock yet." She paused for a moment and then wagged her forefinger at him. "Oh, I get it. This is your idea of a joke, making up a story about me sneaking off to meet someone. Well, it's not funny and I'm really tired so let's just put the groceries away and I'll go make dinner."

"It's not a joke!" Ryan shrieked. "I'm dead serious! You're screwing around with someone else and everyone's laughing about me behind my back! Well that's not funny!" Without any warning, he raised his right arm and heaved the apple into the living room. A loud tinkling sound followed as the fruit projectile hit a crystal vase on the end table, shattering it.

"Why'd you do that?" Jillian asked angrily. "I really liked that vase. And you made so much noise. With you screaming and now breaking all that glass, what're the neighbors going to think is happening here?" They lived in a small apartment building with very thin walls.

"I don't care about the f___ing neighbors!" Ryan roared. "I just care about what you're doin' to me!"

"I'm not doing anything to you," Jillian said, trying to speak calmly and quietly. "But I've never seen you act like this before. It's a little scary." She shook her head again. "Now I'm going to pick up the mess you made and, when I'm doing that, maybe you should go out for a while, take a walk, and see if you can calm down. Then we can talk about this, although I didn't do anything so there's really nothing to talk about."

Ryan gave Jillian an odd little smile and spoke very softly.

"Okay. That's a good idea. I'll go out. But first, let me help you clean up." He shrugged. "Sorry I broke the vase." Dashing into the living room, he picked up a large sliver of glass on the table. "Damn," he muttered, holding up his bleeding thumb so Jillian could see it. "I cut myself. I'm gonna go put a band-aid on it." He marched into the bedroom, still holding the sharp piece of crystal.

As Jillian entered the living room, she noticed two fresh drops of blood on the gray carpet and made a mental note to remember to clean the stain later. Then, very carefully, she lifted the remaining shards of glass and dumped them into the kitchen garbage can. When she had finished, she realized Ryan was still in the bedroom.

"What are you doing now?" she asked, walking into the room just as Ryan closed a small suitcase.

"I decided you were right about going out and calming down." He spoke in a whisper. "So I'm going off by myself for a few days to think things over."

"A few days?" Jillian was shocked. It was Friday in early May and she had been looking forward to spending the weekend with Ryan. "Why so long?"

"I need some time alone."

"Where are you going?"

"Oh, just someplace where I can be alone."

"Can I call you?" she asked, sitting on the bed.

"No. I'm not even taking my phone." Still whispering, he nodded towards the night table where his cell phone still lay. "I'll just be gone for a little while."

"When will you be back?"

Ryan didn't answer. He just smiled strangely at Jillian, lifted his suitcase off the bed, and quietly walked out of the apartment.

Jillian remained seated on the bed, trying to figure out what had just happened. "What was that about?" she murmured. Ryan's odd behavior hadn't made any sense. She thought she understood her boyfriend. But, then again, maybe she didn't. After all, she had only known him for a couple of months.

Their relationship had been what books called a "whirlwind" romance. It had happened that quickly. She and Ryan had met in a graphic arts college extension course. They were both artists, although only Ryan was practicing their profession, freelancing from a home office. Jillian was sending out her résumé, hoping to get a graphics-related job. While she waited, she did filing work for a small law firm near Southvale, the upper Westchester suburb of New York City where they lived.

At Ryan's invitation, they had gone out for coffee one night after class and discovered the two of them had many other things in common besides their vocation. They had both been orphaned at young ages: Jillian's parents had died in a car crash when she was just a toddler; Ryan's parents had been killed in a house fire when he was eleven. Jillian had been raised by her paternal grandparents, both no longer alive; Ryan had been reared by his father's unmarried sister. Neither Jillian nor Ryan had siblings or any other close relatives.

The two of them continued to go out after class, talking about the obstacles they had overcome and confiding in each other. Both were lonely, had few friends, and had trouble forming lasting relationships. They quickly became close. Ryan told Jillian it was the first time he had ever been serious about a girl. She had never gone out with a guy past the third date. He was smart, handsome, and charming—an ideal boyfriend. So when Ryan asked her to move in with him, although she had only known him about a month, it seemed like the right decision.

*But was it?* All of a sudden, after their bizarre fight, she was no longer sure.

Jillian tried to keep busy during the weekend. On Saturday morning, she cleaned the apartment, remembering the drops of blood on the living room carpet, which proved difficult to remove. Even after numerous scrubbings, a slight pinkish smudge still remained.

Following lunch, with the help of a dictionary, she read twenty pages of *Founding Brothers: The Revolutionary Generation*, the nonfiction account of early American history she was working her way through.

Since the afternoon was warm and sunny, she also took a leisurely walk around the neighborhood. But she kept thinking about Ryan. That walk was something the two of them usually did together.

At night, she watched TV and did a few crossword puzzles. But it was lonely without her boyfriend. She really missed him.

On Sunday, she scanned the online job listings and emailed two more résumés. Then she worked on a special card she was designing for Ryan's birthday early next month. In the evening, she read about an important dinner with Alexander Hamilton, James Madison, and Thomas Jefferson in her history book and watched a romantic comedy on TV. There was no sign of Ryan. He hadn't called—but he hadn't said he would call—and his cell phone was where he had left it, on the night table in the bedroom.

By Monday morning, Jillian was in full worry mode. She had to go to work and Ryan still wasn't home. She wanted to phone someone—but who? He didn't have any close friends and she had absolutely no idea who could possibly help her find him. "Guess I'll just have to wait," she murmured as she locked the apartment door.

"Ryan?" Jillian spoke her boyfriend's name aloud when she arrived home Monday after work and opened the door. No one answered. "Damn," she muttered, hanging her jacket in the hall closet.

She walked into the bedroom and saw the phone was blinking. Anxiously, she pressed the "Play" button. But the message wasn't from Ryan. Instead, she heard an unfamiliar male voice.

"My name is Steven Placardo and I'm trying to reach Ryan

Cornell," the man said. "It's important. If he isn't there, then I need to speak to Jillian Keating. Please call me immediately when you receive this message." After the man left his number, the phone clicked off.

Jillian stared at the number she had just written. *Another mystery?* She picked up the receiver and dialed.

"Hello?" a man's voice asked.

"Mr. Placardo?"

"Yes, speaking."

"This is Jillian Keating. You left a message for Ryan Cornell and he's not available right now so I'm returning the call like you asked." She paused. "Can you please tell me what's so important and what this is all about?"

"Where is Mr. Cornell? Do you know?"

"Actually, I don't. He packed a suitcase and left Friday night, just telling me he'd be gone for a few days. I have no idea where he is right now."

The other end of the phone went silent. "I see," Placardo finally said. "Then I really need to meet with you as soon as possible. I have something that I think you should see."

"What is it?"

"It's not a matter that should be discussed over the phone. My office is in downtown Southvale on Spruce Street. When can you be here?"

"What kind of office is it, Mr. Placardo? And what exactly do you do?"

"The firm's name is Rollings, Placardo and Macarelli...I'm an attorney."

This time Jillian was the one who was speechless. "I'll be there nine o'clock tomorrow morning, before I go to work," she said after a lengthy pause. "But what if Ryan's back by then? Should I still come?"

"No," he replied. "If Mr. Cornell returns, then our meeting won't be necessary."

After leaving a message that she would be late for work, Jillian drove to Placardo's law firm. She entered the office, gave the receptionist her name, and then sat nervously in the spacious waiting area. Just seconds later, a distinguished-looking man with graying hair and a neatly-trimmed mustache approached her. "Ms. Keating?"

"Yes." Jillian stood up.

"I'm Steven Placardo," he said, not offering his hand and gazing directly at her. "Let's go inside."

She followed the lawyer into a large office, dominated by an enormous rosewood bookshelf filled with legal tomes. Placardo sat in the black leather chair behind his massive desk and waved her towards the guest chair.

He looked at Jillian and folded his hands. "You're not at all what I pictured."

She stared at him, totally confused.

"Let me explain," the lawyer said. "Then I think you'll understand." He picked up a pen and tapped lightly on the desk. "I had a meeting with Ryan Cornell scheduled for Monday morning at nine o'clock."

Jillian shook her head. "What does that have to do with me?"

"I have been working with Mr. Cornell for quite some time and he has always kept his appointments."

"But I told you on the phone. Ryan went somewhere on Friday night and hasn't come back yet."

"Yes, you did." Placardo leaned back in the chair. "And you also said that you don't know where Mr. Cornell went."

"He didn't tell me. So?"

"So Mr. Cornell told me that he would be here yesterday morning. We had an appointment two weeks ago and, at that time, he gave me a sealed letter. He instructed me to lock the letter in a safe and said, if he did not show up at our next meeting, to take out the letter and read it." The lawyer opened his desk and removed an envelope. "I read the letter late yesterday afternoon, just before I phoned you."

"What does it say?" Jillian inched closer to the desk.

"This is a copy," the lawyer said, opening the envelope. "The original is still in the safe." He handed her a sheet of paper. "Here. I want you to read it."

She glanced at the paper and immediately recognized Ryan's swirling handwriting. The letter was addressed to Steven Placardo and dated two weeks earlier:

> *Dear Mr. Placardo:*
> *If you are reading this letter, it means I did not appear at your office for Monday's appointment. It also means that I am dead. My girlfriend, Jillian Keating, has murdered me.*
> *I don't know how she has done it, only that she has at last succeeded. I have feared for my life for several weeks now, but have been unable to escape. She will tell you that I have "gone somewhere" or that I am "missing," but that is a lie.*
> *Please show the police this letter. I know they will be interested in the life insurance policy on me that Jillian took out last month. Half a million dollars is a large amount of money. I guess it's enough to kill for.*
> *Sincerely,*
> *Ryan Cornell*

After she had finished reading the letter, Jillian held it tightly and looked at the lawyer. "Is this some kind of sick joke?"

"It's no joke."

"I don't understand...Why would Ryan write this letter? He said he loved me." She handed the paper back to Placardo and shook her head. "Why would he make up such awful lies?"

"I don't know. Why would he? And what about that line about the life insurance policy? Is that a lie too?"

"No. That part's true. But the insurance was Ryan's idea. He told me to take out the policy because he wanted to protect me in case something happened to him. I didn't care about the money. It was all his idea."

"Could someone corroborate your story that the life insurance was his idea?"

Jillian thought for a moment. "I don't think so. I didn't mention the policy to anyone...I mean, Ryan's young and healthy so I laughed about it. I didn't think it was important."

"Well you better hope the police don't think it's important," the lawyer said, folding his arms.

"The police?"

"Of course, I have to show them this letter. Ryan Cornell is missing and you say you don't know where he is." He pointed to the sheet of paper and shrugged. "Something strange is going on here."

Jillian stood up. "Yes!" she shouted. But it's all Ryan's doing! I don't know anything about any of this!"

"Tell that to the police," Placardo said. Then, without looking at her, he picked up the phone.

# CHAPTER 2

Ten minutes after Placardo's phone call, a tall angular policeman entered the room, identifying himself as Officer Forsythe. Placardo showed the officer Ryan's letter and briefed him on what had been discussed. Meanwhile Jillian sat quietly, listening, but not contributing anything to the conversation.

"Do you have something to say about all this, Miss Keating?" Officer Forsythe asked.

"Not without speaking to an attorney first," Jillian said. Working in a law office had at least taught her that much.

"Then you'd better call one. I want to question you about Mr. Cornell's disappearance and, at the same time, I'm going to want to check your apartment." The policeman glared at her with piercing dark brown eyes. "You can cooperate or you can wait till I get a search warrant."

"That won't be necessary." Jillian shrugged. "I've got absolutely nothing to hide."

Placardo shoved his desk phone towards her and, with both men watching, she dialed her employer's number. "It's Jillian," she said when the receptionist picked up the call. "I need to speak to

Helene Moskowitz right now. Is she there?" The line went quiet as the woman transferred the call.

"Hi, Jillian. It's Helene."

Jillian sighed, thankful for a small dose of good news. "I'm so glad I reached you, Helene. I've got a big problem and I really need your help."

"What's up, Jillian? You don't sound like yourself."

"That's because I don't feel like myself...Helene, something has happened involving my boyfriend and I'm going to need a lawyer. I want to hire you, but I don't know how I can ever pay your fee."

"Don't worry about paying me. For you, I'll work cheap—you've done me enough favors. But tell me what's going on. You've got me very curious."

"I can't explain right now," Jillian said. Glancing up, she saw Placardo and the policeman staring intently at her. "Can you meet me at my house real soon?"

"Yes. But why there?"

"I'm with a police officer and he wants to talk to me and search my apartment. I live in Southvale, about fifteen minutes from the office. The address is 333 Grove Street, apartment 2C."

"All right, Jillian. I'm starting to get the picture. Go to your apartment, but don't say anything or let the police in until I get there. Got it?"

"Yes. Thanks so much, Helene. Bye." She hung up the phone and faced the officer. "Can I drive back to my house in my own car or do I have to go with you?"

"You drive and I'll follow. But it wouldn't be smart to try anything."

Jillian shook her head. "I won't run away. I just want to get this over with. As I already told you, I haven't done anything wrong so I've got nothing to hide."

Helene Moskowitz was nervously pacing in front of the small apartment building when Jillian arrived. The petite gray-haired lawyer rushed over and hugged the girl tightly. "What the hell is going on?" she asked.

Jillian saw the policeman parking his car so she spoke rapidly. "Ryan ran out of here suddenly Friday night right after we had a short, stupid fight and hasn't come back. He left a letter with his lawyer saying that if he didn't show up for a Monday appointment, then I killed him for the money in a life insurance policy."

Helene released the girl and studied her. "Your boyfriend set you up? Do you have any idea why he would do that?"

Tears started to form in Jillian's eyes. "I thought Ryan loved me. I guess I'm not a very good judge of people."

They stopped talking as the policeman reached them. "I'm Officer Len Forsythe and you must be Ms. Keating's attorney," he said, nodding at Helene.

"Yes," the lawyer said curtly. "Helene Moskowitz."

The policeman pointed to the apartment building. "Let's go upstairs and get started." Without further conversation, the three of them walked up the single flight of stairs, Jillian unlocked the door, and they entered the apartment she shared with Ryan.

The officer sat on the living room couch and crossed his legs. "Now please tell me what happened on Friday night, before Mr. Cornell left," he said, taking a small notepad and pen from his shirt pocket.

Jillian sank into a dinette chair opposite the man and glanced at Helene, who sat next to her. The lawyer nodded so Jillian recounted what had happened since she came home on Friday, trying to be as thorough as possible.

"Did you see Mr. Cornell drive away?" Officer Forsythe asked when she had finished.

"I wasn't looking. I was too shocked by what happened." Jillian shrugged. "He left here with a suitcase so he must have driven someplace."

"We'll check his car. Give me a description and we'll get the license number."

"It's a new silver BMW."

"If it's okay with your lawyer, I'm going to search your apartment now," the policeman said, slipping the pad and pencil back into his pocket.

"Go ahead," Helene said.

"All right then. Let's see what's missing."

Officer Forsythe walked into the small galley kitchen and Jillian heard the opening and closing of kitchen cabinets. As Helene jotted some notes on a legal pad, Jillian sat quietly, observing the man. He entered the hallway and poked his head into the closets. Then, as she watched, he strode into the bedroom.

"Hey, ladies!" he called a few minutes later. "Please come in here. There's something I want you both to see."

Helene and Jillian entered the sunlight-filled bedroom. Although the drapes were open, the lanky policeman knelt on the floor next to the bed, beaming a flashlight on a spot on the floor. "Do you know what this is?" he asked.

Jillian bent down to get a closer view. "It looks like blood," she said.

"Good job," Officer Forsythe replied. "That's exactly what it is and it seems kind of fresh too. Know anything about it?"

"My client doesn't have to answer that question." Helene knelt and put her arm around the girl. "Let's talk about this together first."

"But I've got nothing to hide," Jillian repeated, standing up. "It must be from when Ryan threw an apple and broke the vase Friday night. I told you about that. There're a couple of drops of blood on the living room floor too. I tried scrubbing, but I couldn't clean it completely off." She looked at the tweedy green rug. "This carpet's darker so I didn't know there were any bloodstains here.

Ryan cut himself when he picked up a piece of broken glass from the vase." She shrugged. "It was just an accident."

Officer Forsythe gave Jillian a puzzled look. "Anyone else see this *accident*?" he asked.

"No. We were alone."

"Uh huh." The policeman stood and pointed to the cell phone and wristwatch on Ryan's night table. "Your boyfriend didn't take his phone or watch with him on his little 'trip.'" He pronounced the last word disdainfully as he picked up the two objects and placed them in a plastic bag. "Strange, don't you think?"

"Ryan told me he didn't need a phone because he was only going to be away for a little while and..."

"Jillian, please don't answer any more questions," Helene said. "I'd like to speak to you now." She grasped her client's arm.

"All right." Jillian turned to the policeman and sighed. "But you have this all wrong. I didn't do anything."

Jillian and Helene sat on the living room couch while the officer remained in the bedroom. The lawyer waved her forefinger at the girl. "I don't want you saying another word to the police. You asked me to help you and I can't do that unless you cooperate with me."

"I'm sorry." Jillian shook her head. "But it's so frustrating. He's getting a totally wrong idea about what went on here Friday night."

"After he leaves, I want you to tell me everything you know about your boyfriend. We've got to try to figure out why he did this."

Just then, Officer Forsythe dashed into the living room. Sinking his tall frame into a side chair, he faced Jillian. "Nothing much else missing in the bedroom. Mr. Cornell didn't take many of his clothes with him for this trip, did he?"

Jillian glanced at Helene. After the lawyer nodded, she replied. "I told you I don't know what he packed. When I came into the bedroom, Ryan was just closing the suitcase."

Officer Forsythe smiled slightly. "I looked inside the medicine chest and this is still here." He held up a man's electric razor. "And it doesn't look like he even took a toothbrush or toothpaste." He continued to stare at Jillian with his penetrating brown eyes as he dropped the razor into his plastic bag. "Why wouldn't he take that stuff with him?"

"You don't have to answer that question," Helene interjected.

"I can't answer the question because I've got no idea what Ryan would do and why. None of this makes any sense to me."

"All right," the policeman said, again removing his notepad and pen from his pocket. "Let's talk about something you do know. Give me a description of your boyfriend."

"Ryan has dark brown hair, brown eyes and he's about six foot one and probably weighs one hundred and eighty pounds."

"Do you have a current photo of Mr. Cornell?"

"Yes. In my wallet." Jillian walked to the foyer where she had dropped her bag, reached inside, grabbed her wallet, and pulled out a small picture. "Everything I have involving Ryan is recent. I've only known him a few months and I guess I didn't know him very well." She gave the officer the photo.

He glanced at the picture and put it in his jacket pocket. "Thanks. We'll see if we can find Mr. Cornell." Once again, he gazed directly at the girl with his deep dark eyes. "Of course, that's only if he's someplace where he can be found."

The officer stood and addressed Jillian. "Now I'm going to talk with some of your neighbors to find out what they might have heard on Friday night. Do you happen to know any of them?"

She turned to Helene before responding.

"Okay," the lawyer said.

"There's a retired couple next door. I don't know their names and a single woman in her forties lives in one of the apartments on the other side." Jillian shrugged. "I only moved in with Ryan about a month ago so I really don't know any of the neighbors very well. We just smile or nod when we see each other."

Several minutes later, Officer Forsythe returned to the apartment and dragged a dinette chair closer to the couch. Then he lowered himself into the chair, extracted his notebook, and thumbed through the pages.

"Did you find out anything?" Jillian asked.

"Oh yeah."

The girl gave Helene a quizzical look.

"Miss Keating," the policeman began, staring at his notes. "The lady next door, the one who lives with her retired husband, she said that she heard a loud fight on Friday night."

"Yes. I told you Ryan was screaming. At one point, I even asked him not to shout."

"Did he say something like, 'I only care about what you're doing to me?'"

"Maybe. I don't remember the exact words."

"Well, Mrs. Polanski next door is pretty sure that's what Mr. Cornell said. And after that, she didn't hear anything else. She said she never heard a door slam and she didn't see anyone leave your apartment." He stood and leaned over Jillian, scowling at her. "So what exactly were you doing to your boyfriend? Throwing a vase at him, maybe?"

"That's enough questions." Helene said. "We're getting a lot of innuendo here that I don't like." She rose and moved next to the officer, trying to look into his eyes, which was difficult because he was more than a foot taller than the tiny lawyer. "Are you going to charge my client with committing a crime?" Helene demanded. "If not, then I'd like you to leave this apartment—now."

Officer Forsythe looked at Jillian and then faced Helene. "I don't have enough evidence just yet to arrest Ms. Keating," he said. "But we've got a search out for Mr. Cornell and for his car. And we'll check his cell phone and home phone calls. Let's see what we find." He again gazed intently at Jillian. "In the meanwhile, you'd better not go too far."

# CHAPTER 3

Jillian and Helene sat quietly for a few moments after the policeman left. "So what happens now?" Jillian finally whispered.

"We wait and see if the police find Ryan and his car."

"And if they don't find anything?"

"Then we do our own search."

"How?"

"There are ways," the lawyer said, patting Jillian's arm. "We'll deal with that problem if and when we have to. Right now, I want to hear everything you know about Ryan Cornell." She gazed sympathetically at the girl. "But from what I've just seen and heard, I've got a feeling that what you know won't be very helpful."

Jillian stared at her hands in her lap and spoke softly. "You think everything he told me was a lie?"

Helene nodded. "I'm sorry, Jillian, but it sure looks that way."

"I should've figured he was too good to be true."

"What do you mean?"

"Ryan seemed to really like me, love me even." Still glancing down, Jillian sighed. "No guy's ever acted that way with me."

The lawyer shrugged. "Unfortunately, 'acted' might be a good choice of words...How did you meet Ryan?"

"We took the same graphic arts course last semester. We're both graphic artists."

"Are you sure about that? I mean, have you seen any of Ryan's work?"

Jillian's face registered shock. "You think he lied about that too?"

"Possibly. Did he ever show you any art he created?"

The girl thought for a moment. "No. Actually he didn't. We each have our own laptops. Ryan said he worked at home, but he never told me his password or showed me anything. He knew my password and saw some of my designs—I didn't think it was strange before, but now..."

"Is Ryan's computer still here?"

"I'll check." Jillian stood up and rushed into the bedroom. Five minutes later, she returned, shaking her head. "It's gone."

Jillian sat down again next to Helene, tears welling in her green eyes. "I'm a real jerk," she muttered.

The lawyer put her arm around the girl and gave her a hug. "Don't be so hard on yourself, sweetie. I think this guy spent a lot of time creating an elaborate deception just so he could hook you in."

"But why would he go to so much trouble—and why me?"

"I really don't know," Helene admitted. "But don't worry. I'm sure we're going to be able to figure it out." She patted Jillian's shoulder. "Let's go into the bedroom together and see if we can find out what else Ryan took with him on his little trip. Maybe that'll give us a clue to where he went."

Helene held Jillian's hand as they walked into the bedroom. Then, as the lawyer sat on the queen-size bed, Jillian opened Ryan's dresser drawers and rummaged through them.

"It looks like almost all of his stuff is here. Maybe he took some underwear, but so what?" Turning to face Helene, she spread out her hands.

The lawyer pointed to the sliding door panels along the wall.

"Check the closet. Maybe you'll remember something that's missing in there."

Jillian opened the closet door and began examining the hanging slacks and jeans. "Most of his pants are still here too. I guess he could've taken a pair or two, but I'm not sure."

"Think. Did he have a favorite pair of jeans, something he liked to wear a lot?"

Jillian sat on the bed. "Would that help?"

"It might."

"Okay then..." Jillian thought for a few seconds. "He liked to wear a pair of old, scruffy light blue jeans and a plaid yellow and navy shirt."

"Did you see those clothes in the closet or in the drawer?"

"I don't think so. I'll go check again." Jillian searched for a short while. "Not there. But they could be in the laundry." Darting into the bathroom, she quickly emptied the hamper. "Not in there either!" she shouted before returning to the bedroom. "Does that mean something?"

"I don't know. Do you remember him doing anything in particular when he wore those clothes?"

Slowly, the girl lowered herself onto the bed. "He wore them a lot just hanging around the apartment and he also wore them when he went out to walk and hike."

"Ryan liked to walk?"

"Yeah. He did that a lot." She looked at Helene. "I used to go with him all the time at first. But then he complained that I walked too slow so we just walked around the block and he went hiking by himself...Is it important?"

"Could be." The lawyer nodded her head. "It's the first clue we have about the real Ryan."

Jillian glanced at her watch. "It's almost twelve. Should I go into the office this afternoon?"

Helene shook her head. "You've had too much to deal with this morning. I'll tell Martin about what happened and I'm sure he'll understand. Meanwhile, stay here and think about everything you did with Ryan and everything you thought you knew about him. If something occurs to you, write it down and, if it seems important, call me. I'll give you my cell number." She hopped off the bed. "I'm going back to work now. Let's see if the police can locate Ryan, or, at least, find his car."

"Do you think they will?"

"Maybe they'll find the car. But I doubt that they'll find your boyfriend. He worked too hard to make it look like he's been murdered and that you're the one responsible. He'll have disappeared to a place where he's sure no one will find him." Helene shrugged. "Sorry to be so negative, but I don't want to give you false hope." She grabbed her bag, took out a business card, and handed it to Jillian.

"Will the police arrest me?" The girl scanned the card and frowned.

"It's possible."

"Even without a body? You know I didn't kill Ryan; I didn't do anything to him."

The lawyer nodded. "Yes, I know that. But, unfortunately, the police don't."

Jillian quickly made a peanut butter and jelly sandwich for lunch. Then, taking a sheet of paper and pen, she lay on the living room carpet, thinking about Ryan. She divided the paper in half and headed the left column, "What I Know." Under it, she listed a few basic things she thought she knew about her boyfriend: loves me, graphic designer, not many friends, orphaned, raised by aunt, likes to walk.

She headed the right column, "True or False" and, for the things she knew, wrote "false," "?," "?," "?," "?," and "true." Then, staring at her list, she realized the only thing she was sure of was that Ryan loved to walk. "I really am a total idiot," she mumbled.

*So he loved to walk? So what?* Wondering if that information even meant anything, she snickered to herself. He couldn't walk far enough away to make people think he disappeared and she killed him. He must have taken his car and driven somewhere. Maybe he drove to the airport and hopped an overseas flight or he could have taken a train, ship, or even a bus.

"What's the use?" she murmured. "I don't have any idea where he is. Maybe I'll luck out and the police will find him." She studied her list again, trying to think of something else she knew about Ryan that might be helpful in locating him.

Jillian was still adding things about Ryan to her list—none of them striking her as particularly important—when the phone rang.

"Hi, it's Helene," the lawyer said when Jillian picked up the receiver. "The police just called me. They found Ryan's car."

"So fast? Where was it?"

"That's the strange thing. It was parked right near your house, just a block away. That's why they found the car so quickly."

"Then Ryan couldn't have driven it to an airport or train station."

"No. He must have called a cab or maybe walked to a bus stop. The police are checking the taxi companies and the bus and train depots and airports to see if anyone remembers seeing Ryan Friday night or over the weekend. They're also showing his picture to hotels and motels in the area to make sure he's not holed up in a room somewhere close by."

"Did the police find anything in Ryan's car?"

"No. It was clean and it hadn't been driven in the last few days."

Jillian sighed. "What should I do now?"

"Just continue to think about places where Ryan might have gone. Any ideas yet?"

"No. Most of the things I thought I knew about him were probably lies. Nothing's hit me."

"Well, keep thinking and call me if you come up with something."

"I will."

On Wednesday, Jillian went back to her job at the law firm. In the early afternoon, Helene walked into the storage room where the girl sat on the floor, organizing a large batch of files. "Officer Forsythe just called me. He's coming over now."

"What for?" Jillian asked. "Did the police find Ryan?"

"He didn't say. He just wanted to make sure that you were at work today."

Jillian sighed deeply. "I just hope he's gotten hold of Ryan and this was all some kind of sick joke."

A few minutes later, Helene returned to the storage room. "Officer Forsythe's here," she said.

The girl left the files on the floor and accompanied Helene to the law firm's reception area.

The tall thin policeman nodded to her. "Good afternoon, Miss Keating."

"Do you have some news about Ryan?" Jillian asked anxiously.

"'Fraid not." The man shook his head.

"Then why are you here?"

Officer Forsythe leaned against the wall, crossing his long arms. "We're not getting anywhere with this investigation," he said. "Lots of police officers on the case, but no leads. Checked the phone—nothing there. No activity on Mr. Cornell's credit cards and no one's seen him." He shrugged. "We're just going around in circles, chasing our tails."

Helene stepped in front of Jillian and folded her arms. "What do you want of my client then?" she asked.

Ignoring the lawyer's question, the policeman addressed Jillian. "Do you have your car here, Miss Keating?"

"Yes. I drove it to work this morning."

"Mind if I look at it?"

"Do you have a warrant?" Helene asked, again standing in front of Jillian.

"Do I need one?"

The lawyer turned to her client. "We don't have to allow this. The police have no reason to search your car."

"But, like I keep telling everyone, I don't have anything to hide," Jillian said. "Ryan was never even in my car. We always used his car whenever we went someplace together. He wouldn't even sit in my Hyundai. Said it was too small for him."

Jillian's blue Accent was parked in front of the law office. After the girl unlocked the door, Officer Forsythe peered inside.

"Sorry," Jillian said. "It's got papers all over."

Helene grasped her client's arm. "Quiet," she ordered. "You don't have to make any excuses. It's your car. You're allowed to be messy."

The policeman picked up and glanced at a few of the papers in the back seat before putting them down. Then he pulled up the floor mats and examined each one carefully. Finally, he opened the glove compartment and rifled through the documents. "Nothing here," he mumbled.

"I told you that," Jillian said.

"Open the trunk," the officer demanded.

"Sure." Taking her key, Jillian unlocked the trunk. When the rear panel flew up, she gasped. The interior was smeared with streaks of red.

"What the..." she muttered.

Pushing Jillian aside, Helene stared at the storage area and then walked back to the shaken girl. "Jillian," she whispered, out of earshot of the policeman. "When was the last time you used the trunk?"

"Friday, when I went to the supermarket after work, just before I came home."

"Okay," Helene said. "Don't say anything else. Let me do all the talking now." She returned to the car and waited for the policeman to finish examining the inside of the trunk.

"I'm going to get the lab to run tests on these stains," Officer Forsythe said, lifting his head. "But I'm pretty sure it'll turn out to be blood that matches the stains on the carpet." He closed the trunk and stared at the two women. "Miss Keating's already admitted that was Mr. Cornell's blood."

"I agree it probably will match," Helene said. "But that's only because my client's been set up." The lawyer smirked. "Doesn't all of this seem too pat—the note, a loud argument overheard by neighbors, bloodstains on the carpet, and now this blood-smeared trunk? Does Jillian Keating look so stupid that she would commit a violent crime and then leave so many incriminating clues behind?"

The policeman shrugged. "I don't know about that. But what I do know is that, if the blood matches, then I'm going to arrest Miss Keating for the murder of Ryan Cornell."

# CHAPTER 4

They didn't have to wait very long for the results. Officer Forsythe had the lab rush the DNA tests, which used Ryan's electric razor and his blood on the apartment carpet to confirm that the stains in Jillian's trunk were indeed Ryan's blood.

The policeman returned to the law firm late in the afternoon and, with Helene watching, addressed Jillian. "Miss Keating, you're under arrest for the murder of Ryan Cornell. You have the right to remain silent. Anything you say can and will be held against you in a court of law. You have a right to talk to your lawyer and have her present with you while you are being questioned." Then he took a set of handcuffs from his pants pocket.

"What's going to happen to me now?" Jillian asked, tears flowing down her cheeks, as the officer handcuffed her. "I can't believe I'm going to jail."

"Don't worry," Helene said, putting her arm around the distraught girl. "I'll get you out on bail as soon as I can." After checking her watch, she gazed sadly at Jillian. "But it's too late today so I'm afraid you're going to have to spend tonight in a cell. I'll have you out of there first thing tomorrow morning, I promise." Gently, she squeezed the girl's shoulder. "It'll just be for the one night. You'll be okay. I'm sure you can handle it."

Jillian was still crying as the officer guided her into the backseat of his police car and drove to the station.

Relieved to have the handcuffs off, Jillian massaged her sore wrists as she sat in a hard wooden chair opposite a beer-bellied policeman. The man elicited her personal data—name, age, address, phone number, health issues—recording the information on a form. "Next-of-kin?" he asked.

Jillian shrugged. "I don't have any relatives."

"Then I need the name of someone close to you."

*Until Monday, I would've said Ryan.* Sighing softly, Jillian took out her wallet, found Helene's business card, and gave the officer the lawyer's name and cell phone number.

She was led to another desk where a blonde policewoman told her to empty her pockets, take off her shoes, and relinquish her watch. (She had already surrendered her handbag when she had been arrested.) After making a list of all her possessions, the officer put the items into a wire bin. "Here's your receipt," she said curtly, handing Jillian the stub.

Then, using a digital camera, the policewoman took several photos of her. *My very own mug shots,* Jillian thought as she followed the officer's commands as to where to stand and where to look.

Next, the female officer fingerprinted her using a digital scanner. Jillian was surprised at the technology; she had expected to press her fingers on an inkpad, like in the movies.

Afterwards, the blonde officer took Jillian into a cubicle, closed the door, and patted the girl's body. She was told to spread her legs and then ordered to lift her top. As the policewoman's hands felt inside her bra, she barely suppressed tears.

When the degrading process was finally over, the officer handed Jillian a thin mattress, faded white sheet, and tattered gray blanket, plus a small plastic bag that contained a toothbrush, tiny toothpaste, and comb. Then, walking Jillian down the hall to a holding cell, the policewoman unlocked the door and guided her inside. "This'll be home till tomorrow," she said, slamming the door shut.

Jillian stood at the entrance of the cell, clutching her new belongings, and surveyed her temporary "home." It was a fairly large room with bunk beds bolted to each wall. She counted seven double beds in all, only two of them occupied. The rest of the cell contained no furniture, but it wasn't empty. A tall and obese African-American woman filled the entire middle space, pacing back and forth with arms resting on her massive breasts, and muttering angry words Jillian couldn't understand. Not wanting to upset the imposing woman, she quickly looked away.

Glancing up, Jillian noticed a security monitor mounted on the ceiling and, near the top of the center wall, a small window covered with bars. Sighing deeply, she headed for one of the unoccupied lower bunks.

"Hi," the young woman sitting on the left lower bed said, smiling at Jillian and patting her lumpy mattress. "C'mon over and sit down."

Jillian stopped walking and stood still, unsure what to do.

The young woman called to her again. "Hey, hon. No reason to be scared. I promise I won't bite ya."

With a shy smile, Jillian approached the woman's bed and sat next to her, still clutching her supplies. "Thanks. This is so unreal for me. I've never been in jail."

Jillian's cellmate shook her cascading black, purple-streaked hair and laughed loudly. The woman wore heavy mascara, purple lipstick, and a tight-fitting purple tee shirt. To Jillian, she looked just like a younger purple version of Mistress of the Dark Halloween queen, Elvira.

"Well, jail's mostly real borin'," purple Elvira said. "I've been here for a coupla hours, I think—it's hard to tell with no clock—and there's nothin' to do and I'm goin' outta my f___in' mind." Smiling again, she held out her hand, revealing long purple fingernails. "Hey, 'scuse me for dumpin' on you like that. My name's Cheri—Cheri Orchid."

Jillian stared at her in amazement and then immediately apologized. "I'm so sorry. I didn't mean to be rude, but I've never met anyone with a name like that. Is it your real name?"

"It is now," Cheri said, giggling. "Had my name changed official last year. I used to be Anna Maria Buonoverduccio." She thrust her chest forward with one hand holding her head in a provocative pinup-type pose. "But, since I'm an exotic dancer, couldn't have such a f___in' long name so I came up with this one. 'Cheri' means 'dear' in French, ya know, and orchids are real expensive flowers. I wanted a classy kinda name."

Jillian nodded, not knowing how to reply. She watched the hefty woman who still circled the center of the cell, mumbling as she walked.

"Don't worry about her," Cheri said. "She ain't gonna do nothin' to us. She's just damn mad at the cops about somethin'. It took four o' them to drag her in here a little before you came." She pointed towards the other occupied lower bunk where a skinny woman with matted gray hair and rumpled clothes lay snoring on an unmade bed. "That one's just an old drunk. They probably found her lyin' in the street and brang her in here to give her a place to sleep. They'll throw her out in the mornin'."

"You said you've been here for a few hours." Jillian hesitated before continuing. "Can I ask what your crime was?"

"Sure." Cheri smiled and then shrugged. "Cops caught me and my boyfriend smokin' weed. But my boss'll come down and get me out in the mornin'. He needs me to work tomorrow night." She posed again, tilting her head upward. "I'm the star dancer at the Ooh-La-La Club."

"That's great." Jillian had the feeling Cheri expected a compliment.

"Yeah. Well, I've worked hard to be the best. Moved up the line, ya know." Tossing her mane of black-purple hair theatrically, she grinned at her cellmate. "But I've been doin' all the talkin' about me. What about you? You don't look like someone who's in here for drinkin' or doin' drugs. What'd the cops bust you for?"

Jillian lowered her head and spoke in a whisper. "They think I murdered my boyfriend."

"No shit? Murder!" Cheri loud words caused the giant pacer to stop moving and glare at them. "Sorry," the dancer said, raising her left hand. The large woman nodded solemnly and resumed her pacing. Turning towards Jillian, Cheri spoke very softly. "You whacked him?"

Jillian shook her head. "No. I didn't do anything. But, for some reason, Ryan set me up to make it look like I killed him. Now he's disappeared and he wants the police to think that I murdered him."

"Wow! Sounds like a movie." Cheri leaned back against the plastered dirty white wall and rested her arms behind her head. "I wanna hear the whole story. We got lotsa time so go on and tell me everythin' that happened."

Cheri proved to be a good listener, letting Jillian talk steadily without interrupting. In fact, the girl only stopped her narrative when dinner—if it could properly be called that—was served. The meal consisted of one piece each of American cheese and bologna on two slices of white bread, an apple, and a half-pint container of milk.

Cheri removed the piece of bologna, frowned, and dropped it onto the tray. Then she took the cheese slice out of the sandwich, and slowly nibbled it.

Jillian, on the other hand, discovered she was famished—she hadn't eaten since her quick lunch—so she gobbled all the unappealing food. After drinking the milk, she resumed her monologue, concluding with "...and then the policeman brought me here."

The dancer shook her head. "Wow! What a story! And you ain't got no idea why he did it?"

"Uh uh." Jillian shrugged. "But I'm so dumb. I thought Ryan loved me, while all along he must've really hated me."

"Sometimes guys are tough to figure out," Cheri said, grinning slightly. "I'm lucky I found Rocco. He's a bouncer at my club. He's six-foot-six, three hundred pounds, and looks like some kinda mean giant. Scares the shit outta most people, but he's a real pussycat. Maybe he could beat up your boyfriend, ya know, teach him a lesson."

"If we can ever find Ryan."

"Yeah, right."

The two young women sat silently for a few minutes, looking at the quiet cell. The large mumbling pacer had stopped circling the room and now lay peacefully on a lower bed opposite them. "Are you gonna hafta stay in jail?" Cheri finally asked.

"My lawyer said she'd get me out in the morning."

"That's good. And then what's gonna happen?"

"I don't know. I'm really scared," Jillian whispered.

Cheri put her arm around the girl and hugged her tightly. "Oh honey, don't worry. You didn't do nothin' wrong. I'm sure your lawyer's a real smart lady and she'll know what to do."

"Well, Helene is really smart and she's good. But I don't know if she's that good." Jillian yawned and stood up. "Do they ever turn off the lights here? I don't know what time it is and when I should go to sleep."

"Nah. Them lights are always on. The cops gotta watch us, see that we're not screwin' 'round, hurtin' ourselves or someone else so you just go to sleep whenever." She rolled her eyes and shrugged.

"Oh." Jillian picked up her flimsy mattress, sheet, and blanket and tossed them on the bunk above Cheri's bed. "Then, since I'm so tired, I'll just get ready for bed now. Is that the bathroom over there?" She pointed to a small alcove in the rear, on the other side of the cell.

"Yeah." The dancer nodded.

Carrying her little plastic bag, Jillian walked to the restroom, which consisted of a toilet and tiny sink. Afterward, she climbed into bed and said goodnight to her cellmate. Then, lying on the thin mattress, she covered herself with the sheet and blanket, closed her eyes, and tried to sleep.

"Everyone up!" The policeman's loud shout early Thursday morning woke Jillian and two of the cell's other three occupants. The gray-haired woman continued to sleep.

"What the hell time's it?" The question came from the massive former-pacer, who still occupied one of the lower bunks.

"Time to get ready for court," the officer said as he unlocked the cell door and entered, wheeling a cart with the women's breakfasts. He dumped Jillian's tray on her bed. The meal closely resembled the previous night's dinner: one slice each of ham and cheese on white bread, a mushy banana, and a half-pint of orange juice.

Jillian forced herself to eat the sandwich and part of the banana, just in case she would have to stay in jail.

"Did ya sleep okay?" Cheri called up.

"I guess. But it was uncomfortable without a pillow."

"Yeah. Cops are scared we'll use it to smother ourself or maybe kill someone else in here."

"Oh...What happens next?"

"Go use the john and wash up. In a coupla minutes they're gonna bring us to court."

As Cheri had predicted, the blonde female officer who had processed Jillian Wednesday, opened the cell and handcuffed Cheri, the large—now quiet—mumbler-pacer, and Jillian, ignoring the other rumpled occupant, who still slept. The three women were herded to a police van and, after Jillian and Cheri were placed together in the back, a male officer attempted to guide the large African-American woman into the middle seat.

"Get your goddamn hands off of me, you motherf___er!" the big prisoner shouted, shaking the man away, and falling clumsily into the seat. After maneuvering her large body into a sitting position, the woman began mumbling again.

"I am so scared," Jillian whispered to Cheri, trying not to disturb the large mumbler.

"Nothin's gonna happen. You just gotta post bail. Don't make faces or say somethin' to piss off the judge and it'll all be okay." Cheri had washed her face, removing the heavy mascara and purple lipstick. She now looked much younger and Jillian realized the dancer was probably just in her early twenties, only a few years older than herself.

After a ten-minute ride, the driver parked the van and a hefty male officer slid open the door. He took out the massive mumbler first, and then Cheri and Jillian. Still handcuffed, the three women were led into a courtroom.

"All rise for the Honorable Judge Henry J. Dornmacher," the bailiff announced. An emaciated white-haired man, who didn't look like he had enough energy to even make it to his seat, entered the room. Gingerly, he successfully navigated his way to the bench and adjusted his wire-rim glasses.

"You may sit down," the judge said, his voice remarkably deep and strong.

"First case: 'State against Jillian Keating,'" the bailiff announced.

Judge Dornmacher glanced around the courtroom. "Jillian Keating?"

Still in handcuffs, Jillian rose from her front row seat.

"Do you have a lawyer present?"

"Yes, Your Honor," a petite gray-haired woman said, rising from her seat behind Jillian. "Helene Moskowitz. I am Miss Keating's attorney."

After glancing at his papers, the judge addressed the lawyer. "I see that your client is being charged with second degree murder. I am going to set bail at $200,000."

"Your Honor, my client has no history of violence, no prior criminal record of any kind. She has a steady job and will not flee. I can vouch for her. I respectfully ask that you reduce the bail."

"Your client is accused of murder, not some minor crime, counselor," the judge said, squinting at Helene.

"Your Honor, the police don't even have a body. Right now, all they've got is a missing person and some circumstantial evidence."

Judge Dornmacher again consulted his papers. "All right. I'll lower bail to $150,000. But she'd better show up for the hearing."

"Thank you, Your Honor. She will."

As Helene took care of the paperwork, a policeman uncuffed Jillian. After mouthing goodbye to Cheri, she walked out of the courtroom with her lawyer, a temporarily free woman.

"Hey, Miss Keating, just a few questions!" A middle-aged man with a double chin rushed towards Jillian and thrust a microphone into her face.

Jillian was amazed to find herself surrounded by several TV cameras and a swarm of reporters holding microphones or recording devices. As Helene swatted away the man with the microphone, an auburn-haired woman pushed against Jillian, nearly knocking her over. "C'mon. Tell us what's going through your mind right now. Do you know what's happened to your boyfriend?"

"That's enough." Helene maneuvered her small body in front of Jillian in an attempt to shield her stunned client. "Miss Keating is not making any statement right now, but I will tell you all that my client is innocent. She did not in any way harm Ryan Cornell. Now please let us through. My client has had a very difficult night and she needs to be left alone."

Mumbling to one another, the phalanx of reporters parted like the Red Sea, allowing Jillian and Helene to walk down the center of the sidewalk until, without further interruption, they reached the lawyer's car.

# CHAPTER 5

"But I don't have $150,000 so why'd they let me go?" Jillian lowered her mug as she and Helene sat at a corner table in a coffee shop several miles from the courthouse. No nosy reporters lurked outside.

"Martin took care of it," Helene explained, smiling at her client. "Your boss really likes you and a friend of his, a bail bondsman, owes him a big favor. It's not $150,000 though. The cost is ten percent of your bail and he'd only have to pay the full amount if you run away. Are you planning a quick getaway?"

"No. Of course not." Jillian shook her head. "But that's still a lot of money. I'm really grateful and I'll call Martin and thank him... When do I have to be back in court?"

"Not for at least several months, maybe longer."

"What happens now?"

The lawyer stirred her coffee, studying the swirling patterns before answering. "As I figured, unfortunately the police haven't come any closer to finding your boyfriend so it's time for us to start looking for him."

"How?" Jillian massaged her wrists, which still hurt from the morning's handcuffing. "I mean, if the police can't find Ryan, how're we going to?"

"I've got a guy that I use—Alex Drury, a private investigator. He's very good at digging up info and finding missing people."

Jillian sighed. "If he's that good, he's probably expensive and I don't have the money to pay for an investigator."

Helene took the girl's hand and squeezed it. "Listen, kiddo, you don't have a choice here. We've got to find Ryan Cornell. After we locate your missing boyfriend, then you can worry about how to get the money to pay for Alex because, if we don't find Ryan, you're going to be on trial for his murder." She released Jillian's hand and smiled softly. "But right now, I'm taking you home. After last night, I'm sure you could use a nice hot shower."

Since the police were still holding Jillian's car, Helene had set up their two o'clock appointment with Alex Drury at Jillian's apartment. The lawyer arrived first.

"Are those reporters still outside?" Jillian asked.

"Yes, unfortunately. Just don't talk to them."

"I know. When they stuck a microphone in my face again, after you took me home this morning, I did what you told me and didn't say anything."

"That was good." Helene sat on the couch next to Jillian and patted the girl's hand. "Just keep ignoring them."

"Will they go away soon?"

The lawyer nodded. "When they finally realize that you're not going to talk and give them any information."

"What's Mr. Drury like?" Jillian asked as they continued to wait for the investigator.

Helene laughed heartily. "First of all, he's not a 'Mr. Drury.' Everyone calls him Alex. When you meet Alex, you'll see that there's absolutely nothing formal about him."

A few minutes later, the doorbell rang. "Sorry I'm late," Alex

Drury said, rushing inside as soon as Jillian opened the door. "Got stuck in a goddamn fender-bender on the expressway. A couple of teens with lead feet on the gas pedal. Ought to not let 'em drive till they're at least twenty-five."

Having ended his explanation, the investigator smiled sheepishly at the two women. "Hey, sorry about that. Not even inside the door and I'm already talking about some stupid accident that you two don't give a damn about." He offered his hand to Jillian, who was still standing in the hallway. "And you must be Miss Keating, the one who's in deep shit."

Taking the outstretched hand, she gazed at the handsome young investigator. The man had sparkling blue eyes, curly brown hair, and a dimple in his right cheek when he smiled, as he was doing now.

"Oh, did I say something to offend you?" Alex asked when Jillian didn't immediately release her hand. "You mean you're not in deep shit?"

"Sorry." The girl removed her hand and lowered her face, which suddenly felt very warm. "But you're not at all what I expected."

Helene laughed. "What did you think? That Alex would be a gruff old guy, his pants hanging over a fat stomach, chomping on a cigar?"

"Yeah." Jillian grinned, hoping her face wasn't flushed anymore. "Something like that, I guess."

"I may not look like an old-time P.I., but I'm good at my job." He lowered himself into a chair opposite the couch, took a creased notebook and a pen from his pants pocket, and turned to Jillian. "Helene's given me a quick rundown on this case, but, before I start, I need to know everything that you know about Ryan Cornell." He smiled, again revealing the dimple. "Then I'm going to find that shithead boyfriend of yours and drag him back."

Jillian described her relationship with Ryan—meeting him in the graphic arts class and moving in with him soon afterwards. After giving Alex a photo of her boyfriend, she found the "True/False" list she had compiled about him. "Maybe this will help," Jillian said, handing the sheet to the investigator.

"Listen, kids, I've got to run," Helene said, standing and grabbing her pocketbook. "Got a four o'clock appointment back at the office." She turned towards Jillian and grinned. "Alex will fill me in if he learns something that I need to know. And, of course, you can always call me. You've got my cell number."

"Thanks, Helene." Jillian escorted the lawyer to the door and whispered, "Do I have to talk to him alone?"

"Yes, you do," Helene said softly. "I promise he won't bite. Don't forget, he's working for you—so go on back now." She gave the girl a slight push.

Alex was glancing at his notes when Jillian returned to the couch. "All right. Now where were we? You moved in with the jerk—was the sex that good?"

*Damn Helene!* Jillian lowered her head and bit her tongue.

"Hey, I'm sorry." The investigator pretended to slap his face. "Sometimes I just can't help myself and say stupid things."

Jillian looked up at him, her eyes tearing.

"Listen, I really didn't mean to upset you. I promise I won't ever say anything like that again." He paused briefly. "Please don't worry about me. I've got a strict policy about cases I'm working on to never get personally involved with the client. I only said that because Ryan sounds like such a loser and you deserve better."

She tilted her head down and studied her hands.

"Oh, shit! I've embarrassed you again!"

Jillian tried to force a smile. "No. That's okay. You're right about Ryan. I shouldn't have moved in with him without knowing more about who he really was. But he was so nice and he really seemed interested in me and..."

"Hey, don't beat yourself up over it. Let's get back to what happened. So you moved in with Ryan, and then what?"

"Well, I continued working at Helene's law firm because I couldn't find an art job and Ryan told me he was freelancing at home as a graphic artist."

Alex scanned her "True/False" list. "But he never showed you any of his work?"

"No, and his laptop's gone so I can't check."

"So now you're not even sure he was an artist. You think that could've been a lie too?"

"Yes." Jillian shrugged. "I'm not sure anything Ryan ever told me about himself was true."

"But you know that he liked to walk. You're sure about that." Alex pointed to a line on her list. "It's our only clue right now so I'd like you to think about places he might have walked to and then you or I'll check them out."

"But what good will that do?" She sprang up, spreading her arms. "He didn't take his car when he left Friday and he couldn't have walked far enough away to hide from everyone. I mean, wouldn't the police have found him by now if he was in some hotel just a few miles away?"

"Probably. I agree it's more likely he caught a cab or took a bus to the airport." Alex shook his head. "But if that's the case, we've got to wait till he makes a move—uses a credit card or is recognized."

The girl sat down slowly and lowered her head.

"Hey, don't worry. We'll find him. He can't disappear forever. It'll just take some time. Let's talk about what Ryan told you about his childhood. Maybe something about that will turn out to be helpful."

"Why?" She looked up at the investigator. "It's probably all just a bunch of lies."

"Maybe. But there might be some little nugget of truth in there that can help us."

"All right...Ryan told me that after his parents were killed in the fire, he went to live with an unmarried aunt, his father's sister."

"Did he tell you her name?" Alex asked, scribbling down the information.

"He just called her Aunt Mary. But that could be a lie too."

"Yeah, although it's hard to lie about everything. If she was his father's unmarried sister, then her name would be Mary Cornell." The detective continued to write. "Where did Ryan say his Aunt Mary lived?"

"Someplace in Connecticut near New Haven, but he never mentioned the name of the town." Jillian shook her head sadly. "I'm sorry."

"Not your fault," Alex said. "Is this aunt still alive?"

"Ryan said she died about three years ago."

"Okay. Mary Cornell is supposedly dead so I'm looking for a Cornell family. Did Ryan say he had any brothers or sisters or talk about other family members?"

"According to Ryan, he was all alone, like me." She smiled wistfully. "That was one of the things that brought us together. Neither of us had any family."

The investigator folded Jillian's list, put it into his notebook, and stood up. "I'll get started on trying to track down Ryan and see what I can find out about his Connecticut family. Meanwhile, since you don't have a car right now and aren't working today, go out and take a walk. It's a beautiful day." He reached into his shirt pocket, took out a business card, and handed it to Jillian. "See if something occurs to you that could help us find the missing shithead."

# CHAPTER 6

"What am I even looking for?" Jillian whispered as she stepped out the rear exit of her apartment building Thursday afternoon, avoiding the reporters who still lingered at the main entrance. Dressed in comfortable sneakers and a light jacket, she was ready for a late day walk.

*Did Ryan have a secret hiding place?* She reached into her jacket pocket and felt the Post-It pad she had grabbed on the way out—just in case she remembered something important. However, right now, nothing came to mind.

Jillian sighed and glanced to the left and then to the right. But all she saw were private homes and small backyards, not even another apartment building, and no stores. It was a totally residential neighborhood. Gazing up at the builder-planted row of look-alike maple trees, she wondered if Ryan had somehow transformed himself into a monkey and built a hidden tree house.

She headed to her right, muttering to herself. "Maybe if I could remember where I walked with him. We walked down this street because it led to a deli about ten blocks away. A couple of times, we got sandwiches..." She stood still, shaking her head. "No," she whispered. "Not a help."

Backtracking, she started walking in the opposite direction, hoping no one was watching her erratic behavior. *Let's see,* she thought, *if I go this way...* Again, nothing but single-family homes lined the next several streets. *Wait a minute...* Jillian stopped moving, remembering if she continued left for about a mile, the road led to a park, which contained a small mountain.

"I went there with Ryan once," she murmured. "And we walked around the park." Jillian had enjoyed the experience. But when she had suggested taking the trail up the mountain, Ryan had quickly vetoed the idea. And soon after, he had started complaining she moved too slowly. He began taking most of his long walks without her and she had never gone back to the park or hiked in the little mountain. *Could he somehow be hiding there?*

"It doesn't matter how slow I am now," Jillian whispered as she headed for the park.

About a half hour later, Jillian arrived at the recreation area, which, according to a sign, was named Juniper Park. She entered the green space and followed arrows along a meandering path until she reached the mountainous hiking trail. *More like a big wooded hill,* she thought, surveying the landscape. Then, taking a deep breath, she began climbing the mini-mountain.

The trail was narrow, but well defined, and there was still plenty of daylight left so Jillian walked at a leisurely pace, trying to enjoy her outdoor experience. It was a gorgeous day—sunny, without a cloud in the sky, and with a temperature in the upper sixties. *Better than sitting in the apartment, worrying, and doing nothing,* she thought, listening to a variety of bird chirps and noticing little blue and pink wildflowers along the tree-lined path. Despite the beautiful day, she saw just two other hikers.

After a few minutes of steady climbing, Jillian reached a small clearing. She was getting a bit tired so she took a short break, sitting on a large broken log that lay on the ground. Checking her watch, she saw it was only five o'clock. She still had plenty of time before sunset.

Jillian glanced at the many huge trees, mostly pines, which tightly surrounded the clearing. *But this is Juniper Park—wonder what junipers look like.* One area opposite had a large pile of leaves and branches blocking the view.

*Time to finish my hike,* she told herself. She stood, dusted her rear end, and continued along the trail. *Boring!* All she saw were more trees and no other people.

As she walked, Jillian's mind kept returning to the clearing where she had sat and rested. Something there didn't seem quite right. *But what?* She had to check it out. She turned around and backtracked to the open area with the broken log seat.

Once again, she sat on the log and glanced in all directions. *What's bothering me?* Her eyes focused on the stack of forest rubbish on one side of the clearing. It looked too neat, almost as if someone had purposely created the huge pile of leaves and broken branches to block part of the mountain. *But why?*

*What's that?* Something in the pile glittered in the bright sunshine. Jillian rushed to the debris and picked up the yellow thread that had caught her eye. *From Ryan's shirt?* Now she had to find out what was hidden behind the obstruction. Kneeling on the ground, she began shoving away the debris and, when she had made a big enough dent, she forced her body through the opening.

After wriggling out on the other side, she brushed away the leaves, pine needles, and sticks and found herself surrounded by more large trees. However, to her right, an enormously wide dead trunk jutted at nearly a forty-five-degree angle, rising about six feet out of the ground.

Jillian approached the huge log and examined the imposing structure. Curiously, the dead tree looked solid except for a hole near the top that was covered loosely with branches and leaves. Using her fingers, she started cleaning out the opening, which took some effort. "This is all probably silly," she mumbled. "Just my imagination." But she continued to clear away the leaves in the slanted trunk.

When she had removed most of the stuffing, Jillian was able to push her hand through the hole. The jutting log was completely hollow and the circumference looked even wider than the size of a manhole cover. *I could easily fit through that*, she thought. Peering inside, she saw a tiny ray of light filtering through the other end, maybe ten feet away.

*Doesn't make any sense.* She lifted her head, trying to figure out what could possibly be at the bottom of the dead log. She should have seen total blackness, just earth under the ground. Instead, she saw light, which meant an opening. So the log was a passageway. *But to where?*

Before she had a chance to change her mind, Jillian climbed into the massive trunk headfirst and slithered forward. She maneuvered her way downward within the tube-like structure, moving her arms as if she were dog paddling. Soon she reached the other end.

Jillian crawled out of the hollow log and stood, shaking off flecks of dirt as she examined her new surroundings. This side of the trunk emptied into a small cave and the light she had seen emanated from a four-foot opening. It was very noisy, with a loud roar coming from somewhere just beyond the cave. She crouched and walked outside, entering yet another clearing in the woods. But this clearing wasn't empty. A swirling wind that looked like a mini-tornado—making a swishing sound as it spun—filled the center of the open space.

As she watched in amazement, the strange wind formation continued to rise from the ground into an eight-foot-high spiral, swirling in place like a perpetually spinning, oversized toy top. *Bizarre*, she thought. *What'd it feel like in that wind tunnel?*

"What the heck," she murmured, diving into the twister before thinking it over and losing her nerve. The powerful wind lifted her, tossing her body around several times as if she were in some kind of amusement park ride. Then Jillian pushed herself out of the little whirlwind, falling to the ground on the opposite side of the little cave.

Rising to her feet, she stared at the mini-cyclone, which continued to swirl in the same spot as if nothing had happened. After wiping her clothes, she found a small trail and began following it.

The little path led down the side of the mountain. As she walked, Jillian suddenly felt cold. Somehow the temperature seemed about ten degrees cooler. The day had turned cloudy and patches of sunlight no longer filtered through the trees. She buttoned her jacket and moved faster.

Several minutes later, she reached the bottom of the mountain at the other end of the park. Since this tiny trail ended a few feet in front of the opening, Jillian had to brush aside tree branches before she could step out of the woods. She made a mental note to remember the location of this hidden trail, noticing a pink flowering tree nearby. "Not enough," she whispered. Fumbling in her jacket, she found her Post-It pad and wedged one of the little yellow papers into the dirt next to the trees leading to this path. "In case I want to come back to check out that strange wind tunnel again," she murmured.

As she continued towards the exit, Jillian glanced at her watch. The dial read 5:10. Frowning, she realized the time didn't make any sense. It had to be considerably later. It had been five o'clock when she checked her watch and after that she had walked for a while, gone back to the log, pushed through a pile of leaves, cleaned out the tree trunk, slid into the cave, spun inside the strange swirling wind, and walked down the mountain. *Watch must've stopped working, maybe in that strong wind,* she thought.

When she left the park, Jillian noticed a small pizzeria across the street. Figuring she deserved a dinner treat after all that walking, she went inside, stood at the counter, and ordered two plain slices and a bottle of water. After paying, she waited for her food and looked around. The restaurant was practically empty, which was strange considering it was dinnertime. Then Jillian saw a wall clock on the right side of the room. It read 2:10.

"Excuse me," she said to the stubble-faced counterman. "I think your clock's not working. Can you tell me what time it really is?"

The man lifted his burly arm and glanced at his watch. "I've got two-twelve. What does the clock say?"

Jillian didn't respond. She stood with her mouth agape, staring at the pizza man. "That's impossible," she finally said.

"Look, lady, I don't know what your problem is with the time." The man gazed at the clock and then shrugged. "I mean who gives a shit if it's a minute or two fast?"

"No. That's not what's bothering me." The girl shook her head. "It's got to be much later than that—like about six o'clock."

The swarthy man put both hands on the counter and glared at her. "Listen, here's the deal." He spoke slowly and carefully, as if he were addressing a mentally challenged person. "Today is Wednesday, May 11th and the time right now is...." He checked his watch again. "...two-fifteen in the afternoon, give or take a minute." The man turned around and faced the rear of the store. "Now if we're finished talkin' about the time, I'm gonna go to the oven and get your pizza."

Jillian stood still, not having heard anything the man said after he mentioned the day and date. He had said today was Wednesday, May 11th. But it couldn't be Wednesday, May 11th. That was yesterday, the day she had been arrested and put in jail. Today was Thursday, May 12th. Jillian took her water, walked to a table, and sat down. She needed to think.

The unshaven counterman brought Jillian her order, putting the pizza slices on the table without saying a word and quickly darting away. The girl glanced at the food, but didn't touch it. She was no longer hungry.

*What the hell's going on?* She had taken the mountain trail, gone through the hollow tree trunk to the cave, and spun around in the little whirlwind. Then, when she had emerged from the mountain, the weather had changed significantly. And now she knew why. It was no longer Thursday. Somehow, she had landed in the recent past, nearly a full day behind real time.

Her hike had been different—the log passageway to the cave— but only one thing had been truly strange: that wind tunnel. It didn't make any sense, but the little cyclone must have twirled her backwards in time. "Ryan," she whispered, nodding her head. *That's how he escaped.* He wasn't hiding in some faraway hotel room; he was holed up somewhere in the past. And the key element wasn't where he was. It was when.

Maybe he was living in the same time she was in now, just one day behind. But he could also be hiding at another time in the past. She didn't know if the wind had the power to twirl a person even further back. And if the time Ryan was in differed by just a mere second, she might never be able to find him. "What a mess," she whispered, taking a sip of water.

Quickly, Jillian put down the bottle. Right now, Ryan wasn't her main problem. What about her? Was she stuck here, trapped forever in the wrong time? She jumped up, shoving her uneaten pizza away. She had to find that alternate trail, climb back up the mountain to the hidden clearing, and see if the whirlwind was still there. It was her only chance to return to the present.

Luckily the day wasn't windy and the little yellow paper was still wedged into the ground where she had left it, in front of the trees leading to the hidden path. After pushing away the branches,

Jillian began following the small trail back up the mountain.

She heard the roaring noise of the wind tunnel even before she reached the clearing. "At least it's still there," she whispered. Entering the open space, she stopped and stared at the swirling mini-cyclone. It continued to spin in place, looking exactly as it had earlier. *Here we go again.* She took a deep breath and threw herself into the wind portal.

The little tornado lifted Jillian, twirling her around at lightning-fast speed before throwing her onto the soft ground on the other side of the clearing, near the cave with the hollow log. When her dizziness subsided, she stood and shook her clothes. Then, crouching, she entered the small cave and for the second time wriggled her body through the length of the hollow tree trunk, using the ridges inside the log as ladder rungs. After climbing out of the trunk, she stuffed the opening with branches and leaves to hide the hole. Finally, she stepped over the huge pile of leaf debris, restacked it, picked up the hiking trail, and rushed down the small mountain.

When she reached the bottom and entered the park, Jillian smiled. The weather was again warm and sunny. *A good sign.* Also, the sun was very low on the horizon, meaning it had to be later than mid-afternoon. Checking her watch, she saw it was working again and now read 5:25. Anxiously, the girl walked quickly along the path, searching for someone to talk to. She noticed a white-haired woman sitting on a bench, reading a book.

"Excuse me," Jillian said.

The older woman looked up at her. "Yes?"

"My watch had stopped earlier this afternoon and I was hoping you had the correct time."

The woman glanced at her watch. "It's just about six-forty-five." She smiled at Jillian and waved her book in the air. "Oh, I'm so glad you asked me the time. I am reading such a terrific Dean Koontz novel that I didn't realize it was so late." She closed the book and stood up. "I forgot all about dinner and I've got to get home."

"Me too." Jillian began walking in step with the older lady. "I've got to get ready for tomorrow. Friday is always a busy day at work for me."

"I remember those days." The woman nodded. "But I'm retired now so every day's pretty much the same."

"Do you happen to know today's date?" Jillian asked. "I keep forgetting if it's May 11th or May 12th."

"Oh, I'm sure it's the 12th." The woman chuckled. "It's my daughter's birthday and I called her this morning."

Feeling greatly relieved, Jillian said goodbye to the white-haired woman and began her long walk home.

# CHAPTER 7

Since the police were holding her car for evidence, Jillian had made an appointment to pick up a rental car early Friday morning. Helene had promised to drive her to the agency and she was anxious to show the lawyer her discovery.

"So what is it?" Helene asked as she began driving.

"I can't explain. It's something you've just got to see for yourself."

The lawyer shook her head and grimaced. "Sorry, no can do. I've got a court date right after I drop you off. But why don't you call Alex and show him? Remember we're a three-person team now."

Jillian sighed. "Okay, I guess. But I really don't know Alex at all. I only met him yesterday."

"But I know him very well and I'm telling you that he's someone you can trust." She patted the girl's hand. "Hey, I understand you've just been hurt by a man who you thought loved you, but you've got to take my word and start trusting Alex. Let him help you. He's a very good guy. Just give him a chance."

"All right. I'll call Alex."

After signing the papers for the rental car, Jillian drove the gold Ford Focus home. Contrary to what she had told the woman in the park about having to get ready for work on Friday, she had the day off. When she had called her boss to thank him for taking care of her bail, Martin had said she could stay home until Monday.

"Here goes," she whispered as she picked up the receiver and phoned Alex Drury.

The private eye answered the call on the second ring. "Alex Drury speaking."

"Hi. It's Jillian Keating. Helene suggested I call you."

"Good morning. Didn't expect to hear from you so soon. What's up?"

"I found something that I think is important..."

"Go on...I'm listening."

"It's not anything we can discuss on the phone. I've got to show it to you, as soon as possible. Can you come to my house this morning and wear old clothes and sneakers?"

"Give me about a half hour," Alex said, clicking off.

"Can we talk now?" Alex asked Jillian as he parked his Corolla in the Juniper Park lot and surveyed the small recreation area. "You wouldn't tell me anything except to drive here." He lifted his right foot, showing it to her. "See? I'm wearing sneakers like you said. Now where're we gonna be walking?"

Jillian ignored the questions and waved her arm. "Just look around first. I want you to check the weather conditions before we start."

Alex gazed at the sky and shrugged. "It's kind of cloudy and cool. Maybe upper fifties." He gave the girl a befuddled look. "So why the hell do I have to know the temperature here? Are we hiking up the Himalayas where it'll be freezing at the top?" He smiled, showing his dimple. "You didn't tell me to wear a winter coat."

"No. But it's important for you to remember what it feels like now." She pointed to the mini-mountain. "We're going to hike up that mountain trail."

The detective snickered. "That's not a mountain. Looks more like a damn hill."

"Yeah. It's not real steep so it shouldn't be much of a challenge."

Jillian and Alex walked silently along the narrow uphill trail. At one point, they met another pair of hikers—a middle-aged man and woman—coming down the path and nodded to them. When they reached the clearing, Jillian again sat on the broken log.

After glancing in all directions to make sure no one else was nearby, she smiled. "Okay. Here's where the fun starts."

"What's starting?" Alex asked, spreading his hands. "It's very scenic, I guess, and fun if you like nature, but..."

"Look over there." Jillian pointed to the large stack of leaves and branches that obstructed the view. "What do you see?"

"A bunch of old sticks and leaves. So what?"

"Aren't you curious about what's on the other side?"

"No."

The girl smirked. "Some investigator you are. Good thing *I* was curious and checked it out."

He gave her an incredulous look. "We're climbing through all that shit?"

"Yeah." She nodded. "And we better do it fast, before someone comes along."

They tunneled through the debris and then stood up, brushing away the dirt. Jillian quickly replaced the pile of sticks and leaves.

"Okay," Alex said, studying the densely wooded surroundings. "So we waded through the shit, we're on the other side, and there's nothing here but more trees. Now what?"

"You don't see anything interesting?" Jillian grinned slightly, enjoying the investigator's befuddlement.

He peered in every direction. "Only if you like tall trees.

Are these anything special—some rare type of tree that you've discovered?"

"Nope." The girl shook her head. "They're just regular big old trees. Look again."

"What's this?" The detective walked to the huge tilted log and touched it. "Very large, and it's stuffed full of crap." He turned and stared at Jillian. "Is this like Alice in Wonderland? We're climbing in here too?"

She nodded, smiling at him.

"You gotta be kidding."

"No. I promise it'll be worth it."

Alex snorted, shaking his head. "Only if there's a pot of gold on the other side."

"You've got to go in there to find out," Jillian said, grinning again. "C'mon."

After they cleared away the debris, the girl lowered herself headfirst into the tree trunk and tumbled to the bottom, landing in the little cave. Like the previous day, she heard the swirling wind before she entered the clearing. She wiped dirt off her arms and legs and watched the cyclone while waiting for Alex.

"What the hell's that?" he yelled as he crouched through the cave's opening and saw the small twister spinning in place.

"Hold on," Jillian ordered, grabbing Alex's hand. "Then, when I count to three, we'll go into that wind tunnel together. Don't let go! If we get separated and you land without me, just go back into the twister and fall out on the side by the cave. Okay?"

"We're going into that spinning thing? Why?"

"Just do what I say and you'll see why."

"No pot of gold yet—this better be good."

"Trust me, it is."

On the count of three, holding hands, Jillian and Alex leaped into the mini-cyclone and, after several rotations, she tossed both of them to the opposite end of the clearing. They stood up and each shook off the dirt.

"I want to go inside the twister one more time and land on this side again," Jillian said.

"You think this is some kind of carnival ride?" Alex shook his head. "I've got no idea what the hell you're doing."

She took his hand. "Back into the wind on the count of three."

For the second time, the whirlwind spun the two of them around and around until Jillian pushed them out. They again landed together on the opposite side of the cave.

"Is that enough?" Alex asked, dusting himself off. "Or do you plan to spin around in this wind thing all day?"

"No. That's enough spinning." Jillian stepped onto the small trail that led down the mountain. "Now we just have to walk into the park."

"And then?"

"And then it should get very interesting."

"It better. I'm still waiting for that pot of gold."

Jillian and Alex reached the bottom of the mini-mountain, climbed through the bushes, and she showed him her little Post-It, which was still wedged into the ground.

"So?" he said.

"So we can find our way back to this hidden trail."

"Big deal. It's too small a trail anyway. I'd rather use the regular one."

She smiled. "You may change your mind about that."

They picked up the adjoining path that encircled the perimeter of the park. "Does the weather seem any different here?" Jillian asked.

"Not at all," Alex said, staring at the overcast sky. "It's still cloudy and cool—and why would it be different now? We were only up in the woods for about an hour."

"Oh? You think so. What time do you have?"

The investigator checked his watch and frowned. "That's strange. It says eleven-fifteen. But it's got to be later than that." He stared at the timepiece again. The second hand wasn't moving. "It's stopped. What does yours say?"

She gazed at her arm. "Eleven fifteen. My watch stopped working too, at the same time."

"You don't seem at all surprised," Alex said, studying her.

"That's because I'm not."

"This happened to you the last time you spun around in that wacko wind swirling thing so you knew our watches would stop."

"Yup." She nodded. "Very good, Sherlock."

"Must be because of the strength of the wind."

"If you say so...Let's get outside the park and see what's going on."

"You think something's going on out there?" He nodded towards the suburban street. "It's early Friday afternoon in the middle of May, not exactly a time for lots of action."

"You never know." She shrugged her shoulders.

Jillian and Alex left the park and faced the quiet street. "I'm still waiting for your explanation," Alex said. "Nothing has happened so far unless you count getting dizzy and dirty."

Jillian ignored the detective's comments. "I've got an idea," she said, pointing to the small shop opposite them. "There's a pizzeria. It must be lunchtime by now. Why don't we go inside?"

"Okay. We can grab some slices and you can finally explain what you're doing."

"Fair enough—and we can check the time."

They crossed the street and entered the small eatery where the same burly unshaven man Jillian had talked to stood behind the counter. He noticed her and scowled. "You back again? After you left without eatin' anything, I threw the slices away. Didn't figure you'd be back a coupla minutes later." The pizza man snorted. "Hope you didn't think I'd save 'em all day for you."

Alex stared at the girl. "What's he talking about? You were here earlier today?"

She glanced at the wall clock and whispered, "Look at the time."

The investigator gazed at the clock. It read 2:50. "That can't be right," he mumbled.

Jillian turned to the counterman and smiled at him. "No. Of course I didn't expect you to keep the slices for me. Sorry to bother you again." Then, taking Alex's hand, she led the dazed man out of the pizzeria.

Jillian and Alex stood on the nearby street corner. "Just what the hell is going on here?" the detective asked. "You know it's not three o'clock. It's right around noontime—and what was that guy talking about? You couldn't have been in that pizza shop earlier today. That place's not open for breakfast."

The girl smiled, moving her head in all directions. "I told you this hike would be very interesting. Do you see any store around here that sells newspapers?"

"Why do you want a paper now? You'd only have to carry it through the woods when we walk back to the car. You can buy one later."

"You'll see why." She pointed to a sign on the next block. "Look, there's a deli. I bet they have papers." She gave him a gentle shove. "C'mon. Let's go get a newspaper and find out what's happening in the world today."

As they entered the deli, Jillian saw a selection of newspapers spread out on a lower right-hand shelf and picked up one of the dailies. "Check the date," she said, thrusting the paper in front of Alex's face.

The detective took the newspaper and stared at the front page. "Wednesday, May 11th." He shook his head. "This paper's two days old. Today is Friday the 13th—can't forget that date. Where're today's papers?"

After tossing the newspaper back on the shelf, he stared at the array of dailies and then back at Jillian, totally bewildered. "They're all the wrong day. What's the matter with this place, selling two-day-old papers?"

"You think?" She called to the cashier in the center of the store. "Excuse me. What's today's date, please?"

"May 11th!" the woman yelled back.

"Thanks," Jillian said, nudging the stunned investigator towards the door.

"So maybe our little hike's more interesting now?" Jillian asked as she and Alex walked slowly back to the park.

"Ssh." He waved his arm to quiet her. "Let me think."

They crossed the street, entered the park, and she guided the detective to an unoccupied bench. "Here. Let's sit down and talk about this. Have you figured out what's going on?"

Alex shook his head. "This doesn't make any sense. It can't be Wednesday."

"But it is."

"You're crazy. We can't go back in time—it's impossible."

"Then why don't you tell me what's happening here?" Jillian asked the investigator. "There's no other explanation."

Alex stared at her. "It's goddamn impossible, but..." He pointed his forefinger at the girl. "You found this out yesterday. You went back in time and that's when you were in the pizzeria. Why didn't you tell me first?"

"If I did, would you have believed me?"

"No."

She shrugged. "I told you that you had to see it for yourself."

"I'm assuming you know how to get back."

"I did it yesterday."

"Okay." The detective stood and began pacing back and forth. "You think this is where Ryan disappeared to, somewhere in the past. Why?"

"When I started walking yesterday, I remembered going to this little park with Ryan. But when I suggested to him that we hike in the mountain, he quickly said 'no.' He didn't explain why he didn't want to hike there and I never thought about it again till yesterday. It was right after going here that Ryan told me I walked too slow and we stopped taking long walks together."

"But how'd you figure out to go through those branches and leaves and the hollow trunk?"

"I didn't at first. But then that big pile bothered me—it just looked too neat, like it didn't belong. When I checked it out, I found a yellow thread. It could have come from Ryan's shirt—the one he liked to wear when he hiked. And Ryan acted real weird with me that time in the park so I just decided to follow it up. One thing led to another..." She shrugged.

"Good detective work."

"Thanks." Jillian smiled at the compliment. "But even if he is hiding in the past, we don't know when. I went back one day yesterday and we went back two days today. I have no idea how far in the past we can go."

"He would want to go back much further than that," Alex said, sitting down. "He'd probably go back to a time before he met you, way before he set up his murder and pinned it on you." He stared at the girl. "Then he doesn't even have to hide because no one's looking for him."

"But what's he doing in the past—and why did he set me up?"

"I've got an idea about what he might be doing." Alex smiled slightly. "But I don't know enough about your boyfriend yet to figure out why he hates you so much."

"Please don't call him 'my boyfriend.'"

"Sorry. My bad."

Jillian lowered her head and spoke softly. "You think he really hates me?"

"This ain't true love, honey."

They sat quietly. "You said Ryan took his computer when he left," Alex finally said.

"It's not in the apartment."

The investigator reached into his pocket and took out his cell phone. "Let's see if this works." He stared at the dead phone, tried to turn it on, and then showed it to Jillian. "Nothing—no power, no signal—just like the watches. I bet nothing mechanical or electrical from real time will work here in the past."

"Then why did Ryan take his laptop?"

"Probably so you wouldn't see it and find out he wasn't a graphic artist. And I'm sure he's got shit on it relating to his disappearance."

"Couldn't he just have saved all his data and erased the hard drive?"

"Yeah. But that would've looked suspicious if he was supposed to have been murdered."

"So he just has the laptop with him and isn't using it."

"Maybe."

"But you said you think you know what he's doing here in the past."

"Yup."

"Aren't you going to tell me?"

Alex grinned and shook his head. "I want to find out more about Mr. Cornell first—and after what you did to me today, you deserve to wait."

Jillian and Alex walked through the park until they reached the bottom of the little mountain, relieved no one was nearby. "There it is," the girl said, pointing to her little yellow paper. "See why I needed it?"

"Give me a second before we head back." Without waiting for a response, the detective dashed behind the clump of adjacent trees.

"What are you looking for?"

"If Ryan's been using this same hidden trail, he'd have to have left some kind of marker too." Quickly, Alex examined two of the tree trunks. When he reached the back of the third tree, the private eye smiled and waved to Jillian. "Come here and check this out."

She stood next to him and stared at the hidden side of an ordinary-looking spruce tree. Someone had carved a three-inch long "V" into the center of its trunk.

"I'm sure that's what Ryan used to get back to the trail," Alex said, touching the indentation. "Looks like it was made some time ago, a few months at least. See how dark the notch is?"

She nodded impatiently. "Let's go find the wind tunnel before someone comes. I want to make sure we can get back."

After climbing through the dense woods, Jillian and Alex picked up the little trail and returned to the clearing where the strong wind still swirled. The investigator gazed at the twister. "Okay. You're the expert here. What happens now?"

"Well, yesterday I just went back into the cyclone, let it spin me to the other side, and it was the right time again."

"So you think that's all we have to do?"

"I'm not sure because today the wind twirled us two times first—so maybe it has to twirl us two times again."

"Only one way to find out." Alex grabbed the girl's hand and moved towards the swirl. "Into the wind we go."

The whirlwind rapidly spun the two of them onto the other side of the clearing. Jillian and Alex rose to their feet and dusted the dirt from their clothes.

"Check your watch," the detective said. "Is it working again?"

The girl looked at her left wrist and nodded. "Yes, it is. How about yours?"

"Uh huh. Hope that means we're back where we belong." He

prodded Jillian into the cave. Once inside, he pointed to the massive hollow tree trunk. "Let's jump into the Alice in Wonderland hole and find out."

After climbing through the trunk, they again stuffed it with leaves and branches to camouflage the opening. Then, crawling through the stack of debris, the pair reached the main clearing.

"Good that no one's around," Jillian said as she and Alex reconstructed the large pile of sticks and leaves to hide any view.

"Probably shouldn't try this little trip on nice spring weekends," the investigator said. "Could be many more hikers."

"Yeah. But there are so few people here today. Maybe it's not a popular trail—too short or not challenging enough for serious hikers?"

Alex chuckled. "It's challenging all right, but not in a climbing kind of way."

The duo picked up the regular trail and continued down the small mountain until they reached the park. "I sure hope you're right about us being back," the investigator said, patting his midsection. "My stomach says it's past lunchtime so I'm eating no matter what time we're in."

"Let's check." Jillian approached a ponytailed brunette wheeling a little boy in a stroller. "Excuse me. My watch stopped working. Do you have the time?"

The young woman lifted her arm and looked at her watch. "Yes. It's nearly twelve-forty."

"Thanks...And today is Friday the 13th, isn't it?"

The woman laughed. "It sure is. My daughter's nursery school class is talking about superstitions today. Yesterday, her homework was to cut out photos of black cats and salt shakers and stuff like that."

After thanking the young mother, Jillian returned to the private eye. "Did you hear that? We're okay."

"You may be okay, but I'm starving," he said, grinning. "Let's get the car and go somewhere for lunch."

Jillian finished chewing one of her Chicken Tenders as they sat in a rear booth of Burger King, away from the moms and noisy little kids who occupied most of the seats. "So how do we tell Helene about all this?" she asked her companion.

"I dunno." Alex took a bite of his Whopper before continuing. "Probably gonna have to give her a demonstration like you did with me. Take her out for a little spin." He smiled at his clever choice of words.

"How about you? What're you going to do next?"

The private eye waved the half-eaten Whopper in front of Jillian's face as he chomped on another piece. "Gonna finish eating this. I know it's junk food, but man, I really love it. Could eat this shit seven days a week."

"Do you think anyone else has found the wind tunnel?"

Alex shrugged. "Don't really know the answer to that. I guess it's possible, but, like you said, it's not much of a hiking trail. We only saw a couple of people there today and you said you didn't see many when you went yesterday."

"Yeah—and the wind's pretty hard to find."

"But not for you, my cute and curious client."

Feeling her face flush, Jillian lowered her head and didn't speak until she had regained her composure. "What happens now? If Ryan's hiding somewhere in the past, how're we ever going to find him?"

"Don't worry, I'll track him down. He doesn't think anyone knows where he is so he's not even hiding. But first I've got to learn more about the mysterious Mr. Cornell, what his life was like before he met you, what his interests are. Except for the walking part, everything you know about him is a lie."

Jillian sighed.

"Hey, sorry. Didn't mean to upset you, but I'm only trying to answer your questions."

"It's okay. It's just that talking about this keeps reminding me of how dumb I am."

The investigator shook his head. "You're not dumb. This guy set you up big time."

"But why?"

Alex pointed at Jillian with the remains of the burger. "That, Miss Keating, is the number one question."

# CHAPTER 8

When she returned to her apartment from the supermarket Saturday afternoon, Jillian noticed the light on the bedroom phone was blinking. After pressing the "Play" button, she listened to the message.

"Hey, Jillian. How're ya doin'? It's Cheri." The caller giggled before continuing. "Hope I got the right number. You said you lived with that guy, Ryan Cornell, and this is the only number I found for him. Just wonderin' what's goin' on with you and if the cops ever found your boyfriend. Didn't hear nothin' about it on the news, but I coulda missed it. Gimme a call on my cell when you get in. It's 784-3512. Bye."

After copying the number, Jillian stared at the receiver, feeling guilty. She hadn't thought once about Cheri since Thursday's court experience and didn't even know what the judge had ruled in the dancer's case. She had been too busy feeling sorry for herself. But Cheri had been thinking about her, even going to the trouble of finding Ryan's number and calling.

She picked up the receiver and punched in Cheri's cell number. "Hi," Jillian said when the phone was answered. "It's Jillian. I just got your message and I'm so sorry I haven't been in touch. How're you doing?"

"Hey—glad it was the right number! I'm good. Just chillin' till I got to go to work later."

"What happened with you in court on Thursday?"

"Oh, the judge just made me pay a fine. A hundred bucks. He looked real serious and told me not to smoke weed no more. Wasn't no big deal like with you. All that money for bail."

"Did your boyfriend have to pay a fine too?"

"Yeah. Same deal with Rocco. But everythin's good now. Back to normal."

"I'm so glad, Cheri."

"Hey, anythin' doin' with the missin' boyfriend? Cops ever find him?"

"No. But I don't think they're looking real hard. Remember, they think I killed him."

"Yeah. I remember. What about your smart lady lawyer? She got any ideas on how to find him?"

"Not really. But we're making some progress. Helene set me up with a private eye who's supposed to be pretty good."

"Wow!'" The dancer gasped. "A private eye—that's just like in TV and the movies."

"Yeah. That's my life right now—like a crummy low-budget movie."

"Don't get down on yourself, honey. It'll all work out okay. Didn't wanna call and talk to make you feel bad."

"It's not anything you said, Cheri. I just alternate between feeling sad and mad. I'm still kicking myself for believing that Ryan loved me."

"Hey, I know what that shit feels like. Before I met Rocco, I hooked up with all the wrong guys. But my Rocco's just the sweetest thing—a cute, big, cuddly teddy be-a-a-ar."

"It's good that everything's okay with you, and I really appreciate you calling."

"No sweat. You got a cell number I can reach you at?"

"Sorry, I don't have a cell phone." Jillian didn't mention that she didn't need one because so few people ever called her.

"No problem. I'll use this number. Keep in touch, honey."

"Thanks, Cheri. I will."

Jillian hadn't set her alarm for Sunday morning; she had no reason to be up early. However, when she woke up at five-thirty, she couldn't fall back to sleep. She kept thinking about the strange wind tunnel that somehow transported people to the past.

On Friday, she had agreed with Alex that it would be foolish to climb the mountain trail on spring weekends when more people would probably be using it and someone could follow her movements. But she really wanted to test the time passage again to find out just how far into the past a person could travel. The furthest she had gone back was only two days. However, the detective thought Ryan would have traveled to a time before he met her and the notch he had found in the tree looked old. Could Ryan have spun himself back several months?

*Get to the trail real early and no one'll be around,* she reasoned, jumping out of bed. After gulping a quick breakfast of cold cereal, she put on a pair of old jeans and a jacket, grabbed her wallet, keys, and a few Post-Its, and rushed out of the apartment.

She smiled as she walked to the rental Ford. The early morning was cool and overcast with a light mist in the air, not good hiking weather—and she figured many people would be getting ready to go to church.

As Jillian had hoped, the park was deserted—not even a jogger was in sight—as she made her way to the mountain trail. Quickly, she climbed the path, meeting no one before she reached the first clearing.

After removing the pile of debris, she crawled through the opening and restacked the twigs and leaves to again block the view. Then, pulling the stuffing from the hollow log, she thrust herself headfirst into the cavity. She reached the cave on other side and heard the now-familiar whooshing sound. As soon as she entered the clearing, she took a deep breath and dove into the whirlwind.

This time, Jillian let the wind twirl her for a longer time, closing her eyes and trying to enjoy the spinning experience. *Like a fun park ride.* Then, after about twenty-five rotations, she jumped out of the twister and landed on the soft ground on the opposite side of the cave.

Immediately, she stood up and flung herself back into the little cyclone, again staying inside the whirlwind for many rotations. She repeated her actions three more times. When she had had enough, Jillian sat on the ground, waiting for her dizziness to subside. Then, dusting herself off, she followed the tiny trail down the side of the mountain.

When she climbed out of the mountain, Jillian looked for her little Post-It marking the path. It wasn't there. Reaching into her jeans pocket, she found another yellow sticky paper and shoved it into the dirt. Then, entering the park, she stared at her surroundings. The deciduous trees looked different—some were flowering and others were bare or had tiny buds. She checked the sky, noticing it was another cloudy and overcast day, but much cooler. After buttoning her jacket, she walked quickly to the exit, anxious to discover how far into the past she had traveled.

Jillian headed for the deli she and Alex had found on Friday. She walked in, picked up a newspaper, and looked at the day and date. The masthead read "Thursday, April 7." She had gone back more than five weeks in time.

Jillian put down the paper, trying to figure out what had happened. She had twirled herself five times in the little cyclone, staying in it longer and for many more rotations than she had on the previous two trips. Each twirl today had equaled about a week into the past. She didn't know if a person could travel to an exact day or moment, but at least she now had a rough idea about how the wind portal worked.

*What's the time?* She glanced around the store and noticed a clock on the opposite wall. It read 7:10.

Jillian's eyes widened in surprise. *That late?* It would be getting dark very soon and then she wouldn't be able to find her way back to the wind tunnel. She shook her head, annoyed at herself. After her first two time travel experiences, she had foolishly assumed she would always be transported back to a daytime hour. Now, unless she acted quickly, she would have to spend the night in the past. She didn't have enough cash to pay for a motel room and using a credit card could lead to questions in the future. Also, she had to go to work tomorrow morning.

Jillian approached the woman at the cash register. "Excuse me. Is there a department store near here?"

"No. You looking for anything special?"

"A flashlight."

"Well, there's a convenience store—Meg's Mart—two blocks on the right. They should sell flashlights."

"Thanks," she said as she ran out the door.

Fortunately, the little shop was easy to find. Jillian dashed inside and asked the clerk for flashlights. She chose the most powerful model—with batteries included—paid for it, and rushed out of the store. After tearing off the cardboard wrapping, she tossed the packing material into a sidewalk garbage can. The sky was noticeably darker as she raced towards the park.

When Jillian reached the mini-mountain, she stopped and caught her breath. It was still light enough for her to make out the little yellow Post-It wedged into the dirt. She smiled and took a step towards the woods.

"What'cha smilin' at, sugar?"

The slurred sounds of a deep voice behind her startled Jillian. She turned around and faced two scruffy-looking men in their early twenties. The dark-haired shorter one, with a goatee and potbelly, took a gulp of his beer, spilling the excess foam on his chin and on his dirty gray sweatshirt. The other man, a lanky blond whose bare arms were covered in skull tattoos, waved his bottle and leered at her.

"Nothin' behind you but woods," the tattooed man continued, slurring his words and flashing his yellow uneven teeth.

"Leave me alone." Jillian spoke softly, trying to sound forceful and not reveal how frightened she was.

"And if we don't?" the tattooed blond asked, grinning at her. "Who you gonna call? Ain't no one here but us three."

The man's beefy companion waddled a step closer and spoke for the first time. "Yeah," he said. "We can have a lot of fun together— you and us." Clumsily, he reached for Jillian's arm with his free hand.

"Don't touch me!" she yelled, hitting the man's wrist with her flashlight.

"Oww!" the hefty man cried. "You're not bein' friendly."

The lanky blond stepped next to his buddy, his smile replaced by a scowl. "So you wanna play rough, huh bitch?" he muttered, lunging at Jillian's shoulder.

"No!" she shouted, shoving his arm away. The man tried to grab her hair, but Jillian turned her head and he scratched her cheek.

Moving as fast as she could, she ran into the woods, heading for what she hoped was the path to the wind tunnel. She switched on the flashlight for an instant and then quickly shut it off as she hurried away from her tormentors.

Behind her, she heard one of the men yelling. "What you doin'? Hidin'? Gonna stay in them woods all night?" The words were followed by raucous laughter.

"We'll wait for you!" the other one shouted. "We got nothin' better to do." Then they laughed again.

She heard some more talking, but the words were lower and garbled so she couldn't understand them. Then, trying to calm her racing heart, Jillian moved as quickly as she could along the tiny trail.

Even though the two men didn't seem to be following her, the nighttime trek was still nerve-racking. Afraid that leaving the flashlight on might encourage them to pursue her, Jillian used the beam only in brief spurts. As a result, she was forced to walk slowly in the near total darkness.

The fluttering leaves created scary shadows and, although the birds no longer chirped, the woods were filled with the less recognizable sounds of other animals. She heard a rustling noise behind her and jumped. With her heart pounding, she shined the flashlight in the direction of the sound, hoping the bright glow would frighten the nocturnal creature enough to keep it at a distance. Then, praying she was far enough away from the two drunks, she aimed the light in front of her and continued along the path.

A few minutes later, her foot became entangled in something and Jillian fell face forward into the dirt. The flashlight bounced out of her hand but, luckily, stayed on. She got up, retrieved the flashlight, focused the beam on the trail, and saw she had tripped over a jutting root. She wiped her face and clothes and crept forward again, trying to move with even greater care.

Minutes later, she heard the welcome swooshing noise of the swirling wind. Gripping the flashlight tightly, she entered the clearing and let the small cyclone engulf her. The whirlwind spun her swiftly to the other side and dumped her on the soft ground. When she sat up, she saw the small cave a few feet away. It was daylight again.

Jillian turned off the flashlight as she lowered her head to enter the cave, wriggled through the opening in the huge trunk, and climbed to the other end. Then, after restuffing the log with thick branches and leaves, she forced her body through the stack of forest debris to reach the original trail. She glanced in all directions and, not seeing any hikers, quickly replaced the pile of sticks and leaves to hide any view of the second clearing. Finally, she shook the dirt off her clothing and walked down the mountain, into the park.

Her watch was working again; it read 7:25, but, of course, the time had to be considerably later. As she continued through the park, Jillian saw three joggers in the distance. When she reached her car, she switched on the ignition and checked the clock. The real time was 9:10. It had already been a long morning.

She glanced into the car's mirror and checked her face. It was a complete mess—dirty, with a ragged bloody scratch along her left cheek. *Could've been much worse*, she thought. Then, letting out a deep breath, she drove to her apartment.

# CHAPTER 9

"That's a nasty scratch," Helene said to Jillian, who stood in front of the attorney's desk on Monday morning.

"It's okay. It really doesn't hurt."

"Keep it clean so it won't get infected."

Jillian nodded.

"So you still won't tell me what you found?" Helene continued.

"What did Alex say?"

"Pretty much the same thing you did, that he couldn't explain anything and I had to see it for myself. But you're both making this so damn mysterious." The petite woman shook her head. "Don't forget, I am your lawyer, working hard to keep you out of prison."

Jillian rested both hands on Helene's desk and leaned forward. "Let me know when you have a couple of hours free and I'll show you. Okay?"

"Just what is so important that you can't just tell me? Do you actually know where Ryan is?"

Jillian shrugged. "Sort of."

"Then shouldn't we give this information to the police?"

"No. They'd never believe it and, if Ryan finds out, he'll just run away."

The lawyer rolled her eyes. "I feel like I'm playing a game of twenty questions." She stood and studied Jillian. "You have an idea where Ryan is hiding, but you won't tell me and we can't tell the police. Is he somewhere far away, like in another country?"

The girl pursed her lips. "No. He's kind of near, but very far. None of this will make any sense until I can show you what I found. Then you'll understand everything."

Helene turned the pages of her desk calendar and ran her fingers down an open page. "You've made me very curious, but I've got appointments and court dates through Thursday. Late Friday afternoon is the first free time I have so let me pencil you in for quarter to four." The lawyer looked up. "Will that work?"

"I won't take lunch Friday and I'll ask Martin if I can leave a little early. He's been very supportive so I'm sure he'll let me go." Jillian walked to the door. "But if you get any free time earlier in the week, just let me know. The sooner you see this, the clearer everything'll be."

"You got it."

Jillian sleepwalked through the rest of the workday, thankful her filing chores didn't require any deep thought. Her mind kept returning to the little wind tunnel in the woods, wondering how far back in time Ryan was and what he was doing there.

Early Tuesday afternoon at work, Jillian was in the middle of another daydream about Ryan's whereabouts when the receptionist paged her. She put down the papers she had been sorting and picked up the nearest phone.

"Jillian? It's Alex Drury."

"Hi, Alex. What's up?"

"Well, I'm finding lots of interesting shit about your former boyfriend. Listen, I'm going on a road trip tomorrow and I need you to come with me. I called Helene, but she's busy all day so it's just gonna be you and me. Hope that's okay."

The girl hesitated. "I don't know if I can go. I'm already taking time off Friday afternoon to show Helene you-know-what so..."

"You've gotta come. It's really important. Just tell your boss it involves your case and I'm sure he'll let you go. Helene'll back you up on this."

"Will it be for the whole day?"

"Oh yeah. We're leaving early in the morning and we got a long drive."

"Where are we going?"

"I'll tell you everything tomorrow in the car. We'll have lots of time to talk then. I'll pick you up at seven-thirty. Bye."

Alex rang Jillian's bell Wednesday morning at seven twenty-five. "What happened to your face?" he asked when she opened the door. Even though she had covered the scratch with makeup, it was still noticeable.

"I had a little accident."

"I bet. Wanna tell me about it?"

"No." Jillian shook her head. "I'd rather not."

"Okay. I guess it's not my business. Then let's change the subject and talk about something that is my business—this case. No trouble getting off work, huh?"

"You were right," the girl said, locking her apartment door and walking down the flight of stairs with the private eye. "Martin said anytime I had to leave because of my case was okay with him."

They climbed into the detective's white Corolla, Jillian buckled her seatbelt, and Alex began driving. "You said you'd explain where we're going and why," she said.

"Yup." He nodded. "You ready for all of this?"

"Yeah. I already figured that Ryan must have told me some more lies."

"He sure did, starting with where he grew up. He told you Connecticut so I wasted lots of time trying to find a Ryan Cornell who lived near New Haven." The investigator grimaced. "What a shithead."

"So tell me, what did you find out?"

"Well, after getting nowhere trying to track him down in Connecticut, I started thinking about the name 'Cornell'—what does that remind you of?"

"Ryan's last name? Why does that matter?"

"Usually it wouldn't, unless he changed it."

"Ryan changed his name?"

"Yeah. But let's talk about 'Cornell' first. What do you think of when you hear the word?"

"I know there's an Ivy League college named Cornell."

"Yes, there is. It's in Ithaca, in upstate New York."

Jillian looked at Alex. "Is that where we're going?"

He nodded. "On the outskirts of Ithaca. That's where Ryan is really from."

"You said he changed his name to Cornell. Why would he do that?"

"Who the hell knows? Maybe he liked the school since he lived near it."

"When did he change his name?"

"A couple of years ago."

"What was his real last name?"

"Matthews. He was born Ryan Matthews."

The girl was quiet for a moment. "That sounds a little familiar. I've heard that name before." She pursed her lips.

"You knew a Ryan Matthews?" Alex glanced quickly at his passenger.

"No. Just the name Matthews. But I can't remember where I heard it." For several minutes, they sat silently as Jillian tried to retrieve the hazy memory. "Sorry," she finally said, shaking her head. "It's not coming back to me. Just go on with your story and maybe I'll remember...Who are we going to see?"

"Ryan told you he had an Aunt Mary, right?"

"Yes. He said his father's sister, Aunt Mary, raised him."

"Well, at least this one's fairly close. It's actually Aunt Marie and it's his mother's sister."

"Then her last name wasn't Cornell."

"No it isn't."

"She's not dead?" Jillian asked, her eyes widening.

Alex gave her a quick dimpled smile. "Ryan's aunt's name is Marie Notto and she's very much alive. In fact, she's who we're driving to see today."

They were both quiet as Jillian processed Ryan's latest lie. "How much did you tell her?" she asked, breaking the silence.

"Nothing really. I just said that I was an investigator working on a case and I had some questions about her nephew."

"Does she know Ryan's missing and the police think I killed him?"

Alex shook his head. "I don't think she knows about any of the shit that's been going on down here. She didn't ask so I didn't tell."

"You didn't mention that I was coming along?"

"Uh-uh. Just said it was important that I talk to her as soon as possible. She agreed and we set a date for today at one o'clock. It's about a four hour drive, so even with a stop for lunch—gotta be a Burger King along the way—we'll be okay."

After taking a deep breath, Jillian leaned back in the seat. "This should be really interesting. We'll finally hear some true stuff about Ryan."

"Yup." The detective nodded.

"Maybe I'll find out why he hates me so much."

"Don't count on it. Our mystery man's a very complex character. His aunt might not have all the answers."

"So you're not married?" Jillian asked, sipping a Coke as she sat opposite Alex in a rural Burger King.

"You see any ring here?" he said, waving his left hand in front of her face. "I'm just another lonely single guy looking for the right girl—someone sweet and cute, kinda like you."

"Oh." Jillian, feeling her face reddening, lowered her head.

"Shit! I've done it again. I'm sorry. But, hey, you asked me."

"You're right." She looked up, smiling weakly. "I've got to stop being so sensitive. Let's talk about something else...So why'd you decide to become a private eye?"

Alex finished chewing a bite of his Whopper. "Always loved those old detective shows on TV. When I was a kid, I used to sit and watch hours and hours of 'Colombo' and 'Magnum' reruns till my parents pulled me away. Drove them freakin' nuts." He smiled his charming dimpled grin.

She returned his smile. "Was it just you or do you have any brothers or sisters?"

"I got both—a younger brother and sister."

"Are you close with your family?"

He shook his head. "Not really, mostly because none of them live near here. They're all back in the Chicago area—and I've been on the East Coast for five years."

"That's too bad," she said, examining her drink and twisting the straw. "If I had any family, I'd want to live near them, I think."

"Yeah. It sucks that you lost your folks when you were so young. You said you were three when they were killed. Right?"

"Close. I was only two."

"And your grandparents raised you?"

"Yes." She nodded. "My father's parents."

He eyed her compassionately and lowered his voice. "You look so serious now. Was it that tough for you growing up?"

Jillian examined her hands. "I never felt like they loved me." She raised her head and shrugged. "Maybe they did, but if they loved me, they never told me, and they didn't hug or kiss me very much."

"They could've just not been emotional people," he suggested. "You know, the kind that don't show much, but deep inside, they really do care."

"Yeah, I guess." She gazed directly into Alex's deep blue eyes. "But my parents used to hug and kiss me all the time. Even though I was little, I remember that very well." She wiped her eyes, which were beginning to tear. "Sorry. I shouldn't do the self-pity thing. Other people have much worse childhoods. At least I had a clean home and food and clothing..."

"Wow." Still speaking softly, he interrupted the girl. "A home, food, and clothing—what a bonanza." He reached across the table and gently squeezed her hand.

They finished eating lunch without further conversation. Then, after leaving the restaurant, Alex continued driving along Interstate 86/Route 17 towards Ithaca.

# CHAPTER 10

Alex and Jillian were fifteen minutes early when they reached Marie Notto's house. "Let's give it a try," the detective said, parking in front of the imposing dark gray Victorian and stepping out of the Corolla. "See if she's home. The lady knows we've had a long drive and if, for some reason, she's not able to talk to us yet, she can just tell us to come back later."

The duo walked up the stone path, neatly lined with small boxwood bushes, and Alex rang the doorbell. They waited, hearing no movement inside.

"Do you think she forgot?" Jillian asked anxiously.

"Sure hope not," he said, this time banging heavily on the door. "But we are early and she didn't seem like a ditz on the phone."

They heard footsteps quickly approaching the entrance, followed by a woman's voice calling, "Yes?"

"Ms. Notto, it's Alex Drury. I spoke to you yesterday and we have an appointment for one o'clock. I'm a little early."

"Oh, right," the woman said, unlocking the door and opening it. "The investigator."

Jillian and Alex faced an attractive brunette in her late sixties, wearing a ponytail and a burgundy smock covered with paint stains.

"Just trying to get some work in before our meeting," Marie Notto said, pointing to her clothing. "Give me a minute to wash up and change." After smiling at Jillian, she turned to Alex. "What a nice surprise. You didn't tell me you were bringing a pretty young lady with you."

"Ms. Notto," the detective said, gesturing towards Jillian. "I'd like you to meet my client, Jillian Keating."

The woman's smile immediately vanished and she stared at Jillian for a long awkward moment before grasping the girl's outstretched hand. Then she shook her head. "Forgive me. I'm being rude keeping the two of you standing out here after your long drive." She opened the door and waved them inside. "Come on in and sit down and make yourselves comfy. I'll be right back."

Jillian and Alex walked into a spacious living room, which was sparsely furnished with only a round glass table flanked by a mauve couch and two pale blue wing chairs, all with muted floral designs. However, the walls were covered with Impressionist-style landscapes—a flower-filled meadow, a farm with grazing cows, a sunlit pond surrounded by trees and bushes.

"Why did she look at me like that?" Jillian whispered to Alex as they sat next to each other on the flowery couch.

"I don't know. She smiled when she first saw you. But then when she heard your name..."

"How did she recognize my name? I don't know her and I've never been anywhere near here."

Alex patted the girl's hand and smiled at her. "Don't worry about it. That's what you hired me to do, to find out the answers."

Marie Notto returned wearing a plain navy tee shirt and jeans and faced her visitors. "Can I get you some coffee or soda, or something else to drink?"

"Nothing for me," Alex said. "We just ate."

"I'm fine too," Jillian said, smiling at Ryan's aunt.

"Nice paintings." The private eye pointed to the decorated walls. "Your work?"

The woman nodded. "Thank you. I use my home as an art gallery and hope my guests don't mind too much."

"They shouldn't," Jillian said, gazing at the colorful landscapes. "The paintings are so lovely, very calming and peaceful."

The artist sat on the blue wing chair opposite the couch and crossed her arms. "Okay, enough small talk. You two didn't come all the way out here to chat about my paintings. Now what's this all about?"

"Did you know that your nephew, Ryan, is missing?" Alex asked.

Marie frowned. "Missing? What do you mean?"

"Ryan disappeared nearly two weeks ago," the investigator said, nodding at Jillian. "He told Miss Keating that he was going away for a couple of days and he never came back."

The woman was quiet for a moment. Then, looking at Jillian, she spoke very softly. "Can I ask what your relationship is with my nephew?"

The girl lowered her head and whispered, "We were living together. He was my boyfriend."

"Your boyfriend?" Marie exclaimed. "This is unbelievable!" When she noticed her visitors' perplexed expressions, she stood up. "Don't you know who Ryan is?" she asked Jillian.

"Huh?"

The artist sat down, shaking her head. "No. I guess you don't." She turned towards the girl. "You didn't recognize the name Ryan Matthews?"

"Alex just told me today in the car that Ryan's real name was Matthews. I only knew him as Ryan Cornell. But Matthews sounded familiar somehow. I couldn't remember why."

Marie gave her a sympathetic smile. "Maybe you didn't want to remember," she whispered. "Your parents died in a car crash when you were just a little girl. It must have been terrible for you."

"How did you know that?" Jillian asked, her voice nearly inaudible.

"When Mr. Drury introduced you, I heard your name."

"But what does this have to do with Ryan?" The girl shook her head. "I'm sorry, but I don't understand."

Marie reached over, grasped Jillian's hand, and held it. "The car crash that killed your parents? It killed another two people, also a husband and wife. Their names were Linda and Stuart..."

"...Matthews." Jillian finished the woman's sentence. "Oh my God, that's why the name sounded familiar. It was the name of the couple in the other car." She removed her hand from the woman's grip and looked at her with an expression of sheer horror. "You mean that Ryan..."

Marie nodded sadly. "My sister, Linda, and Stuart Matthews were Ryan's parents. They died in the same terrible accident." She leaned against the chair and turned to the detective. "This can't be just a coincidence, Miss Keating and Ryan."

"No. It's not a coincidence at all. I think this is part of a complex scheme put together by your nephew."

"It's not fair!" Jillian shouted. "He told me they died in a fire!" She jumped up and ran out the front door.

Alex immediately leaped off the couch, saying a quick, "Excuse me" to Marie as he rushed after Jillian. When he reached her, the girl was standing next to his car, sobbing heavily. Alex put both arms around his client and hugged her tightly. "Hey," he said softly. "What's so terrible about this latest news? You know everything Ryan told you about himself was a lie so this stuff shouldn't be such a big deal."

"You...don't...under...stand." She spoke haltingly between sobs.

"I'm getting the picture." He held her shoulders, gently caressing them. "Ryan must've mistakenly blamed your folks for his parents' deaths and that's why he did all this."

Jillian pulled away from the private eye's grasp, gazed at him, tears still streaming down her cheeks, and nodded solemnly. "Yes. I'm sure he did blame them—and he's right."

"What the hell are you talking about?"

She leaned against the car and closed her eyes. "The accident— it was all my parents' fault." Then, opening her teary eyes, she looked at him and spoke very quietly. "My parents were coming home from a party at a friend's house. They both had a lot to drink. My father was driving, and maybe he was talking to my mother or laughing or something, but he wasn't watching the road. He went through a red light and he hit the other car at full speed."

"Okay, so it was your father's fault," Alex agreed, nodding at Jillian. "But the accident happened a long time ago—and you had nothing to do with it. Ryan can't blame you."

"Why not?" The girl focused on the ground. "I blame me."

The detective took her hands and held them as he pronounced his words slowly and carefully. "Jillian, please listen to me. This is nuts. You didn't do anything to hurt Ryan or his parents. That accident was not your fault. You weren't even there. Shit! You were just two-years-old!"

She pulled away from Alex again and shook her head vigorously. "My grandparents blamed my parents. I know they did. I could see it in their eyes. And whenever they looked at me, I could tell they were ashamed—of me, of my parents, of themselves. It was like I always reminded them of what happened." She continued to stare at the wheels of the Corolla. "That's why they didn't love me, because of what my father did."

Gently, the detective began guiding the girl towards Marie Notto's house. "You're all mixed up about this, but this isn't the time to straighten it out. Now we've got to go back in there and talk to Ryan's aunt. She might know some other stuff about him that'll help us." He stopped walking and glanced at Jillian. She was no longer crying, but her eyes were red and puffy. "If you don't feel like you can talk about this, just sit quietly and listen, and let me ask the questions."

"Okay," she whispered. "I'll try."

Alex and Jillian again sat on Marie Notto's mauve couch. "Sorry about that," the detective said. "Miss Keating had no idea Ryan's parents had been killed in the same car wreck. Ryan must have changed his last name so that she wouldn't recognize it."

The woman nodded sympathetically at Jillian. "I'm really sorry. I didn't mean to upset you like that. Ryan told you his parents died in a fire?"

"Yes," she said, staring at her lap.

"Ms. Notto, Ryan lied to my client about everything," Alex continued. "He took an art class so he could meet her and said he was a graphic artist. He told her he was in love with her and convinced her to move in with him. On May 6th, he started a fight and told her he was leaving for a few days. And then he disappeared."

"Why would he do all that?" Marie asked.

"So he could get Miss Keating arrested for his murder."

"What?" The woman held onto the chair and leaned forward. "What are you talking about?"

"That's why I said this was all part of Ryan's plan. He wrote a letter saying if he didn't show up for a meeting with his lawyer on May 9th, a week ago Monday, Jillian had killed him."

Marie stared at Alex incredulously.

"He had convinced Miss Keating to take out a large life insurance policy on him so that it'd look like she had a motive."

"This is unreal," the woman said, shaking her head.

"And there's more. During the so-called fight, Ryan cut his hand and smeared his blood inside Jillian's trunk. The police arrested her. She's out on bail right now."

The artist stood and began pacing back and forth in her living room. "He was always strange, right from the beginning. When he and Danielle came to live with me..."

"Danielle?" Jillian interrupted, looking up wide-eyed. "Oh my God, that's right. There were two children in the back of the car my parents hit. Ryan had a sister."

Marie nodded. "Ryan *has* a sister. Danielle's three years older and she never was a problem."

"But Ryan was," the investigator said, taking a notepad and pen from his pants pocket.

"Yes." The woman folded her arms and gazed at her colorful walls. "He was a difficult child."

"In what way?" Alex asked as he began writing.

"A very angry boy," Marie said, shaking her head. "It was a horrible accident and he was in the car with his sister and parents. I think the children were asleep in the backseat when it happened so they didn't see anything. But losing his parents affected Ryan deeply, much more than his sister."

"Any reason why?"

The woman sat down, put her hands in her lap, and faced the detective. "Ryan was a special child, very bright and talented. Spoiled too, especially by his father. Always the center of attention. It was hard for him to move up here, live in this quiet rural area with me, his eccentric artist aunt who he hardly knew."

"How did Ryan show his anger?" Alex asked as he continued to take notes.

"He was always scowling, unhappy—no matter what I did." Marie shrugged. "Danielle came out of it very quickly. She was a sweet, loving girl, but Ryan..."

"Did you try to get any help for him?"

The woman nodded. "He saw a psychiatrist for six months, but it didn't do anything. The doctor could never get Ryan to talk, to open up and let his anger out."

"Did he have any friends in school?"

"Not really. He was always a loner. Kept to himself. Read a lot. The only person he was close to was his sister."

"Did he do well in school?"

Marie smirked. "With his I.Q., he should have. But, no, he never worked, so he didn't get top marks."

"He changed his name to Cornell, but I'm guessing that he didn't go to college there."

"No. He wanted to. But with his grades, he couldn't get in so he went to Cortland, about twenty minutes from here."

"What did Ryan do for a living? He told Miss Keating he was an artist, but I figure that was another lie."

Marie chuckled. "Now here's the funny thing: He didn't do anything. Imagine that, a smart person like him who didn't want to work."

The detective lowered his pen and looked at her. "Then where'd he get the money to live on?" he asked.

Jillian, who had been following the conversation between Alex and Ryan's aunt without participating, now spoke. "I think I know the answer to that," she said quietly. "From the settlement from the accident." She turned to Marie. "Right?"

"Yes." The woman nodded. "Ryan got access to the money when he reached twenty-one and I'm sure he's been spending it."

"How much money are we talking about?" the investigator asked.

"Each of the children got five million," Marie said.

"Whoo!" Alex inhaled loudly. "Should've been enough to keep him lazy for a long time."

"I'm not so sure," the artist said, shaking her head. "Ryan likes to live well."

"When was the last time you spoke to him?"

Marie paused before answering. "I haven't spoken to Ryan for a long time. I didn't like the way he was wasting away his life and told him so. Of course, he didn't want to hear it. I think the last time

I talked to him was about five years ago."

Alex turned the notebook page. "You said Ryan was close to his sister. Do you think they keep in touch?"

"Probably."

"Does his sister live around here?"

"Yes. Just a few minutes north."

The private eye gazed directly at Ryan's aunt. "Do you think she'd be willing to talk to us?"

"I'm sure she would. If you'd like, I can call her and see if she's available now."

"Thanks. That would be great."

Marie walked into the kitchen and returned a couple of minutes later. "I'm sorry," she said, again sitting on the blue chair. "No answer. I tried her cell phone too."

"That's okay," the detective said, flipping his notebook to a blank page and handing the pad to the woman. "Could you give me Danielle's number and let her know I'll be calling?"

"Sure." She smiled at Alex and Jillian and scribbled a phone number on the page. "Danielle's nothing like Ryan. You'll like her."

Alex tucked the notebook into his pants pocket and stood up. "Thanks for everything, Ms. Notto. You've given us both a lot to digest. It's been very helpful." Then, reaching into his wallet, he pulled out a business card, which he gave to her. "Just in case you do hear from him."

Ryan's aunt took the card and nodded. "I'm glad I helped." She turned to Jillian, who was still sitting. "Miss Keating, I'm terribly sorry Ryan did this to you. But that accident happened so long ago and it had nothing to do with you."

"That's what I've been trying to tell her," Alex said as he continued towards the front door.

"You said Ryan's disappeared. Do you have any idea where he's hiding?" Marie asked.

The investigator glanced at Jillian, who had finally risen from the couch. "Actually, yes, we do have a clue about that. Now we've just got to find him."

"So Ryan really likes money," Alex said as he began the long drive back to Southvale.

"Yeah, and he really doesn't like me." Jillian sat next to the detective, her arms folded, pouting and studying her lap.

"You've got to give it up," the investigator said, glancing at his sullen passenger. "You heard what his aunt said. The guy's nuts— psychopathic even. He doesn't like anyone."

"But he hates me enough to stage this elaborate production just to punish me for what my father did."

"Yes. That's probably true. But I don't think it's the only reason..."

"Why else?"

"I think Ryan's found an easy way to make money."

"What do you mean?"

"Think about it: Someone is able to go back into time. The person doesn't even have to go back very far, just far enough to know a few things that have already happened. It's a no-brainer way to get rich quick."

Jillian sat quietly, digesting Alex's words. Suddenly, she understood what he was talking about. "You mean like the lottery?"

"Bingo!" He pointed at her with his right hand. "And that's not the only way. Ryan could make money on horse races or the stock market too. But I think lotto's the easiest, and from what we've just learned about your boyfriend..."

"Stop calling him 'my boyfriend'!" she said angrily. "It keeps reminding me of how stupid I was."

"Okay, sorry. From what we've learned about Mr. Cornell, he's smart, but very lazy, and people like that always choose the easiest way."

"What're you going to do next?" Jillian asked Alex between bites of her grilled chicken sandwich.

"Gonna call Ryan's sister and work out a time to see her," the investigator replied as he chomped on his Whopper. On the way home, they had stopped at yet another Burger King for an early dinner. "Got any preference as to when we go? I want you to come with me again—and Helene too."

"Try to make it Saturday or Sunday, please. I'd rather not have to take more time off from work, if possible."

"I'll try. I'll call her tomorrow morning to set something up. Should be interesting." He shoved another chunk of burger into his mouth.

The girl glanced at her plate dejectedly.

"What's wrong?"

She shook her head. "I've been such a jerk. You must hate me."

"Why would I hate you?"

"Because I was so dumb, letting Ryan take advantage of me, playing right into his hands like that. What a moron I was." She nodded at him. "But now I'm getting really mad that he used me like that."

Alex pointed the remnants of his Whopper at her. "And don't forget the most important thing: The accident wasn't your fault."

Jillian was quiet for a moment. "I'm trying to convince myself of that," she finally whispered. "But I've spent most of my life thinking it was."

"So where'd you go to school?" Alex asked Jillian as they continued their long ride back to northern Westchester.

"You mean college?"

"Yeah. I went to Michigan. How about you?"

She glanced at the investigator. "How old do you think I am?"

"Twenty-three?"

Jillian shook her head. "People always think I'm older than I really am. I'm only nineteen."

"Really?" He snuck a quick peek at her.

"Yeah and my grandparents never had much money so I just went to community college last year. I had to work as a waitress even to get enough money to pay for that. Then after my grandmother died, I needed a full-time job."

He shook his head. "Tough break."

"It was, but I try to read a lot and take courses at night. I'm through with the self-pity. And that's enough talk about the past." She stared at Alex. "Let's get back to the present. So how're we going to find Ryan?"

"His aunt said Ryan was real close with his sister so I'm hoping she'll be able to give us some more insight into the shithead. I want to get a better picture of him so that we can come up with a plan."

"How're we ever going to catch him if he's somewhere in the past?" She sighed deeply. "It's impossible."

"No. It's not impossible. He's smart, but he's not that smart. There's always a way."

"You're just saying that?"

"No. I really mean it." He pounded the steering wheel with his left hand. "I know we can find him. I'm not saying it'll be simple, but nothing's impossible."

They rode in silence for several minutes, each thinking about the obstacles ahead. "I wonder if there's a way to get to an exact time in the past," Jillian finally said.

"I don't know." Alex shrugged. "In my one experience last week with you, it sure didn't seem like a very precise way to travel."

"Not to the exact minute. But maybe we can go back to a specific day, say three or four months ago."

The private eye glanced at her and grinned. "You planning to go for another whirl in the woods?"

"Yeah," she said, returning his smile. "I'm taking Helene there on Friday so I'll try to pick a certain day to go back to and see how close I can come."

"Sounds like lots of spinning. You'd better warn Helene to be prepared to be dizzy." He chuckled. "Hope she doesn't suffer from vertigo."

"And this time I'm bringing a flashlight with me, just in case." Jillian squirmed in her seat. "I guess I have to tell you what happened when I went back early Sunday morning."

The detective frowned. "I thought we agreed that weekends are a bad time to take the trail because of all the people in the park. Someone could have seen you."

"I know. But the weather was bad Sunday morning and I went really early, before seven, so nobody was around."

"Still, you could have been seen."

"Well, I wasn't."

"And you needed a flashlight because you ended up in nighttime?"

"No, twilight. But it was a cloudy day so I couldn't tell. When I found out how late it was, I had to rush and buy a flashlight or I would have been stuck there overnight."

"Is that when you got that scratch on your face? Did a branch sideswipe you?"

Jillian sat quietly, not answering Alex's question.

"So if it wasn't a branch that scratched your pretty face, how'd it happen?" he continued.

"A couple of drunks saw me when I was looking for the Post-It to go back," she whispered.

"What?" Alex exclaimed.

"It was okay. I hit one of them with my flashlight and the other guy tried to grab me, but he only got my face. Then I ran into the woods and they were both too drunk to follow me."

Alex glanced at his passenger. "You could've been really hurt. You gotta promise that you won't try this again—going back there by yourself."

"Okay," she said quietly. "I promise."

They didn't talk for several minutes. "How far back did you go?" Alex finally asked.

"Over a month to early April."

"What did you do differently?"

"Well I spun around much longer—and I went back into the wind tunnel five times."

He considered Jillian's words before speaking. "So you're calculating that each long spin brought you back about a week in time?"

"Something like that."

"Without using a watch, how do you expect to go back to a more exact time?"

"I'm not really sure yet. But when I'm spinning, maybe I can just try to count."

"Not the most scientific travel plan," the detective said, smiling. "But right now, it's all we've got."

# CHAPTER 11

Ryan Cornell locked the door of his garden apartment and began his walk to the card shop on Flanders Street. It was a fairly long distance—about a mile and a half—but he didn't mind. Ryan loved to walk. The weather was frigid and windy so he zipped his jacket all the way to his neck, put on a pair of woolen gloves, and covered his head with a New York Yankees cap.

Today—Thursday, February 3—he was wearing what he called his "sports fan" clothes—baseball cap, sweatpants, and long-sleeve Yankees jersey, embroidered with the team logo. A shaggy dark-brown wig and wire glasses completed the look, one of his favorites.

He figured he probably didn't need such elaborate disguises, but Ryan couldn't risk being recognized. Anyway, he enjoyed playing various parts. Acting was another of his pleasures.

He walked the familiar Southvale streets until he reached the small greeting card store, located in the middle of a row of specialty shops. After opening the door, he rushed to the register and smiled at the clerk, feigning excitement. "Hey, guess what? That Numbers ticket I bought yesterday, it was a winner." Ryan reached into his pocket and handed the lottery ticket to the young man, who was probably of Indian or Pakistani heritage.

The clerk inserted the sheet into the lottery register, smiled, and nodded his head. "Number 358—a straight play match. Congratulations, my friend! You are a winner!"

Opening the cash drawer, the man counted out the money. "Here you are—two hundred and fifty dollars," he said, handing the bills to Ryan. "Not bad for just fifty cents." The brown-skinned clerk waved his forefinger in reproach. "But you should have played the number for one dollar. Then you would have won double—five hundred dollars."

"Yeah. You're right," Ryan said, putting the money in his pocket. "Hey, next time, if I feel lucky, maybe that's what I'll do." He grinned at the clerk and left the store.

Ryan continued smiling as he walked home, having completed the second part of his brief workday. Earlier that morning, wearing another disguise (blond surfer-dude wig and floppy mustache), he had purchased another winning lottery ticket at a gas station mini-mart.

His aunt had always complained that he didn't work. *Well, Aunt Marie, now I'm working.* Okay, so maybe it wasn't a traditional kind of job, one that she—or most people—would approve of. But the money was damn good. *Just don't be greedy,* he reminded himself.

With his knowledge of all the past winning lottery numbers, Ryan could make as much money as he wanted. He just had to be careful. He didn't want to be a really big winner for two important reasons: He'd be conspicuous and they'd need his personal information for tax purposes. Before going back in time, he'd researched the winning payoffs and limited himself to playing Numbers, Take Five, Sweet Million, Mega Millions, Powerball, and Pick 10, each time winning between $150 to no more than $500. He avoided playing Lotto and Win Four because the prizes were either too large or too small.

In his "job," Ryan rotated between numerous lottery outlets—thirteen so far—all within his walking distance. In the nearly two weeks he'd been living in the past, he had created new disguise combinations for each day and was always coming up with additional ones. Some of his income had gone into clothes for his characters.

He grinned, thinking how strange his closet must look. "But no one's searching it," he murmured. In February—the time he was living in now—Ryan wasn't even missing. And when it became May here and he did disappear, as long as he remained careful, no one would ever find him. Also, a few months after that, no one would be looking for him anymore. They'd assume he was dead and Jillian had killed him.

But after time here caught up with his disappearance, Ryan knew he'd have to make a quick trip to the present. First of all, he'd need a new batch of winning lottery numbers. He'd also want to check Jillian's status—find out when she was being tried, and then sentenced—hopefully put in jail for a very long time. Her father had gotten away with murder, but his daughter would be punished. "Jillian ruined my life and now she must pay," he muttered.

Ryan reached the small garden apartment complex and turned his head in all directions. He didn't want people to notice him coming and going in his various disguises. Seeing no one, he quickly walked to his ground-floor unit, unlocked the door, and entered.

He went directly to his bedroom closet, removed a briefcase from the top shelf, and aligned the three-digit combination. He opened the case, putting most of his latest earnings inside. Then, after locking it, he replaced the briefcase carefully on top of the closet.

Now Ryan was ready for the rest of his day. The choice was up to him; he could do anything he wanted. Today, he had decided to see a movie—a sci-fi adventure—in Mohegan Lake, a nearby town. He planned to find a good restaurant there and eat lunch first.

He regretted abandoning his car. But a dead man couldn't be seen driving the BMW. When he had traveled back to January, he had checked the auto ads and quickly purchased a cheap used Honda Civic from a college kid. Of course, he had paid cash. He wasn't using any credit cards here.

He also wasn't Ryan Cornell. Before going back in time, he had obtained a forged license and ID so, if anyone asked, he was now Bradley Maxwell. That's the name he had used to sign the papers for his car, as well as for the apartment, which he was renting monthly. Bradley Maxwell was another part for Ryan—and he was enjoying this play immensely.

After taking off the baseball cap, wig, and glasses and changing into Brad Maxwell's normal preppy look—jeans and crew-neck sweater—he left the apartment and drove to Mohegan Lake, ready to begin his leisure-filled afternoon.

# CHAPTER 12

"Jillian Keating, please pick up line three!"

When she heard the law firm receptionist's announcement late Friday morning, Jillian rushed out of the file room and reached for the nearest desk phone.

The caller was Alex. "I just spoke to Danielle, Ryan's sister," he said. "Her aunt had told her I'd be calling and she was fine with us coming up to talk to her. You ready for another road trip? I checked with Helene first and she said okay."

"Sure. When're we going?"

"Danielle said anytime tomorrow afternoon was good and I'm getting Helene at nine forty-five, so how about I pick you up at ten? Give you a little more time to sleep."

"That's fine. Thanks."

"Good. Helene said you've got a trip scheduled with her this afternoon."

"Yes. I'm finally going to show her you-know-what."

The private eye chuckled. "That oughta be real interesting. You and Helene can tell me all about it when we're in the car tomorrow. We'll have lots of time to talk."

"Sounds good. I'll see you tomorrow morning then."

"Yup. Bye."

"I'm really curious about all of this," Helene said as Jillian drove the two of them to the park in her rental Ford. "I know tomorrow we're visiting the sister Ryan wasn't supposed to have, but can you at least tell me where we're going now?"

"Sure. We're heading to Juniper Park and we're almost there." She glanced at the lawyer and smiled. "Did you remember to bring a jacket or sweatshirt? It could get pretty cold later."

"What are you talking about?" Helene asked, shaking her head. "It's late May and about seventy-five degrees outside. Just how 'cold' can it get in an hour or two?"

"You'd be surprised. Do you have a jacket?"

"A sweatshirt. I threw it in the backseat."

"Good." Jillian glanced at her passenger again. "And I see you're wearing jeans and sneakers like I asked."

"Yes. I changed at work. What're we going to do in the park?"

"Go for a little hike."

"This is what's so important that you had to show me: a hike in a park?"

"Yes. That's what we're doing this afternoon. We're going for a hike."

After parking the car, Jillian opened the rear door and took out Helene's sweatshirt and her own jacket. Then, lifting the trunk, she removed the large flashlight she had bought on her previous trip to the past.

"What're you doing now?" Helene asked, wrapping the sweatshirt around her waist and eying the flashlight.

"Just being prepared." Jillian wedged the flashlight into her pants pocket and tossed her pocketbook into the trunk.

"It's only late afternoon," the lawyer said. "It won't be dark for another four hours. Just how long a hike are you taking me on? I worked all day and I'm a lot older than you so I'm not in any kind of shape to walk a marathon."

"It's not that long a walk. Don't worry." The girl pointed to the open trunk and smiled. "Go ahead and put your bag in here. You won't be comfortable carrying it in the woods."

Helene unzipped her handbag and removed a couple of items that she quickly shoved into her jeans pocket. Then she handed the pocketbook to Jillian, who dropped it into the trunk and slammed the lid shut.

The lawyer stared at her client, shaking her head. "You're acting very strangely, just like you did in my office earlier this week."

"Be patient," Jillian said, walking towards the little mountain trail. "Very soon you'll understand everything."

Jillian led Helene up the path, moving briskly. They met just one other hiker, an older man who nodded and hurried past them. When the pair reached the first clearing, the lawyer immediately lowered herself onto the large broken log. "I hope we don't have to go much further," she said, breathing heavily. "I haven't done this much walking in a long time."

"Don't you exercise?"

Helene shrugged. "Not really. I'm too busy at work and, when I'm off, I just like to chill."

After looking in all directions to make sure no one was nearby, Jillian separated the large pile of sticks and leaves.

"What're you doing?"

Anxiously, the girl motioned to the lawyer. "C'mon, quickly, before someone comes. We've got to crawl through this. We can talk later."

"The mystery continues. Glad I'm wearing old jeans...You first." After Jillian climbed through the opening, Helene squatted on her knees and clumsily followed.

Jillian restacked the leaves and sticks while Helene stood up, brushed the dirt off her clothes, and surveyed the surroundings. She immediately noticed the hollow tilted trunk. "That's some huge log."

"Yeah," the girl agreed as she began removing the branches and leaves she had stuffed inside the log's cavity. "It sure is."

Helene walked over to join her. "Why are we doing this?" she asked as she pulled out chunks of debris.

"You'll understand everything very soon." When she had cleared the opening, Jillian stood up straight. "Okay," she announced. "We're ready."

"Ready for what?"

Ignoring Helene's question, the girl pointed to her watch. "What time do you have?"

"Why? Isn't your watch working?"

"It's working fine. I just want to know if yours is."

The lawyer looked at her wrist. "I've got four twenty-five."

After checking her watch, Jillian smiled. "So do I."

"All right. Now we both know the correct time. What next?"

The girl pointed to the opening in the log. "Next we climb through here."

Helene stared at her. "You've got to be kidding."

"Not at all. We're going into the trunk headfirst and when you get to the other end, we're going to do everything together. Okay?"

The woman exhaled deeply. "Okay—but I don't understand what the heck you're talking about."

"Don't worry. You will."

After lowering her body into the hollow log, Jillian again heard the whooshing sound of the wind even before she reached the cave on the other side. When she wriggled out of the log, she waited for Helene to emerge. "C'mon," Jillian said, gently pulling the lawyer towards the cave's opening.

Helene entered the clearing and gazed wide-eyed at the whirlwind, still swirling in place. "What is that thing?" she yelled. "It looks like some kind of miniature tornado!"

"It's much more than that!" Jillian called as she moved next to the woman. "Like I said, we're going to hold hands now and dive into the funnel. If we get separated, go back through the spinning wind to the side of the cave with the hollow log. Ready?" She reached for Helene's hand.

The lawyer pointed to the swirling wind. "Why on earth do we have to spin around in that?" she asked.

"You've got to trust me on this. I'll explain later. Please!"

"I just hope you know what you're doing." Helene grasped Jillian's outstretched hand and allowed the girl to throw both of them into the small cyclone.

As they spun, Jillian counted slowly to a hundred. Then she tossed herself and the lawyer out of the whirlwind and they both landed opposite the cave.

"Did we have to be in that spinning thing for so long?" Helene asked, sitting up and holding on to the ground with both hands. "Now I'm really dizzy."

"Sorry, Helene. But we've got to go back into that wind tunnel seven more times and each time I'm counting to one hundred before I toss us out."

"Why are you doing that?" the lawyer asked, a look of confusion covering her face. "What's going on here?"

"Just be patient till we're finished and then, I promise, everything will be perfectly clear."

Jillian took Helene's hand and continued twirling in the wind tunnel. After one of the spins, they landed in total darkness.

"Are we getting a thunderstorm?" Helene asked.

"Maybe." Jillian switched on her flashlight and rushed the lawyer back into the spiral before she could ask any more questions.

When they had completed eight lengthy spins, the girl threw both of them to the ground and they crept away from the spinning funnel.

Helene lay on the ground and didn't stir. "That's it, right?" she asked. "We're done? We better be because I'm too dizzy to take any more." She started to sit up, but immediately fell down again. "I hope you're not in any hurry to continue this wacky hike because I really can't move yet."

Jillian clutched her knees, trying to regain her equilibrium. "No. That's okay. We can stay here until we're both ready to walk the rest of the way down the mountain. And while we're waiting, look at your watch. Is it working?"

Still lying on her back, Helene lifted her arm and gazed at her left wrist. "No." She frowned. "It says just past four thirty, but that can't be right." With great effort, she managed to sit up and face Jillian. "You knew this would happen. Is it because of the wind?"

"Yes. That's a very powerful wind." She smiled at the lawyer. "Much more than you realize."

After their dizziness had subsided, Jillian and Helene wiped the dirt off their bodies and continued walking along the tiny trail that led down the mountain.

"Feels cooler here, doesn't it?" the girl asked, unwrapping her jacket and slipping her arms through the sleeves.

"Yeah," Helene agreed as she hurriedly put on her sweatshirt. "It sure does. Temperature must've dropped more than fifteen degrees. How'd you know that would happen?"

"You'll see." Jillian smiled again, enjoying the lawyer's confusion.

When the two of them reached the end of the path, they cleared away branches and stepped out of the trees and into the park. The girl glanced at the landscape and pointed to a section of woods. "Look over there. Don't some of those trees look like their leaves have changed colors? Yes! And a couple of them are even bare."

The lawyer followed Jillian's finger and shrugged. "Must be some kind of tree disease."

"Perhaps." She touched the woman's shoulder. "Wait here for a second, Helene. I just want to check something." Jillian looked at the area around the entrance to the trail, but saw no yellow Post-It in the ground. Then, quickly, she scanned the trunks of nearby trees facing the woods. No notch on any of them. She had gone even further back in time than Ryan. She took out another yellow sticky paper and wedged it into the dirt.

"What're you doing?"

"Marking this little trail so we can find it again."

"Why's that so important? We can always walk back through the park to reach the car." Helene exhaled deeply. "Besides, going through the park sounds like a better idea to me anyway. I'm not sure I'm in condition for another hike in the mountain."

"We have to go back the way we came as you will soon understand."

The woman smiled. "You mean the mystery's almost over?"

"Yes."

When they reached the edge of the park, Jillian pointed across the street. "There's a little deli a couple of blocks that way. Let's go there."

"Good idea," Helene said, hugging her shoulders. "I could use a cup of coffee. It really is cold—and windy too. And it was so dark at one point back there. How could the weather change so drastically? We were only in the woods for less than an hour."

"If you say so." Jillian suppressed a grin.

Jillian and Helene entered the small deli and the lawyer immediately darted to the food counter. "I'm getting my hot coffee." She rubbed her cold hands together. "You want anything?"

"No. I'm fine." Jillian nodded towards the magazines. "I'll just look at today's paper." She headed to the now-familiar lower right-hand shelf, picked up one of the dailies, and checked the date. According to the newspaper, it was Thursday, October 14 of the previous year.

She began calculating how far into the past they had traveled. Today was Friday, May 20 so they had gone back more than seven months. But she had made eight lengthy spins, each approximately one hundred seconds, hoping to arrive at a date close to late September.

When Helene returned, sipping her coffee, Jillian was still in deep thought, holding the newspaper. "Ah," the lawyer said. "That feels good. I was really freezing out there bef...." When she noticed the girl's serious expression, she altered her words in mid-sentence. "Why are you frowning? Is something wrong?"

"No, not really. I'm just trying to figure something out." She placed the paper on the shelf and turned to the lawyer. "Okay, now we're going to talk, but close your coffee first."

"Why?"

"I don't want you to choke."

"Why would I choke?"

"You might get upset."

After putting the lid on her hot coffee, Helene looked at Jillian. "The never-ending mystery continues. All right, I'm ready. Shoot."

"Look at the newspapers, Helene." The girl waved her hand over the shelf. "What's the date on all the daily papers?"

The lawyer studied the piles of newspapers and then faced Jillian. "This makes no sense," she whispered. "They all say Thursday, October 14 of last year. What's going on here? Is this some kind of a trick—or are you trying to make a joke?"

The girl shook her head. "No trick or joke. Now I want you to listen to this." She addressed the cashier. "Excuse me. My watch has stopped. Do you have the right time, please?"

"Yeah." The man glanced at his wrist and then looked up. "It's five to three."

"Thanks."

Helene stared at Jillian. "That time can't be right." She gazed at her arm. "Our watches stopped at about four thirty."

"Let's go outside." She took the lawyer's hand and led the dazed woman out of the deli.

They stood in front of the shop while Jillian waited for her companion to recover. "This makes no sense," Helene repeated, shaking her head. "It's absolutely impossible."

"I don't understand how this could happen either. But it's a fact. We're back in last October." The girl looked in both directions and noticed a middle-aged man in a navy suit, carrying an attaché case, approaching them. "You want more proof? I'll ask him."

Jillian smiled at the businessman. "Can you tell me the correct time?" She pointed to her watch and shrugged. "It suddenly stopped."

"Sure." The man lifted his left arm and gazed at his wrist. "It's exactly two minutes after three."

"And today is Thursday, October...?" Jillian paused and waited.

"It's the fourteenth," he said, filling in the date.

As the businessman continued past them, the girl turned to Helene. "See? The time here's three o'clock and it's October 14th. We're the ones who're out of place."

"I need to sit down." Helene leaned against the storefront.

"Okay," Jillian agreed. "Let's go back to the park and find a bench." They headed for Juniper Park, moving quickly. As they walked, the girl shoved her cold hands into her jacket's pockets. "I don't know how long we'll be able to sit," she said. "It looks like a storm's coming." The sky had blackened, the wind had gained force, and the temperature seemed to have dropped another ten degrees.

As soon as they entered the park and sat on one of the benches, rain, aided by swirling winds, began pelting them. Jillian stood up. "Sorry, Helene, but we can't sit here and talk. I've got a flashlight with me, but no umbrella." She nodded towards the small mountain.

"Like I said before, we've got to go back the way we came. Otherwise, we'll be stuck in the wrong time. C'mon. Let's get out of here before we get soaked and frozen."

Without speaking, the lawyer stood, and, still carrying her closed cup of coffee, followed the girl to the mini-mountain.

At the base of the hill, with heavy rain continuing to fall, Jillian frantically searched for her yellow Post-It. "It's not here!" she cried, turning to Helene, who, with her short gray hair, resembled a wet mop. "This wind must've blown it away."

"What now?" The lawyer stood under a nearby tree, shivering as she tried to keep dry. "You're in charge of this bizarre expedition."

The girl shook her head. "I'm not sure. Without my marker, I don't think I can find the trail in the rain and, I'm afraid if someone sees us in the woods in this weather, it'll look really weird. Do you have any money on you?"

"A little. I shoved my wallet in my pocket. But I mostly use plastic."

"We can't use credit cards and leave a paper trail that we were here. But we're going to need someplace to stay until the rain stops, maybe a cheap motel..."

"Wait a minute," Helene said. "It's the middle of October, right?"

"Thursday, October 14."

"That's Columbus Day week—and I'm in San Francisco."

"You mean the you back then is away?"

"Yeah, a combination business trip, vacation. I come home Saturday night."

"We can stay at your house?" Jillian asked. "Oh shoot. How do we get in? We left our handbags in my trunk."

Helene reached inside her pants pocket and smiled. "I always carry my keys. Come on. Let's get moving before we catch pneumonia. We're going to have to find a cab."

As they stood in the pouring rain outside the park, Jillian and Helene spotted an empty taxi and flagged it down. Twenty minutes later, the cabbie pulled up in front of the lawyer's condo. The meter read $24.80.

"Do you have enough cash?" Jillian whispered.

"I think so." The lawyer opened her wallet and quickly checked. "Yeah. I've got it." They stepped out of the cab and Helene handed the driver thirty-five dollars. "No change." Then, still standing in the rain, she spoke quietly to the bearded man. He nodded, took a pen from his dashboard, and wrote something in a small notebook. Helene stepped back and the cabbie smiled and waved at them before driving away.

"What were you talking to the cab driver about?"

"I arranged for him to pick us up early tomorrow," Helene explained as she guided Jillian towards her condo and they hurried to the door. "We're going to need a ride back to the park. That's why I gave him a big tip and promised him an extra twenty bucks tomorrow."

"Smart move." Jillian stopped and glanced at the row of identical two-story gray-shingled attached houses. "Will anyone notice that you're back home ahead of schedule?"

"No. I'm not real friendly with my neighbors and they're used to seeing me come and go at strange hours." She gave Jillian a gentle shove. "We can talk inside. It's cold and wet out here." She took out her key ring and unlocked the front door.

"First thing we're going to do is get out of these wet, dirty clothes," Helene said, slipping out of her soaked sweatshirt and unlacing her sneakers. "Take everything off so I can put them in the washing machine. I'll go find you a bathrobe." She rushed into her bedroom while Jillian stood in the hallway, water dripping onto the floor as she removed her jacket, jeans, and shirt.

"Underwear too," the lawyer called. She returned wearing

a white terrycloth robe and holding an identical robe, which she handed to Jillian. "Since I'm doing laundry anyway, might as well clean everything."

"Sorry I'm making such a mess." As she put on the robe, the girl stared at the puddle she had made on the floor.

"No problem. That's why I've got ceramic tiles everywhere. Easy to clean." Helene scooped up Jillian's discarded wet clothes and dashed to the washing machine.

After they had both taken showers, Jillian and Helene, still wearing matching terrycloth robes, snuggled into facing leather loveseats in the lawyer's modern black-and-white living room, sipping mugs of hot chocolate. "This is so bizarre," Helene said, shaking her head. "We're in the past and you think that's where Ryan's hiding?"

"I'm sure of it—and Alex agrees."

"But we don't know the exact date he went back to."

Jillian took a taste of the hot chocolate and shrugged. "Even if we did, I don't think we could travel to that specific time. This little wind tunnel time machine doesn't seem to be very precise."

"Is that why you counted to a hundred?"

"Yeah. I couldn't use a watch and I wanted to see if we could spin back to a certain day. I was aiming to go back eight months to September 20th, but I was off by about three weeks."

As she sipped the hot drink, Helene thought about the girl's words. "We'll figure out a way to track him down," she finally said. "The three of us working together are smarter than he is. And Mr. Cornell has no idea that we're onto his scheme." The lawyer stood and smiled at Jillian. "I'm warmer now, but hungry after all that exercise. How about you?"

"I guess I could eat something. But you weren't supposed to be here this week so do you have food in the house?"

Helene grinned. "I hate to cook. One of the reasons I got

divorced more than twenty years ago. Hubby wanted Helene Homemaker, but instead he got me, the queen of frozen dinners. I always have a pile of them so let's go check the freezer and see what I've got in stock."

Jillian munched on roasted turkey with sweet potatoes while Helene ate a linguini and shrimp dinner. "We've got to be back tomorrow morning for that trip upstate with Alex," the lawyer said between bites.

"That's right. I forgot about us driving to talk to Ryan's sister."

"Do you think we can find the trail in the morning?"

"We'd better be able to," Jillian said. "It should be a lot easier if it's not pouring rain. If we can't find it, we'll be stuck here, at a time before Ryan's even done anything." She shook her head. "I don't want to think about that."

Helene twirled some pasta on her fork and frowned. "I wonder what happens if we run into ourselves in the past. Can we co-exist— or do we explode or merge together or does something else strange happen?"

Jillian took a sip of water and considered the lawyer's question. "I never thought about that. But maybe it would be dangerous. I guess we probably should avoid meeting our past selves." She giggled. "That whole idea sounds very weird. I mean, what would you say to yourself? 'Hi Jillian, I'm Jillian too.'"

"Okay," Helene said, chuckling. "Then we won't have a party with ourselves. But we should go to sleep early so I'll set the alarm since all the clocks here work fine." She stood up quickly. "That reminds me. Before I forget, I'm going to find an extra watch to take with me when we go back. We'll need it tomorrow and I want to see what happens." She headed to her bedroom and soon returned, waving a small bracelet watch. "I'm leaving this right here on the table. Let's both remember to take it tomorrow morning."

Jillian nodded.

After finishing her dinner, the lawyer picked up the remote. "It's too early to go to sleep so we may as well watch TV for awhile. Okay?"

"Sure."

Helene switched on the television and ran through the stations, stopping at a baseball game. "You a sports fan? Want to watch this?"

The girl shook her head. "I do like baseball, but I don't want to see this game because it's from last year's divisional playoffs and I remember who won."

"Oh. I don't follow baseball much. Which team won?"

"The Phillies."

The lawyer flipped through the channels once more and again turned to her guest. "I don't see anything that I want to watch. How about a DVD?"

"That's fine."

Helene rummaged through a shelf under the TV and took out a handful of movies. "Here," she said, dumping the pile of DVDs on the kitchen table in front of Jillian. "Find something you like."

The girl glanced at several of the titles and shrugged. "I don't know any of these. They're too old. Why don't you choose one?"

"Okay." After examining the movies, Helene picked up a DVD. "Here's a good one. Let's watch *The Sting*. It's about a couple of con men, Paul Newman and Robert Redford, tricking bad guy Robert Shaw big time."

"Sounds like fun. Maybe we can get some ideas."

"You never know," Helene said, smiling.

At five-fifteen in the morning, the persistent ringing of the alarm clock woke both Helene and Jillian. Quickly, they sipped coffee and ate a couple of breakfast pastries Helene had discovered in her frozen food stash.

Before leaving, they carefully cleaned the condo, removing all traces of their overnight visit. "I don't want to frighten myself when

I come home and see evidence that someone stayed in my house, even if it was me," the lawyer said with a grin.

A half hour later, they stood in front of the building waiting for the cab driver. "I hope he shows up," Jillian said, gazing at the clear dawning sky. "At least it's stopped raining."

"Yeah, and we're not freezing like yesterday," Helene added. Both of them wore heavy sweaters in addition to their newly-laundered clothes. The lawyer studied the street and nodded. "That guy'll be here. Extra money always helps, and besides, we're early." She lifted her left wrist, which now held two timepieces, and checked the bracelet watch. "I told him to be here by six o'clock.

"Hey, if you think about it, we don't have much of a choice," she continued. "Since I'm not supposed to be here, I couldn't make a phone call from my house to a cab company, so the only other thing we can do if he doesn't come is walk to a main intersection and try to hail a cab that way. But I still think that driver'll be here. It's my job to understand people and I know...See?" Helene pointed to a car approaching on the right.

The white cab continued towards where they stood and the bearded driver pulled up next to them. "Hello, ladies," the cabbie said in heavily accented English, giving them a broad smile. "Good morning. I come back to drive you."

They stepped into the rear seat of the taxi and the driver headed to Juniper Park.

The park was empty as Jillian and Helene walked quickly to the base of the small mountain. "I think the trail's somewhere around here," the girl said, gesturing towards a group of trees to their right and glancing at the ground dejectedly. "It would help if I could find the Post-It. Then at least we could be sure the path was nearby."

"Well, you can look for the paper if you want. But I'm going to start checking the woods before hikers and joggers start showing up here." Helene stepped between two trees, separated a tangle of branches, and eyed the ground.

Jillian kicked the damp earth with her sneakers, loosening the dirt near the edge of the mini-mountain. But no yellow Post-It appeared. "I give up," she muttered, climbing into the dense woods to join the lawyer.

For several minutes, the two women wandered amidst the trees and bushes along the periphery, not seeing any sign of the narrow trail. Then Jillian noticed a little opening between two evergreen trees and began following it. "Helene!" she called. "Come here! I found it."

Jillian and Helene walked rapidly along the narrow path. "Listen," the girl said, cocking her ear. "Do you hear that? It's the whooshing noise of the wind tunnel. We're going to be okay."

"Are you sure?" Helene asked as they reached the clearing.

"It's always worked before. All we have to do is jump into the spiral and fall out on the other side, by the cave." The girl turned to her companion. "Ready? Let's do it."

Holding hands, they both dove into the swirling wind, which spun them to the opposite end of the clearing next to the cave with the hollow log. Jillian sat up and immediately checked her left arm. "Is your watch working?"

After brushing the dirt off her body, the lawyer looked at her wrist. "Well, that depends on which one you're talking about. Now the bracelet watch's stopped working. It's stuck on six thirty-five." She grinned at the girl. "But the other one's started ticking again. I wonder what time it really is."

"Well, when we landed in October 14th, it was nearly an hour and a half earlier than when we left." Jillian glanced at the sky. "So I'm figuring it must be morning here too, about eight o'clock. We'll check the time in the car to make sure. If I'm right it means that, if we hurry, we'll have enough time to get ready for our trip upstate. Want to come to my house or should I drive you home?"

"Drop me back at the office since that's where I left my car yesterday. Anyway, I need to go home and change." Helene tugged at her jeans and sweatshirt. "These aren't exactly the clothes I want to wear when we meet Ryan's sister. I'll call Alex from the car and ask him to pick us up a few minutes later." The lawyer smiled as she and Jillian entered the cave, removed the filling from the hollow log, and prepared to climb through its opening. "I'll just tell him that we got stuck with a problem from the past."

# CHAPTER 13

Ryan completed his daily lottery "work" by early Saturday afternoon and decided he wanted to make even more money. *Good time to go to the racetrack.* "Yeah, try my luck," he whispered, chuckling at his clever choice of words.

Going to the track on a Saturday night appealed to him because he knew it would be more crowded than on weekdays, making it less likely someone would notice him—especially if he was careful to pick up his winnings at different windows. He wouldn't even need much of a disguise.

Of course, Ryan always had the option of going to Off Track Betting to wager on horse races, but he found the OTB gambling parlors depressing—full of losers who liked to talk to you, grumbling about their bad luck. If Ryan won big there, he would definitely be noticed. Those gamblers would pretend to be his friends, hanging around him, wanting to know his secret for choosing winners. *Like I'd really help them!*

The track would be fun—a night out, watching and rooting for the horses. Quickly, he dashed back to his garden apartment. After making sure the front door was locked, he hung up his jacket and immediately headed to his bedroom closet.

He took his briefcase from the top shelf, entered the combination and opened it, adding most of his latest lottery winnings to a large envelope that contained a rapidly-growing wad of bills. After rummaging through a second compartment, he removed a folder labeled "Horse Racing."

"Let's see," he murmured, thumbing through several sheets of paper. "Aha!" Lifting a page, he pointed to the heading: "Yonkers Raceway Results for Saturday, February 5."

He closed his briefcase and carefully returned it to the closet shelf. Then, holding the piece of paper, he lay on the bed to review the payoffs for each of the night's upcoming races.

Ryan drove to Yonkers, reaching the lower Westchester city two hours before the scheduled seven-ten start time. After eating a leisurely gourmet dinner at a nearby Italian restaurant, he arrived at the track shortly before seven o'clock.

Since the races would begin soon and the temperature was already in the low thirties, he chose valet parking rather than walking or waiting for a shuttle bus. Most of the parking lot served the adjoining Empire Casino, which had opened in 2006 and drew many more people than the raceway.

Ryan saw no reason to play slot machines, games of chance in which he didn't know the results. He was in Yonkers to make money, not to gamble. In the afternoon, he had compiled a list of winners and carried the valuable paper in his pants pocket. His plan was to win most of the races, but not all—just in case someone was watching.

Tonight, as he entered the field level of the racetrack, Ryan was playing the part of a young executive. He wore a black woolen overcoat with plaid scarf over a gray sports jacket, white pinstriped shirt, and charcoal dress slacks. A small pasted-on mustache completed the look.

Even though he didn't need it, Ryan bought a racing program for a couple of dollars, figuring it would make him look more like the casual gambler he was pretending to be. Then he headed to the automated ticket machines.

After purchasing a voucher for forty dollars, he put it into the left-hand slot and touched the screen to select his winners for the first race: a two-dollar triple, 5-6-2. He planned on skipping the second race because all the favorites were going to win and the payoffs would be very small. Besides, he would be making a lot of money; he didn't need to be overly greedy and arouse suspicion by winning every race.

The machine printed Ryan's betting slip and the voucher minus the cost of his pick. After examining the ticket to make sure it was correct, he grinned and put the winning slip in his wallet. Although the evening was clear, it was much too cold to stay outdoors to watch the races, so he moved inside.

"Good luck," a bald security guard said as he entered the building.

*Luck.* Ryan snickered as he rode the escalator to the indoor grandstands. *Don't need it.*

He passed the second floor of the racetrack complex, an enclosed restaurant section where bettors could dine comfortably while watching the races since each table was equipped with a TV screen. But he had already eaten a luxurious dinner and wanted a place where he'd be less conspicuous.

On the fourth floor, he stepped off the escalator and walked past a windowless concourse filled with TV monitors showing horse races across the country. A row of manned ticket windows lined the entire left wall and automated betting machines covered the opposite side. In between, a crowd of OTB-type patrons sat or shuffled around. Some stood on line placing bets while others stared at their programs or at one of the televisions. *Losers!* He smirked and continued past the seedy characters to the doorway on the right that led to the grandstands.

Ryan entered the two-tiered enclosed area, which was filled with stadium-like orange and green seats. "Perfect," he muttered. People were scattered throughout the lower stands, munching on hot dogs and drinking beers. They seemed to be a genteel crowd, more like folks just enjoying a leisurely Saturday night out than degenerate gamblers desperate to win lots of money.

After heading down a side aisle, Ryan searched for a quiet section, one without too many people. He especially wanted to avoid nosy types and blabbermouths. "Ah," he murmured, noticing a place on the far left, four rows down. An elderly couple sat three seats away and no one was behind or in front of them. In fact, although the night's races were just about to begin, the entire area was empty and quiet. He sat down, opened the racing program and scanned it, pretending to be interested.

"Should be fun tonight, eh?" the old man nearby called to him.

*Shit. Still not far enough away.* Faking a smile, Ryan nodded to the white-haired man. "Yes. It'll be fun."

"We don't usually go to the track," the frizzy-haired woman next to the old guy said. "We go to the casino. But we always lose so much money there that we thought this would be a nice change."

"And cheaper," the man added, chuckling. "We'll just lose a little on each race."

Ryan smiled at them and stared at the racing brochure again, pretending to be deep in thought.

But the old man continued talking to him. "Got any hot tips?" he asked. "We could use a winner."

Ryan lifted his head and examined the elderly couple more carefully. The man's brown jacket was splattered with white stains and the woman's long black coat had a torn side pocket. *Old assholes could really use a winner.* "No hot tips," he lied. "I don't know anything about harness racing." He shrugged his shoulders. "I just ate dinner near here and happened to notice the track. Always have bad luck with the horses. Never win."

"Oh," the man said, frowning slightly. "Sorry to have bothered you."

"That's okay. Sorry I couldn't help," Ryan shook his head in a mock expression of sadness.

～

Three buglers—Ryan couldn't tell if they were male or female— outfitted in orange vests, white shirts and pants, and black boots, stood in front of the grandstands playing their instruments to signal the start of the first race. They were followed by a group of horses that pranced in both directions around the track in preparation for their races. Each horse wore a number on both flanks and was harnessed to a driver who sat behind in a small, open two-wheeled cart.

At quarter past seven, the first race started with eight horses and tethered drivers beginning their mile-long trot two times around the oval.

"Come on Willoughby!" Ryan shouted, cheering for the number five horse, which he knew would be the winner, followed by Curious Simon (#6) and Don't Lie to Me (#2). Ryan didn't want to openly root for all three of his horses because then the snoopy couple sitting near him would know he'd won the triple.

"Let's go Sticks & Stones!" The old lady's frizzy gray hair bounced as she bobbed her head up and down, shouting encouragement to her horse. Her male companion put his arm around the woman and smiled at her.

Ryan smirked at them, knowing Sticks & Stones wouldn't even finish in the money. "Couple of losers," he muttered as the race came to an end. The winner was Willoughby, followed by Curious Simon and Don't Lie to Me. The 5-6-2 triple paid $552 for Ryan's two-dollar bet.

Without saying a word to the elderly duo, he made his way out of the aisle and headed up the ramp to the inner atrium to collect his winnings.

At the first ticket window on the left in the crowded interior hall, a heavyset bearded clerk put Ryan's stub through the machine and smiled at him. "You won the triple! Good for you!"

The words were spoken much too loudly for Ryan's comfort. "Thanks," he said, shuffling his feet and reluctantly returning the man's grin. Then, glancing quickly in all directions, he realized none of the bedraggled gamblers seemed at all interested, even the short guy wearing glasses on line behind him. They were all preoccupied—either at a machine concentrating on placing bets, at a window talking to a clerk, checking the TV monitors, or staring at racing programs, trying to come up with a long-shot winner.

Ryan sighed thankfully, grateful no one was watching. As the bearded man handed him his winnings, Ryan quickly stuffed the bills into his wallet and stepped away from the line.

He remained in the busy open area, strolling to an automated machine to place his bets for the rest of the races he planned to win. He had plenty of time; there was at least a fifteen-minute intermission between each race and he wasn't even betting the next one. When he finished, he intended to find another seat in the grandstands, hopefully this time without nosy neighbors.

Before leaving the betting vestibule, Ryan carefully deposited the rest of his winning tickets—soon to be worth thousands of dollars—in his wallet. He reached the grandstands just as the second race ended.

"Damn it!" a chubby blonde woman shouted, almost knocking Ryan onto the ground as she angrily pushed past him. "Dumbass three horse."

He found a new seat in what seemed to be a quiet row. A tall middle-aged man sat by himself two seats to Ryan's left, scowling at the track, and, three seats to his right, an older acne-faced woman studied a racing program. The floor was already littered with losing tickets.

Ryan took out his program, again pretending to be absorbed in evaluating the upcoming trots. When he heard the buglers, followed by the announcement signaling the start of the third race, he closed the booklet and joined the crowd in watching the horses and carts on the field.

"Way to go, Prince Wesley!" a man behind Ryan yelled.

"Move your goddamn butt, number seven!" a woman screeched, the sound of her voice irritating Ryan's ears.

*Stop wasting your time yelling*, he wanted to say, wishing he could confront the screechy screamer. Her horse wasn't going to win. But, of course, Ryan couldn't tell her the winner of the third race would be #3, Hasty Pudding, followed by #8, MoonOverMexico. The winning exacta (3-8), which he had, would pay $792 for his four-dollar bet.

This time, Ryan didn't even bother rooting for his horses. He leaned back in his seat, just listening to the call of the race. When it ended nearly two minutes later, the winner was Hasty Pudding and the second place horse was MoonOverMexico. He stood up and returned to the betting concourse to claim his winnings.

By the time the last race of the night began, Ryan was thoroughly bored. Although he was happy to be pocketing lots of money, he was finding it impossible to cheer for horses he already knew were destined to win.

His fellow gamblers, however, were completely caught up in the excitement, thinking this could be their lucky moment. All around him, people were on their feet, jumping and screaming as they passionately willed their chosen trotters to win the race.

"Faster Bardolino!" yelled a stubble-faced young blond guy in the row in front of him.

"Hold on, boy!" the skinny African-American man on Ryan's left shouted. "You're almost home! Don't let 'em catch you, Go 4 Broke!" He waved his bony hand forward in encouragement.

*He's gonna be happy*, Ryan realized. Go 4 Broke, a ten-to-one long shot, was going to hold on and win the race. He reached into his shirt pocket and pulled out his ticket slip. In this race he had the triple and the winning combination of 1-6-3 would pay him $624.

After tucking the valuable ticket away, Ryan decided to practice his acting skills. He checked the racing program and quickly found the name of the number eight horse. "C'mon Yellow Rose in Bloom!" he shouted. "You can do it!" Of course, the horse couldn't do it; the nag was dead last, forty lengths behind Go 4 Broke. *Let 'em think I lost.*

As the race ended, most of the crowd crumpled their losing tickets, tossed them on the floor in disgust, and headed to the exit. Ryan, pretending to be upset like them, shook his head in apparent frustration. Then, walking briskly, he stopped at the ticket window on the far right, which he hadn't yet visited, to collect his final winnings.

"Straight triple," the thin-faced brunette ticket clerk said, smiling at Ryan. "Good way to end the night." She counted out his money.

He grabbed the bills and immediately stuffed them deep into his pants pocket since the money no longer fit in his wallet.

"See you hit the triple."

Ryan looked up and faced a fat, slovenly-looking bald man.

"Better to be lucky than good," the man continued. "If the driver of Misconception don't get tangled up with the five horse, Go 4 Broke loses by ten lengths." The obese gambler smirked at Ryan, dismissing him with a wave of his hand. "You don't know nothin' about racing."

*Don't have to know racing, you f___in' loser.* Ryan bit his lip, forcing himself not to reply to the irate man, and continued to the valet parking desk to retrieve his Civic.

Ryan drove directly to his apartment. He glanced to his left and right as he entered the small complex, relieved no neighbors lurked nearby—not that he expected company since it was nearly two a.m. and bitterly cold.

Quickly, he unlocked the door, stepped inside, and again immediately locked and chained the entrance. He tossed his coat on the chair, sat on the couch, and took out his wallet. He hadn't added up his winnings at the track and was anxious to find out exactly how much money he had earned.

His wallet and pants pockets bulged with the plethora of bills, mostly twenties and hundreds. First he arranged the money in piles according to denomination. Then, carefully, he counted the loot.

When he had finished, Ryan leaned back and grinned. *Very profitable.* After subtracting the two hundred dollars he had taken with him to the track, most of which he had spent on his gourmet dinner, the total was $6658.50. "Not bad for a night's work," he muttered as he gathered the bills and took them into the bedroom to add to his other winnings.

# CHAPTER 14

Jillian had calculated the time correctly so she and Helene were ready when Alex picked them up for their Saturday morning road trip. The lawyer insisted Jillian sit in the front seat for the first part of their long drive to Ryan's sister's house saying, "You should be the one to brief him on our extended trip to the past since you're more familiar with the weird whirlwind."

As the detective drove, Jillian recounted what had happened to her and Helene the previous day. "...And I tried to time the spins, counting to a hundred, but I couldn't get to the date I was aiming for. I was off by three weeks. So even if we know what day Ryan went back to, how're we going to find him if we can't get to a particular day in the past?"

"Don't worry," Alex said, glancing at her. "We'll find a way. Let's see what his sister tells us. Everything new that we find out about the shithead will help."

Helene leaned forward and whispered in Jillian's ear. "Alex is very creative. When he's ready, I'm sure he'll come up with something clever."

The girl shook her head and sighed. "We don't even know if

Ryan's stayed in this area or gone someplace else."

"Oh, he's still living around here," the private eye said, nodding several times. "I'm sure of that."

"Why?" Jillian asked.

"There's no reason for Ryan to leave because he thinks no one's looking for him in the past. Besides, if he wanted to travel back to another time or return to the present, he'd need access to that wind tunnel so no way he'd go far from here."

The three travelers stopped in yet another rural Burger King for lunch, waiting on line with the weekend midday crowd, mostly families with young toddlers and noisy groups of teens.

"Doesn't he ever eat anywhere else?" Jillian whispered to Helene as Alex placed his order.

"For fast food, I don't think so," the lawyer replied. "Please just humor him. Trust me, he's the best private detective you can have."

"Okay. Then I guess I'll have chicken again." Jillian stepped to the counter and ordered her meal.

The two women took their trays to one of the few unoccupied tables in the rear of the restaurant, joining Alex who had just sat down. "Isn't this food great?" the investigator asked, unwrapping his Whopper and taking a large bite.

Helene, munching on a fry, grinned at him. "I wouldn't call it great food, but it fills the tum." She patted her small midsection.

"Yeah, I guess." Jillian tried to sound enthusiastic as she nibbled her grilled chicken sandwich and looked at her two companions sitting opposite. "I'm curious. How did you guys meet?"

The lawyer poked Alex gently in the arm. "Tell Jillian the story. Then maybe she'll understand why I'm always saying that you're so good."

"In bed?" The investigator feigned shock. "You really want me to tell her about our affair?"

"Alex!" This time, Helene gave his left shoulder a hard punch.

"Ow! I was only kidding!" The detective rubbed his wounded shoulder before turning towards Jillian. "A couple of years ago, I was hired by a lady who owned a travel agency. She had a policy of giving a small discount to customers who booked trips and paid with cash, which her agents would put into a special envelope that she'd total and deposit each week. I guess the idea had worked well for her, bringing in business, but all of a sudden, the lady found she was missing cash. Not too much—maybe a hundred or two hundred bucks. But it was happening every week so she knew one of her people was stealing from her."

He pointed to his chest. "That's where I came in. I'd just started my business and she'd seen a newspaper write-up, took a chance, and hired me. I found out who the thief was real fast."

"How?" Jillian asked.

"Easy. I had a bank connection check the accounts of all the travel agents and one of them had been making cash deposits in amounts that closely matched the missing funds." He gave the girl his dimpled grin. "But we still needed proof so I posed as a customer and booked a trip to Aruba with the suspect. When she told me about the cash discount, I acted all excited and told her I would go to the bank and get the money—and I did, only they were marked bills. So when the agent tried to deposit two hundred dollars, the bank notified the cops, and she was arrested." He leaned back in the chair and smiled. "No sweat."

"Good story," Jillian said. "But I still don't understand how you met Helene."

The lawyer reached over the table and touched the girl's hand. "Annie Treadwell, the owner of the travel agency, she's my best friend."

"Oh."

The three of them continued eating without further conversation. After finishing her salad, Helene turned to the detective. "How much longer till we get to Danielle's house? What's her last name?"

"It's Danielle Coogan and we should be there in about two hours. In fact, I'm gonna call her now and give her a heads up." Alex took his cell phone from its case, and punched in a number.

"Hello, Ms. Coogan? Yeah, it's Alex Drury." He gazed at his watch. "Just wanted to let you know that we should be there at just about three-thirty." He listened for a few seconds. "Okay. That's fine. Didn't want you to have to stay home, just sitting around and waiting for us." As he heard the response, he grinned. "Yeah, thanks. See you then."

"What'd she say?" Jillian asked.

"Just that she had nothing important to do today and that she was very interested in meeting me and whoever I was bringing along." Alex glanced at his companions. "Seems her aunt just told her I would be calling, but wouldn't tell her why, so she's real curious about what's going on."

Danielle Coogan's home in Cayuga Heights, a little village in northern Ithaca, was a sprawling red-shingled ranch surrounded by a large landscaped lawn. Two kids' bikes blocked the right side of the driveway, which also featured a hopscotch game drawn in several pastel colors of chalk.

Alex parked on the street and he, Jillian, and Helene walked along the entranceway, passing several clay flowerpots filled with marigolds, petunias, and pansies. The investigator pressed the doorbell.

"Who is it?" a woman's voice called.

"Alex Drury, Ms. Coogan."

The front door opened immediately and an attractive curly-haired blonde in her early thirties smiled at the threesome and waved them inside. "Come on in. I'm dying to hear what this is all about."

She directed Alex, Jillian, and Helene to the living room, which included a pair of facing brown leather couches separated by a beige Parsons table. "Please sit down and make yourselves comfortable. Can I get you something to drink? Soda or water maybe?" She smiled softly. "I know you've had a long ride."

"I'll take some water, please," Jillian said, sitting on one of the sofas.

"Me too," Helene said, continuing to stand. "And if I could use the bathroom?"

"Of course." Danielle pointed to an open door in the hallway. She turned towards Alex, who still stood in the cozy living room. "Can I get you anything?"

"No thanks. I'm fine." He sat next to Jillian, sinking into the soft leather.

Danielle smiled at the detective and darted into the kitchen, quickly returning with two bottles of water.

"Very nice house," Jillian said, taking one of the waters and nodding at her host. "We saw the bikes outside. How old are your children?"

"Thank you. Emma's six and Bobby is almost four." Ryan's sister sat in the couch opposite her visitors. "My husband took them to the park for the afternoon so we'd be able to talk without the kids constantly interrupting mommy."

"Very considerate," Alex said, smiling at the woman.

"Yes. He's a great guy." She leaned forward, staring at Alex and Jillian. "So now please tell me what's going on."

"All right," the investigator said, glancing first at Helene, who had just entered the room and taken a seat next to Danielle, and then at Jillian. "Let me start by introducing these two lovely ladies. Ms. Coogan, I'd like you to meet Helene Moskowitz. She's an attorney."

"Nice to meet you," Helene said, smiling at Danielle.

"Same here."

"And the young lady sitting next to me is Helene's client," Alex continued. "Her name is Jillian Keating."

"Oh." Danielle's smile vanished and she stared at Jillian in shock. "I don't understand..."

The girl spoke quietly. "Yes, I am that Jillian Keating and I'm so sorry to upset you like this. I felt the same way a couple of days ago when I met your aunt." She tilted her head towards the investigator. "Alex will explain everything and then it'll all make sense."

Danielle's face was somber as she turned towards the private eye. "Please go ahead then, Mr. Drury. What's this all about?"

He quickly summarized Jillian's predicament while Ryan's sister listened intently without interrupting. When he had finished, Danielle stared at Jillian sympathetically. "I'm so sorry about all of this, Miss Keating. That terrible accident was not your fault."

The girl lowered her head and nodded slightly, biting her lower lip.

"That's what I've been trying to convince her," Alex said. "Your Aunt Marie suggested you may be able to help us because she thought you were still in contact with your brother."

Danielle leaned against the couch and exhaled deeply. "I do speak to Ryan occasionally. But I haven't heard from him recently."

"When was the last time you spoke to him?" the detective asked, taking the notepad and pen from his pants pocket.

The woman thought for a moment. "About a month ago—and he was very mysterious, even for Ryan."

"How so?" the investigator asked, scribbling in his pad.

"Well, he said I may not hear from him for a long time and when I tried to ask him where he was going and why he couldn't call, he wouldn't give me any kind of an answer."

"Sure sounds like someone who was planning to disappear," Helene said.

Danielle shrugged. "I really didn't think anything of it at the time. He always talked like that."

"So Ryan liked being mysterious?" Alex continued.

"Oh yes. He always loved drama." She smirked. "My brother

should've been an actor."

None of them spoke for several seconds. "Can you tell us what you remember of Ryan as a child?" Helene finally asked.

Danielle stared at the ceiling as she contemplated the question. "He was a spoiled kid. My father thought he was special and made sure everyone knew it."

"How was he special?" Jillian asked.

"Ryan was very smart—taught himself to read before he even turned four. And then, of course, there was his flair for the dramatic." She smiled slightly. "He would watch TV and pretend he was on a show, imitate the characters. For a little kid, he did a great job."

"What happened after the accident?" Alex asked.

Danielle gazed sadly at Jillian. "His world fell apart. And I don't think Ryan's ever recovered."

No one said anything for nearly thirty seconds. Jillian took a sip of water before breaking the lengthy silence. "Your aunt said that you were able to adjust."

Ryan's sister nodded. "It was different with me. I was used to being in the background and I was okay with it and still am. I don't need to be the center of attention." She gave a little shrug. "Of course, I was really in bad shape after losing my parents, but..." Her voice trailed off.

"You saw a psychiatrist?" Helene asked.

"Yes, for a couple of months."

"Did it help?" the lawyer continued.

"Not really." Danielle shook her head. "Ryan saw the doctor for much longer and it didn't help him at all."

"How do you know that?" Alex asked.

"He acted even angrier after seeing the doctor."

"In what way?" the investigator said.

"Screaming, yelling, having fits. He'd even throw things at Aunt Marie."

"Wow!" Jillian exclaimed. "That must've been real tough."

"Yeah. But then, suddenly, he stopped acting out."

"Do you know why?" Alex asked.

Danielle lifted her head, again examining her ceiling. "I think he finally realized it wasn't going to get him anywhere and he was stuck living with Aunt Marie, like it or not. I convinced him that it was better to stay with her than to get put in a foster home, which is where he would've ended up if he kept making it impossible for her to keep him." She lowered her head and made eye contact with her visitors. "But Ryan was still just as mad."

"How can you be sure of that?" Alex asked.

Danielle hesitated for several moments. "Did my aunt tell you about the pictures?"

"No." Alex put down his pen. "What pictures?"

"The ones that Ryan taped all over his room." She glanced at Jillian. "They all had to do with accidents."

Alex continued taking notes as they waited for Danielle to explain. Ryan's sister rubbed her arms absentmindedly and stared into the empty hallway before speaking. "Every day he would check the newspaper that was delivered to my aunt's house and cut out pictures of car accidents." She spoke very softly. "That's what he decorated his walls with, smashed up cars and—if they were in the paper—photos of the victims, injured or dead." She shook her head. "It was horrible—all those gruesome pictures."

"Did your aunt try to stop him?" Jillian asked quietly.

"She checked with the psychiatrist and he told her to let Ryan do it, that it was his way of dealing with the deaths of our parents, getting his anger out. But I think the doctor was wrong. All it did was to keep reminding Ryan about what had happened and it made him even angrier."

"How long did this go on?" Helene asked.

Danielle shrugged. "I don't think it's ever stopped. After a few months, Ryan took down the newspaper clippings without anyone telling him to. But he kept saving those awful accident pictures. He put them in boxes at the bottom of his closet. I know, because one time I went into his room to borrow a sweater and I saw a partly-opened carton filled with piles and piles of photos. He had at least four other ones."

She looked at Jillian before continuing. "Then, when he was a teenager, Ryan started collecting information about our parents' accident and, especially, about you."

"Me?"

"Yes. He used the Internet to find out everything he could about what happened." She gazed sadly at Jillian, shaking her head. "I knew he was obsessed with you, but I never thought he would do something like this. I'm so sorry."

"Thanks," the girl whispered.

"Your aunt mentioned Ryan didn't work much in school," Alex said, changing the subject. "Can you tell us anything about that?"

Danielle smiled at him. "My brother hated school. He never liked work of any kind—or being told that he had to do something."

"So he got by just because he was so smart?" Alex asked.

"Yeah, pretty much."

"And there was nothing at all in school that he liked?" Alex continued.

Danielle looked at the investigator, considering his question. "Well, there was one activity he did participate in—school plays. Like I said, he always loved acting and he was actually very good. Starred in a lot of the shows through high school. It gave him a chance to dress up in costumes and perform, always his favorite thing."

She let out a little chuckle. "I think Ryan would've liked to have been a professional actor. Might have even been a success. But actors have to audition and they work really hard to get jobs." She shook her head. "Too much effort for my little brother."

Jillian twirled her bottle of water and spoke softly. "Did Ryan have any friends?"

"No. He always kept pretty much to himself."

"What about girlfriends?" Jillian continued.

Ryan's sister hesitated for a moment. "I remember him going on a few dates...But he never talked about any of them. I don't think he ever had a real girlfriend, you know, someone he went out with for a long time." She looked at Jillian sympathetically before speaking again. "But from what I've heard today, you were living with Ryan so..."

"That doesn't count," the girl whispered, staring at her lap.

They all sat quietly until Alex spoke. "How about hobbies? Anything else your brother was interested in besides acting?"

"Well, he liked to read. He stayed in his room a lot, reading books, mostly novels, I think."

The investigator wrote something in his notebook, then he closed the small pad and rose. "So to sum up Ryan: His interests were acting and reading, plus an obsession with Jillian and the accident that killed your parents. He avoided any close relationships and didn't want to work."

"I guess that's pretty much it," Danielle said, shrugging her shoulders.

"Your aunt mentioned something about you and Ryan getting a large settlement from the accident," Helene said. "She thought that's what Ryan's been living on."

"Yes. He was living on it. But, a few months ago, he told me he'd run out of money."

"He used up five million dollars?" The lawyer stared at Ryan's sister in amazement. "How'd he do that so fast?"

"Ryan likes to spend money. He eats in the best restaurants, buys expensive cars, wears the finest clothes, and takes lots of vacations." She smirked. "Why not? His whole life is one big vacation; he doesn't have a job to go to. I tried to tell him to save his money, you know, invest it, or at least cut down on his spending, but he wouldn't listen."

"It sounds like you still have the money from the accident," Helene said.

"Oh yes. Doug and I have a financial advisor who helps us." Danielle smiled at the lawyer. "We want to save most of the settlement money and use it for our kids' education and for when we retire."

"So what does your husband do?" Alex asked, again scribbling in his pad.

"Doug's the manager of the Bank of Cayuga Heights—soon to be named vice-president." She nodded at the detective. "You know, I worked too, before I had children. I was a second grade teacher. I never understood my brother's attitude towards having a job, why he refused to work."

The four of them were quiet again until Helene spoke. "Mrs. Coogan, if we go to trial, would you be willing to testify about the things you told us about Ryan—his obsession with Ms. Keating, the photos of accidents, the phone conversation when he said you wouldn't hear from him for a long time?"

Danielle turned towards the lawyer. "Yes. Does that mean you think the police will find my brother soon?"

Helene shook her head. "They're convinced my client killed him so they've pretty much called off the search."

"Ryan's hiding somewhere and you think no one'll be able to find him?"

"That depends." Alex leaned against the living room wall and spoke softly. "We've got a good idea about where he is."

"Then why didn't you tell the police?" Danielle frowned at him. "I don't understand."

"It's kind of complicated," the detective replied. "But we're hoping to find him ourselves."

"Good luck," Danielle said. "I love my brother, but I've always known there was something seriously wrong with him. And now that he's done this..." She shook her head. "If I can help you, please let me know." She smiled slightly at Jillian. "Miss Keating, I am very, very sorry about what my brother has done to you."

The girl nodded. "Thank you. Now that I know more about Ryan, at least I understand a little about why he did it." Then, staring at her lap, she continued in a whisper. "And my father was responsible for the accident."

"Your father," Ryan's sister repeated. "But not you."

# CHAPTER 15

"I got a winner," Ryan said, handing his Take Five card to the woman behind the Customer Service counter at the A & P supermarket.

After putting the ticket into the lottery machine, the moon-faced clerk with huge hoop earrings hollered in surprise. "Wow! You sure do! You won $387! That's pretty damn good." As she walked back to Ryan, earrings spinning, she smiled at him. "Did you know it was that much money?"

"No," he said, shaking his head. And, for a change, he was telling the truth. He only knew he had picked four out of five numbers correctly, giving him the second place prize. He hadn't bothered to check how much the actual payout was. That didn't really matter; the prize money always ranged between $300 and $500.

Today, February 9th, Ryan was hardly disguised—no wig or strange outfit. In fact, he was wearing his favorite walking clothes—the light blue jeans and plaid yellow and navy shirt he had taken with him into the past. But he had styled his hair a little differently, applying mousse to give it a tousled, somewhat unkempt appearance. To complete the look, he had added black-framed glasses.

"Wait here a second, hon," the cashier said. "I've got to go in the back and get your money." Again she grinned broadly. "We don't usually get such big lottery winners."

Ryan nodded, but didn't smile. He wasn't thrilled with the woman's fawning attention. She was too surprised by his win—and much too loud. When he got home, he'd make a note not to play the lottery again at this supermarket or, if he did, to make sure a different clerk was manning the desk. *Maybe I shouldn't do Take Five anymore...*

"That's real cool," said a sultry feminine voice behind Ryan, interrupting his thoughts. When he turned around, he faced a pretty brunette in her early twenties.

"I mean about you winning the lottery," the young woman continued. "I'm waiting for a rain check so I couldn't help hearing you and her talking." The brunette shrugged. "The most I ever won was twenty-five dollars on a scratch-off."

"Yeah. I sure was lucky." Ryan forced a smile. All the conversation about his lottery success was making him uncomfortable. "First time I ever won so much."

"Well, you enjoy it." The girl grinned, showing off her perfect white teeth.

"Here's your winnings!" The clerk had returned from the office, shouting and waving a wad of bills. Placing the stack on the counter, she tabulated the money. "Three hundred and eighty seven dollars! Congratulations!" Still smiling, she handed the cash to Ryan.

"Thanks," he said, quickly shoving the bills in his wallet. Then he had a sudden thought. The girl in the supermarket was attractive and she must like him since she had initiated the conversation. Ryan hadn't been out with a girl since Jillian and that relationship didn't count. This was a perfect opportunity—as long as he was very careful.

"Hey." He smiled at the young woman standing behind him. "You know what? I've just come into some money. How about celebrating with me by going someplace for lunch?"

The brunette returned his smile. "Yeah," she said, nodding her head. "I'd really like that."

Ryan and the girl settled into a booth at the Chinese restaurant she had recommended, only a short block from the A & P. "So I'm Sara," she said, smiling at him. "What's your name?"

"Brad," Ryan lied, returning her smile. "I'm glad we met."

Sara nodded. "Me too. What kind of work do you do, Brad?"

Ryan thought quickly. It was just after noon on Wednesday, a time when most guys his age were working at a job. Luckily, he was wearing nondescript clothes. "Oh, I'm a struggling artist. Trying to make a living's been tough so today helps."

"I'll bet," Sara said, staring directly into his deep brown eyes. "I've never met a real artist. So what do you do—draw, paint...?"

"Paint, mostly landscapes." He mentioned the first thing that came into his mind, thanks to his Aunt Marie.

"Oh, I'd love to see something you've painted. Is your work at one of those places that sells art? I can't think of the name."

"You mean 'gallery'? No, not right now. I'm between shows so, sorry, there's nothing you can see."

"Too bad." She reached for a fried noodle and dipped it into the bowl of duck sauce.

"What about you?" Ryan asked. "What do you do?"

The girl chewed her food before answering. "I'm still going to school, studying history. And I work part-time in Sears too."

A thin young Asian waiter with spiky black hair approached the booth and asked for their orders. Ryan and Sara picked up the glossy one-page menus and glanced at the lunch offerings.

"Choose something special," Ryan suggested.

The girl grinned at him. "Okay, thanks. I will." She lowered the menu and turned to the waiter. "I'll have the lobster Cantonese."

"Me too," Ryan said, handing his menu to the waiter.

The young spiky-haired man flashed a big smile. "Two lobster Cantonese," he said in accented English, not writing the order on a notepad. "Very good choice. You will enjoy."

"What do you think?" Ryan asked as he and Sara ate their food.

"The waiter was right." She lifted her head, smiling at him. "This lobster is really good."

"Yeah. It is. Thanks for suggesting this place."

"And thanks, Brad, for taking me to lunch. I don't usually get to eat such fancy stuff. You know, I just grab a slice of pizza or a burger or something quick like that."

"Me too." Of course, Ryan was lying again. He liked to eat well and generally treated himself to expensive meals, even for lunch. "So what're you doing this afternoon?" He didn't have any plans and the young woman was pleasant company.

Sara tilted her arm and checked her watch. "Well, I've got a class in twenty-five minutes." She shrugged at him. "I gotta be there because this professor takes points off your grade if you cut."

"I remember teachers like that." Actually, he didn't. He had only attended college classes when he wanted too, never thinking about any of the consequences.

The girl stood up, placing her cloth napkin on the table, and smiled at Ryan. "Thanks again for lunch. It was real nice meeting you, Brad." She stopped talking and looked at him.

*Shit! She's waiting for me to ask for her phone number or email.* He took out the prepaid cell phone he had bought after arriving back in January and returned her smile. "What's your number, Sara? I'll give you a call and we can get together sometime soon."

"It's 384-9867—I'd like that."

# CHAPTER 16

Following their Saturday afternoon visit to Ryan's sister, Jillian, Alex, and Helene sat at a round table in a cozy restaurant along Interstate 86/Route 17, sipping mugs of coffee after eating a leisurely dinner. The investigator had wanted to stop at Burger King again, but both women had vetoed his choice.

"Anyplace else," the lawyer had pleaded.

"Yeah," Jillian had agreed. "You can even pick the restaurant. We don't care what it is as long as it's not Burger King or some other kind of fast food."

As he leaned against the velvety seat, Alex took a sip of coffee and continued talking about their number one subject. "So according to what we know about Ryan from his aunt and sister, we can figure he's winning money using his knowledge of the past and probably disguising himself to keep from being recognized."

"Lottery mostly," Helene said, resting her mug on the table. "It's the easiest way for someone as lazy as Ryan to make money."

"And he loves acting so much," Jillian added. "He probably plays a different role each time." She shrugged her shoulders. "This is all just a game to him—even what he's done to me."

"He's one very sick dude," the detective said, shaking his head. "But he's also very smart. We're gonna need a really good plan to get him."

"Any ideas yet?" Helene asked.

Alex nodded at the lawyer. "Yeah, a few. But I want to do some more research. I'm gonna travel back to sometime in February so I can see firsthand what the shithead was doing then."

"You're going to follow Ryan into lotto stores in his disguises?" Jillian asked. "I thought we'd just agreed that was too dangerous, that we wouldn't go into stores showing people his picture because he'd get suspicious if he knew someone was looking for him."

"Nope," Alex said, smiling at the girl. "That's not what I meant. I want to follow the original Ryan, the one you met in the art class, to see how he spends his time. You don't know what he did during the day—remember? You thought he was working as a graphic artist, but, of course, he wasn't. So I'm curious. What the hell did he do with all that free time?"

"Beats me," Jillian said.

"Do you think it can help us?" Helene asked.

"Hey, it sure can't hurt," Alex said.

Jillian stared at the private eye. "You shouldn't go back by yourself."

"Why not?"

"It's dangerous. Look what happened to me and Helene last time when we were trapped and nearly got stuck in last October. I've had the most experience with the wind tunnel so I'm going with you."

Alex shook his head. "Bad idea. Ryan doesn't know me from beans, but he'd recognize you in a second."

After glancing first at the investigator and then at Helene, the girl smiled. "Not if I disguise myself. I'd like a chance to dress up and do some acting too—how'd you think I'd look as a ditsy blonde?" She touched her hair lightly, put one hand under her chin, and giggled.

"I don't know..." Alex said.

"Please let me come. Ryan's gone to so much trouble to try to hurt me. I want to be involved in everything we do to find him and bring him back." Jillian turned to Helene, who sat quietly, listening to the conversation. "And Martin said I could take time off work if I needed it, right?"

"Yes. He did."

Alex exhaled deeply and then shrugged. "Okay, I guess. But it would be a lot easier if I went alone." He pointed his index finger at the girl. "If you come—even if you're wearing a disguise—you've gotta stay far away from Ryan. I don't want you anywhere near that slug."

"I'll be careful. I promise. I just want to be part of this."

After a momentary silence, the detective spoke again. "We agreed that the park's too crowded on spring weekends to take a chance climbing the mountain so I'm planning on going hiking first thing Monday morning."

Jillian smiled at Helene, who nodded. "Okay," the lawyer said. "You leave Martin a voice mail that you need the day off and I'll stop into his office Monday morning to confirm that you're out working on your case. He'll be fine with it, I'm sure."

"Be ready at eight o'clock Monday," the investigator said.

"I'll be waiting by the door."

True to her word, Jillian was ready when Alex rang the doorbell early Monday morning. When she opened the door, he stepped back in amazement. "What did you do to yourself?"

Shaking her hair, which was now honey blonde and curly, the girl grinned. "I told you I could change the way I look enough so that Ryan would never recognize me. It's just a wig." She lifted a curl near her right ear, revealing a strand of dark hair underneath. "See?" Then, unsnapping her shirt pocket, she removed a pair of brown-rimmed glasses and put them on. "How's this?"

"Very different. But if we find Ryan, I still don't want you getting anywhere near him. That shithead's been stalking you forever, so even if he doesn't recognize you from the way you look, he could still identify your voice."

"I'll be good and just stay in the background and observe. I promise." Jillian raised her hand as if she were taking an oath.

As they walked to the detective's car, the late May weather was already warm and humid. Nevertheless, Alex had tied a sweatshirt around his waist and Jillian carried a jacket. In addition, the girl had shoved her trusty flashlight into one jeans pocket and, because of her recent time travel experience with Helene, she had stuffed a small folding umbrella in the other pants pocket.

"Hot day for a hike, huh?" the investigator said as he drove them to Juniper Park.

"Not for long though." She smiled at him. "As I remember, we had a pretty cold February."

Alex parked the Corolla and he and Jillian headed to the mini-mountain, passing two sweaty joggers. They walked silently along the trail, meeting no other hikers. When they reached the first clearing, the duo made sure no one was in the vicinity, removed the pile of debris that camouflaged the other side, and quickly crawled through. After restacking the leaves and sticks, they approached the mammoth tilted log.

"Looks just the same as I remember," Alex said quietly as he pulled branches and leaves from the trunk's cavity.

"Let's hope the wind tunnel's the same too," Jillian said. Reaching inside the opening, she helped him remove the stuffing and then climbed headfirst into the hollow trunk. Like all the other times, she heard the whooshing roar of the wind even before she crawled out of the log and into the cave on the other side. She entered the clearing and watched the little twister spin in place as she waited for Alex.

When he crouched through the cave opening, the detective shouted at Jillian. "It's still here!" Anxiously, he reached for her hand. "C'mon! Let's do it—into the whirlwind at the count of three!"

Holding hands, Alex and Jillian threw themselves into the funnel and let the strange wind twirl them. Earlier, they had agreed to count to 120 for three lengthy spins and then count to 25 for a final, shorter whirl. Based on what she had discovered on her previous treks into the past, the girl hoped her calculations would land them back sometime in February.

"I'm really dizzy," the investigator said, lying on the ground after their second long spin. "Can't we rest some more before we go back into that twister?"

"Why? We're only going to get dizzy again." Jillian sat next to him, hugging her knees. Then, playfully, she swatted at his shoulder. "Don't be such a baby."

Grumbling, the detective staggered to his feet, grasped her hand, and leaned forward until they were both sucked into the little cyclone.

After their fourth and final spin, the pair hurled themselves out of the swirling wind and fell to the ground. But they couldn't see anything. The landscape was completely dark.

"What the hell?" Alex exclaimed.

"Not to worry." Jillian dug into her pants pocket, retrieved the flashlight, and turned it on. "I've been prepared for this after I almost got stuck at night here that other time—and it happened with Helene too...Better?"

"Much," he agreed, reaching for the girl's left hand. "But we're not walking through the woods like this. Let's go back into this thing and find some daytime."

Still holding the investigator's hand, Jillian clicked off the flashlight with her other hand and shoved it into her pocket. Then they both stood and again dove into the wind portal. After a short spin, Alex pushed them out. This time, as they tumbled to the ground, they were able to see where they were landing.

"That last spin shouldn't make too much of a difference in time, should it?" the private eye asked as he propped himself up, shaking off his dizziness.

"I don't think so. But even though I've done this a few more times than you, I'm still no expert on the way this wind tunnel time machine works." Jillian stood and wiped the dirt off her clothes. "Are you okay to walk yet? I'm curious to find out today's date."

The two time travelers began following the tiny path down the mountain. "Does it feel colder here?" Jillian whispered.

"Yeah. It sure does." Alex stopped walking and untied his sweatshirt. "Hold on a second while I put this on."

"Me too," the girl said, buttoning her jacket.

Wearing their extra clothing, the hikers continued the rest of the way through the woods. After peeling away the final branches, they stepped out of the little mountain and into the park. The day was crisp and clear, brightly sunny with a sprinkling of fluffy clouds. A few people were visible in the distance, but no one was anywhere near them.

"Look at the trees," Jillian said.

"Yeah. Lots of them without any leaves so it's gotta be sometime in winter." Alex pointed to the left. "Hey, isn't that a pile of snow over there?"

"You're right. It is."

The detective walked to the small group of nearby trees. "First step, I wanna see if time traveling Ryan's back now—here it is." Alex pointed to the three-inch "V" he had discovered on his first trip into the past.

"See?" He touched the notch as Jillian climbed over a bush and stood next to him. "It looks different than before, much lighter. Ryan's hiding here, but he hasn't been back very long, so the time's gotta be at least a couple of months earlier."

Before they left the park, the girl took a yellow Post-It from her pocket and knelt to shove the paper in the ground.

"What're you doing?" Alex asked.

"Marking the entrance to the trail, like I did before."

"Forget it." The investigator shook his head. "Didn't work last time you tried it, from what you told me, and it's not necessary. I'm not gonna forget where this notch is and this tree's not gonna disappear. "C'mon." He yanked Jillian's arm, pulling her towards the park exit. "Let's get this show on the road."

Jillian and Alex crossed the street and strode rapidly towards the small deli. After opening the door for the girl, he rushed to the shelf with the newspapers. "Tuesday, February 8th," he said, waving the paper in her face as she caught up to him. "We did good. Should be able to see the slug in his planning stage." The detective returned the newspaper to the shelf and headed towards the exit. "Time to get started."

"What are we going to do first?" Jillian asked as they walked in the direction of the main intersection.

"We'll take a cab to Ryan's apartment. Check what time it is too. Wanna make sure we've got enough daylight left." Alex glanced at the sky. "Sun doesn't look too high, but it is February so the days are still pretty short."

The investigator flagged a taxi and gave the driver Jillian's Grove Street address, which in February was just Ryan's apartment. "Gotta assume he'd been living there when he was working out his plan to convince you to move in with him. No reason for him not to."

Jillian nodded in agreement and then spoke to the cab driver. "Excuse me. Do you have the time?"

The driver, a skinny unshaven young man with stringy brown hair and rumpled clothes, stole a quick peek at his watch. "It's quarter to twelve," he muttered.

"Thanks."

"Good," Alex said softly. "Gives us over four hours."

"What if Ryan just stays inside the whole time?" the girl whispered. "Then we won't learn anything."

"Hey, think positive. It's a beautiful winter day. He's got no job, nothing he has to do. I'll bet he goes out—and when he does, we're going with him."

"Stop here." Alex ordered the driver to pull over just before the taxi reached the apartment building on Grove Street. "This corner's fine." Still sitting in the backseat, he took out his wallet and counted out the nine-dollar fare, adding a ten-dollar tip.

"Thanks!" After taking the bills, the young driver turned and smiled at his generous passengers.

"How much would you charge to just let us sit here in your car for a half hour?" Alex asked.

"Huh?" The cabbie gave him a puzzled look.

"We're waiting for someone to come out of the building and we don't want him to see us."

"Yeah," Jillian added. "It's a surprise."

"Oh, sounds cool." The driver thought for a minute. "I guess twenty bucks should do it."

After reaching into his wallet again, the detective handed the slovenly cabbie the money.

"Okay." The driver pocketed the bill and looked at his watch. "You got till twelve-twenty." He leaned his head against the seat and closed his eyes.

"What if he doesn't come out of the house by then?" Jillian whispered to Alex.

"Then we'll get out of the cab and wait."

"What if he's not even home?"

"Then we'll wait till he comes back."

"Maybe we should have rented a car."

Alex shook his head. "Couldn't do it. Requires ID and would take too long. This is the only way." He stretched his long legs and massaged them.

"This is so boring," Jillian said, glancing at the apartment building.

"Welcome to the wonderful world of the P.I." Alex settled deeply into the seat and continued to stare through the window.

As she gazed at her future home, Jillian tried to occupy her mind. *Wonder what he's doing right now?* she thought. *Probably thinking up some new way to hurt me. Or figuring how to get me to move in with him, like Alex said.* By February 8th, she and Ryan had already met in the graphic arts course and, thanks to his diabolical plan, were seeing each other after class.

"I was such a jerk," she muttered.

"Huh?" The investigator glanced at her.

"Sorry. Just sitting here thinking about what an idiot I was with Ryan."

"I thought you were finished beating yourself over the head about all that shit," Alex said, again shifting his attention to the apartment building. "He stalked you and then he lured you into his den like some kind of a wild animal. You were an innocent victim. You had no idea about what he was doing."

The girl shook her head, sadly. "I should've been smarter and figured it out."

"No," the detective said, keeping his eyes focused on the building's entrance. "You couldn't have known he was a fraud. His plan was too well thought out."

"Still, if I..."

"Time's up," the cabbie announced, turning around to face his passengers. "It's past twelve-twenty and I gotta get going." He smiled at Alex. "I can stay longer if you wanna give me some more money."

"No. Our friend's not out yet, but we can wait for him in the street." Alex pointed to the young man's cell phone, visible in his shirt pocket. "But give me your number. We might call you to come back here and drive us in an hour or two."

"Sure." The cabbie grabbed a pen, scribbled some numbers on the back of a card, and handed it to the investigator. "Call me and I'll come."

"So what now?" Jillian asked as she and Alex stood on the sidewalk opposite Ryan's building. "It's too cold to just stand here for hours."

"We'll wait a couple of minutes more and then walk around the neighborhood."

"Okay. But what if he comes out and goes to his car and drives off?"

"Then we're screwed." The detective smiled his dimpled grin. "But it's a gorgeous winter day and we know our guy loves to walk so I'm hoping we can follow the dirtbag on foot."

As they stood behind parked cars, Jillian and Alex shuffled their feet back and forth to keep warm while they continued to study the apartment building. Ten minutes later, Alex poked the girl softly on her side. "Look," he said, pointing across the street.

"It's him!" Jillian exclaimed in a whisper. Ryan had exited the building wearing a black suede jacket, gray slacks, and a gray and black plaid scarf draped around his neck.

"Looks like he plans to walk," Alex said. "C'mon. He's moving fast."

After Ryan crossed the street, Alex and Jillian followed, remaining about thirty feet behind him.

"What if he turns around and sees us?" the girl asked softly as she hurried to keep pace with her companion.

"So what? At this distance, with your blonde hair and glasses, he won't recognize you and he's never even met me. Besides, he's got no reason to think anyone's following him. Remember, this Ryan belongs here. No one's looking for him yet and he's not the time traveler."

They walked for nearly a mile through quiet suburban streets until they reached a commercial strip. After crossing the busy thoroughfare, Ryan headed towards a small brown building with a gold sign on top that read "Coachman's Restaurant."

"I remember this place," Jillian said as she and Alex stood opposite the eatery, watching Ryan open the door and step inside. "I once ate here with him."

"Was the food good?"

"I didn't think it was all that great." She faced the detective and shrugged. "The people were snobbish and the food was overpriced and nothing special. But Ryan loved it."

Alex glanced at his watch. "He's gonna be in there a while enjoying his fancy lunch so there's nothing for us to see. It's after ten thirty our time and must be past one o'clock here. Let's go grab something quick to eat." He smiled at the girl. "I saw a good place a couple of blocks back."

Five minutes later, Jillian sat in yet another Burger King watching Alex wolf down a Whopper. "How can you eat such heavy stuff so early?" she asked. "I'm not at all hungry." She took a sip of hot coffee, but just twirled the lettuce in her salad with a fork, not putting any of it in her mouth.

"Always time for a great burger." He took another large bite, chewed it, and smiled at her. "Works for me. Just call it an early lunch. Besides, we may not have a chance to eat later on. That's another important part of being a P.I." He waved the rest of his Whopper at Jillian. "Gotta grab food whenever you can."

"Well, then I guess I wouldn't be a good private detective." She stopped playing with her lettuce and looked at him. "I can't force myself to eat something if I'm not hungry."

"You're not gonna have that?" Alex pointed to the uneaten salad.

"No." She shook her head. "Do you want it?"

"Sure."

Jillian slid her salad across the table. "Do you know the old movie, *The Sting*?" she asked as she watched the investigator devour her food. "I saw it with Helene when we were stuck at her house Friday night."

"Yeah. A couple of con guys trick a British crook with a horse race scheme."

"Could we do something like that to Ryan?"

Alex stopped eating and smiled. "Interesting idea—you want a production, something on a big scale?"

"Yes." She returned his smile. "That would be awesome."

"Let me think about it. See what I can work into my plan." He nodded. "But I like it: a big con job."

Quickly, the detective ate the rest of the salad and wiped his mouth with a napkin. "Okay. Let's buy a couple of cups of coffee to go and then get back to our post and wait for our subject to finish his fancy lunch."

This time, helped by the hot coffee and the afternoon's warmer temperature, they were both much more comfortable standing across the street waiting for Ryan. Nearly a half hour later, their quarry stepped out of the restaurant. "We're up," Alex said, nudging Jillian.

They walked briskly in a direction away from his apartment building, following Ryan at a safe distance through the mostly residential streets. The man moved rapidly, never once turning around.

"He's...not...going...back...home," Jillian said, gasping between each word as she struggled to keep up with her former boyfriend's fast pace.

"Like I'd hoped," Alex said, speaking normally since he had no problem matching Ryan's foot speed. "We lucked out by traveling back to this particular day in February. Today's weather's too nice for him to just sit home so I figured he'd go out walking somewhere."

They continued to follow Ryan for another mile, reaching an industrial area with a small shopping center and a gas station. On the next block, he entered a large windowless one-level brown building. The massive overhead sign read "SECURE SELF-STORAGE."

"Interesting." The investigator reached for his pad and pen and nodded his head.

"Why?" Jillian asked.

"Should have some fascinating shit stored in here." Alex wrote both the name of the storage facility and the street—Wildwood Road.

"Like what?"

"Like maybe that's where he's gonna stash his laptop before he disappears. And remember what his sister told us—all those boxes filled with newspaper clips about you and scenes of gory accidents." He pointed to the storage building with his pen. "Ryan's not keeping any of that shit in his apartment. It's gotta be stored here—and when we get him, he'll have a key to a room in this building. Then we'll have proof that he was hung up over you."

Jillian and Alex again waited while Ryan remained inside Secure Self-Storage. "Boring," Jillian complained, shuffling her feet while she kept her eyes focused on the entrance.

"Yeah. Isn't it fun being a private investigator?"

"It's much more exciting on TV."

"They lie."

Ten minutes later, Ryan opened the door, crossed the street, and headed straight towards them.

"Quick," Alex ordered. "Just follow my lead." He began walking slowly, head slightly lowered, moving in the same direction as Ryan. Jillian strolled next to the detective, trying to imitate his casual demeanor.

Their well-dressed target, holding a large yellow envelope, rushed past like a black and gray streak, not glancing at either of them. When Ryan was fifty feet ahead of them, Alex put his hand in front of Jillian, motioning for her to stop.

"Are we just going to let him go?" she asked.

"Too dangerous for us to follow him now that he's seen us."

"But he didn't even notice us."

"We can't be sure of that and if he'd turn around and see us now, he'd know we were following him because we were walking so slowly, we should have been out of his sight...Understand?"

"Yeah, I guess. So what're we going to do?"

Alex looked at the sky. "We got here about noon and the sun's a lot lower now. We've been here a few hours so it's gotta be close to four o'clock. Remember, this is February and it'll get dark early. First we'll look around for a taxi, and if we can't get one, I'll find a phone and call that cab driver we used before to take us back to the park."

"What do you think he's got in that yellow envelope?" Jillian asked as she and Alex sat in the back of the cab they had flagged down near the storage facility.

"Probably some clippings with details about you that he'll use to make up a bunch of lies to convince you how much the two of you have in common."

"Seems like a complicated way to get information." After taking off her brown-rimmed glasses, she turned to face Alex. "Why doesn't he just go to the library to do research?"

The investigator shrugged. "Who knows? From the way his sister described him, Ryan might be paranoid about not wanting anyone to see what he's doing. In the library, people are always around. Besides, he's collected so much shit about you, he's like a regular library anyway. Maybe he even catalogued all the papers.

Lord knows he had the time."

They sat quietly until Jillian spoke softly. "He planned this whole thing with me so thoroughly."

"Yeah. Lazy bum had nothing else to do—no job or school demands that everyone else has."

"What a waste." She shook her head. "He's so smart and..."

Alex tapped his chest and interrupted Jillian. "But, unlike me, he's not a nice guy. Ryan's a spoiled brat who grew up to be a spoiled man whose only interest in life is to punish you for something you didn't even do." The investigator turned towards her and grinned. "But, I promise you, we're gonna get the lowlife."

The cab driver dropped his passengers at the entrance to Juniper Park and, after Alex paid the man, he and Jillian walked rapidly towards the mini-mountain. The late afternoon temperature had gotten considerably cooler and the wind had picked up. She buttoned the top of her jacket and stuck her hands into the pockets as she strode forward.

They passed a group of teen boys playing baseball and a couple of puffing joggers, but when they reached the wooded hill, no one was nearby. The detective dashed into the clump of trees and soon found the notch. "Over here," he called, motioning to Jillian.

Moving silently, they picked up the tiny trail and, walking single file, followed the path up the small mountain. "I hear it," the girl said as they approached the clearing that housed their swirling time machine.

After peeling away the branches, Alex, with his companion right behind him, stepped into the open area. Then, holding hands, they threw themselves into the mini whirlwind and let it toss them to the other side of the clearing next to the cave.

Jillian sat up and immediately checked her watch. "It's moving again," she said, smiling. "We're back."

# CHAPTER 17

Ryan was bored. He'd already done his work for the day—buying a Sweet Million ticket and pocketing $483 in lottery winnings. As he walked to his apartment, he realized he was wearing his black-framed glasses with the moussed-hair—the same simple disguise he had worn the previous week when he'd met that pretty college student, Sara.

Thinking she might be free, he took out the prepaid cell phone, stepped under the awning of a grocery store, and called Sara's number.

"Hi," he said when she answered the phone. "It's Brad Maxwell. Remember me? We met last week at the supermarket and then went out for Chinese food."

"Oh, the lottery winner. Of course, I remember you."

Ryan could piture Sara smiling. She was glad he called. "Hey, I'm taking a break from my painting right now and was wondering if you'd like to have lunch again. I know you said you're going to school and working, but I didn't know your schedule."

"Well, it's Wednesday so I had classes this morning. But I've got a little time now before I gotta go back so I'd love to meet you for lunch."

Ryan chose a moderately priced Italian restaurant nearby for his lunch date. Since he was playing the part of a struggling artist, he couldn't very well select a more expensive, gourmet eatery. Besides, he had invited Sara so he would be paying for her meal and Ryan didn't like to spend money on others.

Fifteen minutes after he had phoned her, Sara bounced into the restaurant. "Hi," she said, grinning broadly as she spotted Ryan standing in the vestibule and joined him. "Thanks for calling. I'd been thinking about you, but you didn't give me your number or even your email."

"Then I'm glad I called you," he said, returning the girl's smile. "I was working all morning, finishing a large landscape, so I needed to get out of the apartment and clear my head. Went for a walk and decided, since I was already out, to treat myself to lunch and then I thought of you." He nodded towards the hostess standing behind the small counter. "Let's go grab a table."

The blonde hostess seated them in a small alcove in the front of the restaurant and they both studied the menu quietly.

"Have you eaten here before?" Sara asked.

"No," Ryan lied. In fact, he had been to the restaurant once, wearing his baseball fan disguise.

"Well, I'm gonna order the chicken parm." She closed the menu, unfolded the burgundy napkin, and placed it on her lap.

"I'll have penne pasta with shrimp." Ryan smiled at the girl and rested his menu on the table. "So what've you been doing since I saw you?"

The young woman shrugged. "Nothing special. You know, I go to school, go to work, go to school. Not much time for much else." She grinned at him. "That's why I was so glad you called. Breaks up the day. Makes it a little different."

"A cute girl like you—bet lots of guys ask you out."

Sara stared at her lap and frowned. "Not really," she whispered.

Then, raising her head slowly, she looked at him. "I've got some issues."

"Oh." Ryan glanced quizzically at the girl, trying not to appear angry. *Shit*. He didn't want to hear a sob story; he just wanted good company for lunch. "You don't have to talk about it," he suggested.

Sara gazed directly into his eyes. "I think I'll feel better if I tell you, Brad."

"Then go ahead," Ryan said, faking a sympathetic smile. "Tell me."

"Well, okay then...My parents divorced last year." She lowered her head again and spoke very softly. "It was real rough at home. My father drank too much and used to hit my mom, and sometimes me and my little brother if we got in his way."

"Too bad." He hoped it wasn't a long story. *Who the hell cares about her stupid family?*

"Yeah. My mom finally got a court order to keep him away. But by then she was such a wreck that it didn't even matter."

"I'm sorry." If she didn't finish this soap opera soon, he was going to make up his own story about forgetting an appointment and cancel lunch altogether.

"She got so depressed that she just took pills and lay around the house all day, sleeping and not doing anything. Then she stopped eating." Sara looked up at Ryan with tear-filled eyes. "Mom died three months ago."

"Very sad." He forced himself to look unhappy, but it took all of his acting skills. *Who needs to hear this shit?*

"So now I gotta take care of my brother and my dad's back in the house again." She paused briefly. "So far, he hasn't hit us, but I think he's still drinking and..."

Ryan couldn't stand listening to any more of the girl's troubles. "Gee, that's a terrible story," he said, interrupting her. "But, like you said, this is your lunch break." Smiling, he reached for Sara's hand. "Forget about all that sad stuff for now and just try to enjoy yourself."

He stroked her arm sympathetically.

She nodded at him, managing a slight grin. "You're right, Brad. I'm sorry to lay all this on you. Let's talk about something else—tell me about the painting you just finished."

Ryan barely suppressed a cheer. With the conversation now focusing on him, he launched into a detailed description of his mythical landscape. "I once saw photos of a large vineyard in France," he began. "I loved the vibrant colors and the lush purple grapes so I tried to recreate that scene in my painting. It's very colorful, with different shades of greens and yellows contrasting with the purple tones of the grapes."

Sara placed her elbows on the table and rested her head in her hands. "That sounds totally awesome. Can I see it?"

He shook his head. "'Fraid not. I don't like anyone seeing my paintings until they're shown in a gallery."

"Well, then when's your next show? I'd like to go check it out."

"I haven't scheduled one yet. Still gotta finish a couple more landscapes." Ryan smiled at the girl. "But I'll be sure to let you know...Hey, our lunch is here." He pointed to a swarthy young man who was approaching their table.

They watched quietly as the waiter set a food-filled platter in front of each of them. "Looks good," Ryan said.

"Yeah," Sara agreed, reaching for her fork. "I didn't realize how hungry I was."

"Me too." He began eating his shrimp pasta and, after a few bites, turned to the girl. "So you've gotta go back to school after lunch?"

She nodded. "It's my ancient history class. I think I told you last week, this professor takes points off your grade if you cut, so..." With a shrug, she lifted a small piece of chicken parm with her fork.

"That's too bad. We could've spent the rest of the afternoon together celebrating my finished landscape."

"Maybe next time," she said, smiling encouragingly.

They ate the rest of their meal without further conversation.

"Want any dessert?" Ryan asked as the busboy removed their plates and the waiter offered them two small menus.

Sara glanced at her wrist. "Uh uh. Not enough time. Besides, I'm really full. I don't usually eat big lunches like this." She rose to her feet, tossing her linen napkin on the table. "I'm sorry, Brad, but I think I gotta leave. This teacher also doesn't like it if you show up to his class late."

He shrugged.

"If you call me earlier, we could work it out so we could get together for longer."

*What the hell? Telling me what to do?* "Okay," he said aloud, faking a smile.

"Thanks again for the great lunch." Sara took two steps towards the exit and turned around. "Oh, and one more thing. Next time, Brad, I'd really like to see that painting of the vineyard."

# CHAPTER 18

Tuesday evening after work, Jillian and Helene sat in Alex's small office waiting for the investigator to speak. "Okay," Helene finally said. "You're the one who called this meeting, saying it was important, and we're both hoping you're ready to tell us about a plan to get Ryan." She looked at him quizzically. "But it's almost dinner time and we're so cramped in here. Why not move our meeting to a restaurant?"

Alex leaned back in his swivel chair, rested his arms behind his head, and smiled. "Don't want anyone else hearing this. It's too damn brilliant."

Jillian rolled her eyes. "Enough with the suspense. Please tell us your brilliant plan."

Alex stood, placed his hands on the paper-filled desk, and leaned forward. "Here's what we're gonna do," he said. "We're going back in time, of course, and we're gonna lure the shithead into a trap."

"How can we do that if we can't go back to a specific day?" Helene asked.

"Aha!" the detective shouted. "That's the beauty of my scheme.

We don't need to go back to a particular day because Ryan's gonna come to us."

Jillian looked at him, a confused expression on her face.

"Yup!" Alex said, nodding his head. "We're gonna hold a big contest—and Ryan's gonna wanna be the winner."

Both Jillian and Helene stared at the investigator. "Don't worry," Alex said. "I've got it all figured out." Again he smiled at them. "The only thing missing is the exact time this contest will take place. But we'll take care of that little detail once we go back to the past."

Still grinning, he turned towards his client. "Jillian wanted a major con, like in the movie *The Sting*, and I've granted the beautiful lady's wish." He bowed deeply to the girl, whose face reddened.

"And just when are you planning on doing all this?" Helene asked.

"I was hoping to do it soon. We're all gonna have to spend a week in the past setting up this operation, and with the Memorial Day weekend coming up, it might be a good time to..."

Jillian, having recovered her poise, interrupted him. "If it's a major con, don't we need some more people?"

"Yeah." The detective nodded. "I was gonna get to that. We need two more that we can trust. I want a big strong guy and another hot-looking girl. But I'm sure I can find them."

This time Jillian grinned. "I know two people just like you described who I think would really like to do this. Do you want me to call them?"

"If you're sure they can be trusted."

"I'm sure," Jillian said, smiling at the detective. "The girl already knows all about what Ryan's done to me. When should I tell them we're going on this 'trip'?"

"I'm flexible and you can always get time off," Alex said. He turned to the lawyer. "How about you, Helene? You've always got so much stuff happening. What do you say?"

"Call your friends and see if they can get a week off on short notice," she told Jillian. "If everyone else is in, then I'll rearrange my schedule and we can leave on Thursday."

Jillian used Alex's office phone to call Cheri. The dancer picked up immediately. "Hello, who's this?" she asked, sounding confused.

"Hi, Cheri. It's me, Jillian. How are you?"

"Oh, Jillian. You got a different number. What's up with you and the shitass boyfriend?"

Jillian smiled. "That's why I'm calling. I'm sitting here with a couple of people who are working with me to find him. But I can't explain anything on the phone, just that I need a huge favor from you—and from your boyfriend."

"Rocco? I filled him in on everythin' and he'd be glad to help. What do ya want us to do?"

"Can you get a week off starting on Thursday? We're all taking a trip to find Ryan and bring him back here. But you'll have to be away with us all that time."

"Sounds cool—a real adventure! Are you gonna travel far?"

Jillian glanced at Helene and Alex and giggled. "Yeah. It's kind of far. But it's also kind of near."

"Huh?"

"Cheri, do you think you and Rocco can get the time off to come with us?"

"Yeah. I'm sure we can. I got vacation days coming and Rocco does too. Ooh-La-La Club won't give us no problem." The dancer paused for a moment. "They wanna keep me happy."

"I remember. You're the star—Cheri, will you do it?"

"Of course! Now whatta me and Rocco gotta do?"

Less than an hour later, Cheri and her boyfriend joined the others in Alex's little office. The investigator had ordered Chinese food for the occasion, set out paper plates, and the five of them tried to find adequate space to sit and eat. It was especially difficult for Rocco, who was as tall and beefy as Cheri had described. With his shaved head, bushy mustache, and muscular physique, the bouncer resembled a fearsome mob hit man.

"Here, let me get rid of this," Alex said, picking up a magazine rack to give Rocco a little more legroom.

"That's okay." The burly giant waved the detective away. "I'm used to havin' to squeeze myself into tight places. I'm good just sittin' here." He gobbled some beef and broccoli from his paper plate and smiled. "Good Chinese."

Cheri sat in a folding chair wedged against Jillian, holding a bottle of water, but not eating. "This is so-o-o excitin'!" she exclaimed. "Like one of them spy movies. I can't wait to go after that creep who done this to you."

"Me too," Jillian agreed, scooping some chicken and pea pods into her plate. "But it's going to be a lot of work."

The dancer took a sip of water and smiled at Jillian. "Yeah, from what this guy Alex says, it'll be like puttin' on a play, actin' out parts."

"Did you ever see an old movie called *The Sting*?" Jillian asked. "It's with Paul Newman and Robert Redford."

"No." Cheri shook her head. "Never heard of it. How old is it?"

"From the early seventies, I think. I watched it at Helene's house, not too long ago. It's a great con story and it's something like we're gonna do to Ryan."

"One of my favorite movies," Helene said, pointing her fork at the dancer. "Great fun."

"Cool." Cheri smiled at the lawyer. "Maybe I'll see it when we get back."

After dinner, Alex resumed the meeting. "I want everyone at the Juniper Park main entrance, Thursday morning at nine. And don't drive there. Take a bus or a cab. We don't want to leave a bunch of cars sitting in the parking lot for a week because it'll look too suspicious."

"We're goin' to a park?" Cheri asked, giving Jillian a questioning look.

"That's where we'll begin, with a little hike," Jillian said, patting her friend's hand. "But, don't worry. It'll get much more interesting."

The detective faced Cheri and Rocco, and continued. "Don't bring your cell phones, iPods, laptops—or any other kinds of electronic devices—with you."

"No cell phones?" The dancer stared at Alex.

"They won't work where we're going," Jillian explained.

"You mean we're goin' somewhere that don't have no Internet—or electricity?" Rocco asked, frowning at Jillian.

"No electricity—like someplace in the goddamn jungle?" Cheri stood up quickly, shaking her black, purple-streaked hair. "Uh uh." She glanced unhappily at Jillian and squeezed the girl's arm. "Sorry, honey. I really wanna help you, but I need to blow dry my hair."

Jillian smiled at her friend and gently pushed the dancer back into the folding chair. "Sit down. Where we're going, you'll have electricity and even Internet. We just can't take our phones and computers there. You'll see why when..."

"Speaking of your hair," Alex interrupted, pointing to Cheri's eye-catching tresses. "You'll need to tone it down for most of our trip. No purple, and less makeup, please. We don't want anyone to recognize you."

The dancer nodded.

"Another important thing," the investigator continued, again addressing Cheri and Rocco. "Don't bring any credit or debit cards. We'll just be using cash on this trip." He grinned at the perplexed couple. "In fact, don't even bring your wallets or IDs because I'll be paying for everything. Think of it as an 'all expenses paid,' free vacation."

The dancer smiled at him. "I don't understand any of this shit. But I like the 'free' part."

"And one last thing," Alex said to the couple. "You can't tell anyone anything about this trip except that you'll be away for a week and won't be able to be reached."

Rocco, leaning against the wall, nodded his head solemnly.

"Okay, I guess," Cheri whispered.

The five of them sat quietly until Helene spoke. "We're going away for a week, Alex, but how're we supposed to pack? We don't have any room for suitcases."

Cheri turned to the lawyer. "No room for suitcases?" she asked. "Why not?"

"You'll see," Jillian said, patting the dancer's shoulder. "As you're learning, this is a very different kind of trip."

"Sounds more and more wacky," Rocco said, chuckling.

The detective rested his elbows on the desk and nodded. "Helene's right though. We all have to take some basic stuff with us." He smiled at the dancer. "No hair dryer though. You'll buy one when we reach our destination. And I gotta take some things that we'll need to catch Ryan so..." He glanced at the other four. "Everybody got a backpack?"

Helene, Jillian, and Rocco nodded affirmatively.

"I don't." Cheri shook her head.

"Go out and buy yourself a real big one," Alex said. "Then I want everybody to put only the stuff you can't live without for a week in the backpack—and leave some room. I'm gonna be bringing the supplies we'll need for the parts we'll be playing." He grinned at his small audience. "Trust me, it's gonna be lots of fun."

# CHAPTER 19

Ryan checked his appearance in the mirror, running his fingers through his freshly moussed hair to give it the proper toussled look. He was dressed casually in a blue sports shirt and black jeans. After all, he was playing the part of a struggling artist. Adjusting his black-framed glasses, he smiled at the idea.

Tonight—Saturday, February 19—he had a date with Sara. Although he hadn't liked the idea of the girl telling him what to do, Ryan was becoming increasingly lonely living in the past. He couldn't even contact Danielle because he was afraid he wouldn't be able to keep his facts straight and his sister would realize something was strange. "Can't take the chance," he mumbled, putting on his black wool jacket. Then, grabbing his keys and wallet, he locked the apartment door.

Ryan was picking up Sara at her home and he wasn't looking forward to the experience. "Don't give a shit about her family," he muttered, angry at the thought of having to make small talk with either her younger brother or drunken father.

But he did like the girl. She was good company—pretty and smart. As long as she didn't get too nosy about his paintings, the evening would work out just fine.

Sara lived in Southvale's working-class neighborhood, about ten minutes from Ryan's more upscale garden apartment complex. Her street was lined with small single-family homes, bunched closely together. Although most of the pastel-colored houses were well cared for, a couple of front lawns were littered with junk—a broken baby carriage, tire rims, rusted pipes.

Relieved that Sara's home was not one of the latter, Ryan walked past the neat lawn, climbed three concrete steps to the front door, and rang the bell.

"Who's it?" a male voice asked.

"Brad Maxwell. I'm here to see Sara."

The door opened slowly and Ryan faced a gangly long-haired teenager who frowned at him. "She ain't ready yet," the boy snarled. "Ya gotta wait."

"Thanks." Smiling at the surly kid, he entered the hallway and continued to the worn plaid couch in the living room. "I'll just sit here, if that's okay?"

The teen shrugged, followed his guest inside, and stared at him. "So how'd ya meet Sara? Ya look too old for her."

Ryan, trying to maintain his composure, continued smiling. "We met in the supermarket when we were both standing on line."

As he leaned against the wall opposite the sofa, the boy snickered. "Real romantic. Set it up so she'd talk to ya, huh?"

Ryan shook his head. ""No. Actually, I was on line ahead of your sister and she spoke to me first."

"Yeah. I bet." After a toss of his long brown hair, the teen again stared hostilely at the visitor. "Whaddyer do?"

"You mean for a living?"

"Yeah. What kinda job ya got?"

"I'm an artist. I paint landscapes."

"Pictures of grass and trees and that nature shit?"

"I guess you can call it that." Ryan forced a grin. "But I like to think of my paintings in more positive terms—green pastures and rolling meadows."

"It's still all grass and tree shit to me." The boy folded his arms. "And that ain't a job where ya make lots of money—just sittin' around paintin' stupid pictures."

Ryan shrugged. "Well, if you mean I'm not rich, then you're right. But I do okay. As a matter of fact, I've sold a number of..."

"Oh, are you two guys getting to know each other?" a feminine voice asked, interrupting Ryan's latest lie. He and the teen stopped talking and turned towards the girl, who stood at the bottom of the staircase.

Sara entered the living room and smiled at Ryan and her brother. She was wearing a pale blue turtleneck sweater and a pair of tight black jeans that accentuated her shapely rear.

Ryan stood and grinned at the girl. "You look great."

"Thanks, Brad." She approached the scowling teen, who continued to lean against the wall, and put her arm around his shoulder. "Everything okay, Mikey?"

"I guess so." The boy looked at Ryan again, this time not quite as angrily. "Where're you guys goin'?"

"Dinner and a movie," Sara said, tapping her brother's shoulder playfully. "Hey, have you been checking out my date?"

"Why not? Dad should be doin' it."

"Yeah, right," the girl said, smirking. "Lotsa luck with that idea. I'm just glad he's not here. He'd be cursing and screaming at everyone."

*Dad sounds like a barrel of laughs.* "Okay," Ryan said, glancing at his watch. "I think we ought to get going if we want to catch that eight o'clock movie."

"You're right." Sara smiled at her date and headed towards the entrance closet. "I'll get my jacket."

For dinner, Ryan had chosen a popular steakhouse with a salad bar, figuring they wouldn't have time for a lengthy meal before the movie. Even though he had made a reservation, the restaurant was crowded and he and Sara still had to wait for a table. They stood in a small vestibule until, ten minutes later, a young nose-ringed woman called, "Brad!" and, holding two menus, stared in their direction.

Sara stepped forward, but Ryan didn't immediately react. After giving him a puzzled look, she poked her date softly in the ribs. "Brad, what's the matter? The girl just called your name."

"Oh, sorry," Ryan said, smiling at Sara as the two of them walked behind the hostess. "Must've been daydreaming."

They were ushered to a small table overlooking bare trees and a half-frozen stream. "I bet this view looks beautiful in the spring," Sara said.

"Yeah," Ryan muttered, still annoyed at himself for not remembering his own name.

"Something wrong?"

"No. I just realized I forgot something." For a change, he was telling the truth.

"Oh, was it important?"

He grinned at the girl, shaking his head. "Not at all." Ryan picked up one of the menus and opened it. "I hope you're hungry because this place gives you lots of food. Let's order and hit the salad bar."

After dinner, Ryan drove Sara to the movie triplex. They had decided to see a new spy thriller that had gotten good reviews. He bought popcorn and soda for both of them and they found aisle seats near the back of the theater. "You can see the screen better from here than up front," he said.

"You think?"

"Yeah. It's a fact." Although Ryan didn't know if it was indeed a fact, his opinion was worth far more than the average person's.

After numerous commercials and several previews, the movie finally began. Ryan put his arm around his date, and she snuggled next to him. Cozily, they watched the action-filled thriller, which held their attention.

"How'd you like the movie?" Ryan asked when the lights came on.

"It was terrific!" Sara stood and put on her jacket, smiling at him. "I love that kind of picture, with lots of chase scenes and exploding bombs. But I haven't been to many movies lately. Thanks so much for taking me."

"You're welcome," he said, returning her smile as they strolled out of the theater. "I'll take you home now."

She stopped walking and stared at him seductively. "It's not that late. Why don't we go back to your apartment first? This way, you can show me your paintings. You know how much I've been wanting to see them."

Ryan waved his forefinger at the girl. "Uh, uh, uh. Remember what I said—I don't show my work to anyone until it's ready and in a gallery."

Sara grinned. "Yeah. But I thought you could break that rule for me, just this once—and we'd be all alone."

Smiling, he shook his head. "Sorry. No exceptions."

# CHAPTER 20

On Thursday, May 26 at nine-fifteen in the morning, the five members of the newly-formed search party stood at the main Juniper Park entrance. Each person had a jacket or sweatshirt tied around his or her waist and wore a backpack. Alex's shoulder gear had an oddly shaped bulge.

Cheri and Rocco had been the last to arrive. "Sorry we're late," Cheri said sheepishly to Jillian, Alex, and Helene as the bouncer paid the cab driver. "I was tryin' to stuff some extra shit into this thing." She indicated the huge blue backpack strapped tightly against her body.

The detective frowned at her overloaded satchel. "I thought I asked you to leave some room for the supplies we need."

Cheri shrugged, looking slightly embarrassed. "Sorry 'bout that." Then, shaking her now brown ponytail—minus the purple streak—she smiled at Alex. "But see, I remembered 'bout my hair and makeup. I just kinda forgot the leavin' room in the bag part."

As Rocco reached the others, he heard his girlfriend's comment and turned around to show off his black backpack. "Hey, I got lotsa room in mine, Alex. Just dump everything in here."

"Fine," the investigator said, removing several filled plastic bags from a large trash bag and shoving them into the big man's backpack. "That oughta do it." He picked up the black garbage bag and hoisted it over his shoulder. "Everybody ready for our trip?"

"Yeah," Cheri said. "But you still ain't told us where we're goin'."

"And why we gotta take a hike in the park first," her boyfriend added.

Helene smiled at the couple. "It'll be a surprise, like a mystery cruise."

Jillian moved closer to the dancer and began talking rapidly. "We'll start walking and, I promise, you'll both find out what's happening right after we leave the park. Until then, the rest of us won't know everything either."

"Huh?" Cheri stared at her friend and Rocco scowled, making him look even more ominous.

"C'mon." Jillian gave her friend a playful shove. "Let's go."

It was a beautiful late May morning—not too hot or humid—perfect weather for walking. With their heavy backpacks, the group resembled a serious hiking expedition, which didn't make much sense considering they were just climbing a small mountain and Juniper Park didn't offer overnight camping facilities.

Immediately after the backpackers began climbing the trail, two young men, walking rapidly, dashed ahead of them. After the groups nodded greetings to each other, Alex held out his hand, signaling his people to stop. "Let them go," he whispered. "We'll stay here for five minutes and then continue."

They stood in single file on the narrow path, waiting for the investigator's signal to move again. The woods were silent except for an occasional bird chirp and the soft rustling of tree branches. "Pretty out here," Rocco, who was last in line, finally said. "Never did much hikin', but this is kinda fun."

Cheri, directly in front of him, turned and jabbed her boyfriend playfully in his stomach. "Dodo-Roc, we only hiked about twenty feet. How could ya even know you like it?"

"I just know. It's so quiet like."

Alex looked at his watch and then called to the others behind him. "Okay. That's long enough, folks. Let's get going again."

The little band walked without further interruption until they reached the first clearing. "This is real good," Cheri said, rushing to the broken log seat. "A place to sit and rest. My backpack was gettin' damn heavy."

"That's because you stuffed it with so much crap," Rocco said, sitting next to her.

"They said we was gonna be away for a whole week and I need lotsa shit for...Hey, what're you guys doin'?" Cheri stopped her explanation as she noticed Alex and Jillian busily clearing away the pile of debris that blocked the view of the other side of the woods while Helene stood guard, making sure no strangers were watching.

"Now the fun starts," Jillian said, turning towards Cheri and Rocco and waving them forward. "C'mon. We continue this way."

The couple stood and headed towards the newly-created opening. "Why're we goin' through here?" Cheri asked. "This ain't on the road."

"No, it's not," her friend agreed. "We're going a special way."

After all five of them had crawled through the opening, Alex, Jillian, and Helene quickly replaced the pile of leaves and branches so the clearing was no longer visible from the other side.

"How come you're doin' that?" Rocco asked. "We're only gonna have to move that stuff again when we come back."

"Think of it as a secret passageway that we don't want anyone else to find," the private eye said.

Cheri scanned the new surroundings, which contained only the massive tilted dead log, and frowned. "What's so special about this place? There's nothin' here but lots more trees."

"True," Jillian said, walking to the gigantic hollow trunk, and tapping it. "But this one is very special." She began removing the leaves and thick branches that filled the cavity. With help from the others, the trunk was soon clear of debris.

"You guys sure like playin' with sticks and leaves," the bouncer said, chuckling as he wiped his hands on his jeans. "What now?"

"You see how big this opening is?" Jillian indicated the circumference of the hollow trunk. "We're all climbing through."

"Why?" Cheri asked.

"You'll see when you get there," the girl replied.

Rocco stared at her, dumbfounded. "You gotta be kiddin' me. I ain't gonna fit in that thing. I'm way too big."

"You should fit," Alex said, smiling. "But take off your backpack and I'll slide it down, just in case."

The bouncer shook his head. "I dunno. I don't wanna get stuck in there."

Cheri stepped up to her boyfriend and gave him a quick hug. "Don't worry, Dodo-Roc. If you get stuck, I'll push you out."

Jillian had heard enough. "Nobody's getting stuck!" she exclaimed, pointing emphatically at Alex. "Look, he's a big guy too and he's been in there a few times and never had a problem— C'mon!"

One by one, each of the backpackers climbed headfirst into the gaping cavity of the dead trunk, with Alex tossing the large plastic bag and Rocco's backpack down the chute before taking his turn. The bouncer was the last person to maneuver his body through the opening and slide to the other end of the hollow log.

"Jesus!" he shouted as he joined the others outside the cave and stared at the little wind swirl. "What the hell's that?"

"Think of it as a train, boat, or plane," Jillian said. "It's our transportation to Ryan."

Yeah," Alex agreed as he stashed the black plastic bag behind a tree next to the cave.

Cheri and her boyfriend looked totally mystified.

"You'll see," Jillian continued, grasping the dancer's wrist. "Rocco, put on your backpack and then we're all going to hold hands and spin around in that wind tunnel together. If your hand slips and you get separated, go back to the side near the cave and wait for the rest of us. Okay?"

Still mesmerized by the spinning wind, the bouncer strapped on his backpack and he and Cheri nodded their heads.

"Okay!" Jillian yelled. "Let's go!"

Holding hands, they all jumped into the whirlwind. As they spun, Jillian, Alex, and Helene counted to 110 and then pushed the couple out of the little twister.

"What was that all about?" Rocco asked, lying on the ground. "Now I'm so damn dizzy."

"I thought it was kinda fun," Cheri said, sitting up and hugging her knees. "Like one of them spinnin' carnival rides." She made a twirling motion with her index finger.

"I'm glad you liked it because we're not finished yet," Jillian said. "We're going back into that wind two more times."

"A total of three spins, right?" Alex asked.

The girl nodded. "Yeah. That's what we decided. With a shorter count than we did Monday, let's see what happens."

"This isn't an exact science," Helene said. "Luckily, we don't need to arrive at a specific time."

"What the hell are you all talkin' about?" the bouncer asked, staring at the three of them. "Where are we arrivin'?" Still lying on his back, he glanced in all directions. "We're just in a goddamn park!"

"Time to get up," Alex said, without responding to the man. "We're going into that wind tunnel again."

"We're done," Jillian announced after their last twirl and they all inched away from the whirlwind, remaining on the ground to rid themselves of any lingering dizziness.

"How's everyone doing?" the detective asked, standing and flexing his legs.

"I'm good." Cheri stood too, brushing bits of dirt from her clothes. "I hope I didn't break nothin' in my bag though. You didn't tell us we'd be spinnin' 'round in some strong little wind thing."

"Sorry," Jillian said, smiling. "But even if I did, you wouldn't have understood."

"Understood what?" The dancer stared at her friend. "You promised it'd all be clear by now, where we're goin' on this trip." She looked at the dense woods. "A bunch of trees in a park—it's still all the same."

"Oh, really?" the girl said, continuing to smile. "Do all the trees really look the same? I see some without any leaves. Pretty strange for this time of year, huh?"

After taking another brief glance at the foliage, Cheri touched the needles of a towering pine. "I dunno. Most, like this one, still got leaves."

"That's only because there are lots of evergreens right here," Jillian said. Then she pointed to her wrist. "Check your watch. Is it working?"

The dancer stared at her faux diamond-studded timepiece. "No. How'd you know that?"

"Mine ain't workin' either," Rocco said, sitting up.

"How about the weather?" Helene asked, walking up to the couple. "Does it feel any different?"

"Yeah," Cheri said. "It's kinda chilly." As she rubbed her arms, the dancer turned towards Jillian. "Why's that? It was lots warmer out when we started."

Jillian nodded. "You're right, Cheri. It sure was." She unwrapped her jacket and slipped her arms through. "But the temperature's going to be cool during our trip so you'll have to dress warmer."

The others untied the sweatshirts or jackets they had been

carrying around their waists and put on the outerwear. Then they again formed a single line and Alex led everyone down the other side of the small mountain.

After they parted the branches, the backpackers stepped out of the tiny trail into an empty Juniper Park. Cheri looked up at the cloud-filled sky and frowned. "It ain't sunny no more."

"Yeah," Alex agreed. "Cool and cloudy here."

"What d'ya mean 'here'?" Rocco asked. "We're still in the same park. It's just a lot colder now."

"Pretty strange weather for the end of May, huh?" Jillian said, smiling at the bouncer. "I see more trees without any leaves—and how about the grass?" She gazed at the ground. "Doesn't it look pretty dead?"

"Why's that?" Cheri asked. "Don't this park take care of the grass?"

Rocco pointed at the investigator, who had darted towards a clump of nearby trees and was carefully examining the back of one of them. "What's he doin'?"

"Looking for a notch...Is it there?" the girl called.

"Yup," Alex said, smiling as he dashed back to the group. "And it doesn't look brand new either so our timing should be pretty good."

"Huh?" Cheri stared at Jillian and then at the detective with a perplexed expression. "What the hell are you two talkin' about?"

Helene grasped the dancer's arm and began leading the confused young woman towards the park exit. "After we walk out of here and check into a motel, you and Rocco will understand everything."

# CHAPTER 21

Sara walked quickly to her car late Wednesday afternoon on February 23, clutching a scrap of paper. As she scanned the sheet, she mouthed the address to herself, trying to memorize it: "27 Corview Street, Apartment 12."

She knew dropping in on Brad uninvited wasn't the right thing to do, but her curiosity had been building since she first met the artist. They had gone out four times and on every date she had asked to see his paintings. Each time, he had refused. On their last date—lunch at a diner—when he had gone to the restroom, she had rummaged through his jacket, found a letter addressed to him, and scribbled the address. Then she had googled the driving instructions.

Sara didn't buy Brad's excuse about his landscapes needing to be completely finished and in a gallery before anyone could see them. She was sure there was another reason for his reluctance to let her visit him. Something about this guy she was dating seemed a little bit off. Sure, he was attractive. But she had practically told him she'd be interested in a physical relationship and all he'd done so far was kiss her goodnight at her front door.

*Gotta be some reason he won't ask me into his apartment.* "Maybe he's married," she muttered, shifting the Volkswagen into gear. "Or gay." *Maybe the paintings were stolen? He's some kind of crook?*

Sara shook her head. No. It didn't fit. He was secretive though, definitely hiding something. As she drove, she tried to figure out exactly what Brad Maxwell was keeping from her.

Sara reached the garden apartment complex and parked across the street. Then she raced to the door of Apartment 12 and boldly knocked.

"Who is it?" a man asked, his voice somewhat muffled.

"Surprise! It's me, Sara."

He didn't respond immediately. "Sara?" he finally said, still not opening the door. "What're you doing here? How'd you know where I live?" He didn't sound happy at all.

"Oh, I'm sorry if I'm disturbing you, Brad, but I really wanted to see your paintings. Can I come in, just for a moment? I promise I won't stay." She waited, hearing movement inside that sounded like he was rushing back and forth. "Hey, you don't have to clean for me," she called.

Brad, wearing a winter jacket, opened the door and stepped outside, immediately closing and locking the door behind him. "Sara, you really shouldn't have come here," he said, frowning and glancing in all directions.

"Why? What's wrong?" She stared at him and realized he looked a little different. *His hair.* Today, it was neatly combed, without the usual moussed look.

"We can't talk here. C'mon." He prodded the girl towards the street. "Where's your car?"

She pointed to the Volkswagen.

"Let's go for a ride." He took her arm and led the confused girl to her car.

"Where are we going?" Sara asked as she sat in the driver's seat.

"Back to your house."

"Why?" She glanced at Brad.

"Because that's where you belong."

"Oh." She sat quietly, not starting the ignition. "What about you? How'll you get home?"

"I'll take a cab." He continued to frown at her. "You know you really shouldn't have come here."

"I just wanted to see your paintings, Brad. Can't you understand that?" She gazed sadly at her passenger. "I thought artists like you are proud of their work."

He nodded solemnly. "Yeah. I am proud. But like I told you, I don't show anyone my paintings until they're in a gallery." He smiled at her. "I'm arranging for a show right now so you'll be able to see them soon."

"Really?" Sara put the car into gear and began driving slowly.

"Yeah. We're just finalizing the details."

"When's the show gonna be?"

"Sometime in late March. I'll let you know everything when we get it all set."

"Okay." She gave him a weak smile. "I'm sorry I barged in on you like that. I didn't think you'd mind so much."

"Now you know I do mind so don't ever do it again."

They spent the rest of the ride to Sara's house in an uncomfortable silence.

Ryan sat in the backseat of a cab, reviewing his disturbing little episode with Sara. It had been a close call. Luckily, he hadn't been wearing one of his elaborate disguises and just had to add the black-framed glasses to look like Brad. His hair wasn't styled, but that didn't matter since she had shown up at his door without an invitation.

*Not good.* She was too curious about his goddamn paintings. He'd done such a great job of lying. And how'd she find his address?

He knew he hadn't given it to her.

He shook his head and sighed. The girl was attractive and good company, but he couldn't go out with her again. It was too dangerous. *We're done.* He wouldn't call her anymore. She didn't have his cell number—the number was blocked—and he didn't have a phone in the apartment.

She'd give up when he didn't call and she couldn't reach him. Ryan leaned back in the cab, resting his arms behind his head. Her loss—she'd certainly miss him. *Serves her right for being so damn nosy.* He'd have to be more careful about making friends here in the recent past.

Better to just wait it out and concentrate on making money. Work a little harder—buy two winning lottery tickets a day. Maybe go to the track more often. Of course, he'd have to keep a good record of which disguises he wore to which stores, but it was all doable, especially for a smart guy like himself.

Ryan closed his eyes and pictured Jillian in handcuffs, being arrested and jailed for his murder. She was wearing orange prison garb, her hair was matted, and she was sobbing. *All worth it,* he thought, smiling at the satisfying image.

# CHAPTER 22

The small band of time traveling backpackers began walking from the park to the nearest motel, which Alex had found when he had researched their trip. "Don't use your real names when you check in," he instructed Cheri and Rocco.

"You mean like an alias?" the dancer asked.

"Yeah." The investigator smiled at her. "We're starting our little play now."

"Cool!"

Alex turned to Jillian and pointed to her head. "Go put on the wig and the glasses so you're already wearing that stuff when we reach the motel."

Jillian nodded, ducked into a nearby side street, undid her backpack, and found the disguise. Quickly, she put on the brown-rimmed glasses and covered her dark hair with the honey blonde wig.

"You look so different!" Cheri squealed when she returned. "I wouldn't have known it was you."

"That's the idea," Alex said.

"Is the wig on straight?" Jillian asked.

Helene appraised her appearance. "It's a little crooked," she said, reaching over and tugging on the curly hair until it was centered on the girl's head. Then the lawyer stepped back and admired her work. "Much better."

After a twelve-block walk, the group reached the Shady Elms Motel, an unpretentious two-story white building with about fifteen rooms. The neon sign leading to the rear parking lot flashed "Vacancy."

"Won't we look suspicious just walking in here without any car?" Jillian asked.

"Nah," the investigator said. "They won't give a shit. They'll just be happy to get some business. I don't think this place does real well. And if anyone asks, we'll just tell them the truth—that we're a group of hikers and we were out hiking in Juniper Park."

The modest motel featured a tiny lobby that contained only a pale blue love seat, two navy upholstered chairs, and a small wooden table with a coffee pot, Styrofoam cups, stirrers, and sugar packets. According to the wall clock, the time was 1:35.

When the backpackers reached the registration desk, Alex asked the buxom white-haired clerk for three rooms: one for Helene and Jillian, another for Cheri and Rocco, and a third for himself.

The lawyer signed in as "Mrs. C. Moscow and daughter," the dancer registered herself and Rocco as "Mr. and Mrs. Rick Flowers," and Alex entered his name as "Alan Ketcham." Then he gave the clerk a cash down payment for seven nights.

"Thank you," the woman said, beaming as she counted the bills. "Glad you folks will be staying with us all week." After printing a receipt, she smiled at her new guests. "I've got three rooms together at the end of the hall. Is that okay?"

"Fine," the detective said, nodding.

The clerk reached under the counter and produced five swipe cards, which she placed into a small machine. "Here you go," she said, handing Alex the newly configured keys. "Rooms 114, 115, and 116. Just turn right. And we've got coffee available in the lobby all day. Please feel free to help yourselves."

"Thanks," the investigator said, smiling his dimpled grin. "Do you sell newspapers someplace here?"

"'Fraid not." The clerk shook her head. Then, a few seconds later, she raised her hand. "Hold on. I think the morning guy left today's paper in the office. Let me check." She walked into the back room and quickly returned, clutching a newspaper. "Here," she said, thrusting the paper at Alex. "You can have this one."

"Thanks a lot." He turned towards the hallway, gripping the paper.

"Glad to help," the woman said. "Enjoy your stay at Shady Elms."

The five travelers easily found their three rooms near the end of the short hallway. "Let's all go in here for a quick meeting before we settle in," Alex said, sliding the key into his door.

After tossing their backpacks on the thin green carpet, Jillian, Helene, Cheri, and Rocco sat together on the queen-sized bed. The detective placed the newspaper on the small desk and pulled out the chair underneath. Then, before lowering himself into the seat, he turned on the TV.

"Why'd you do that if we're gonna talk?" Rocco asked.

"I bet I know," Cheri said. "It's so no one can hear what he's gonna be sayin'." She smiled at the investigator. "Right?"

"Yup." Alex nodded his head and addressed the couple. "Okay. This'll only take a few minutes. We're just going to brief you and Rocco about what's happening here." He scooped the newspaper from the desk, waving it in the air. "Anyone want to guess the date on this?"

"Whaddya mean 'guess the date'?" the bouncer asked. "It's today's paper so it's May 26th."

"Wanna bet?" The private eye grinned at him.

"I hope it's some time like March 15th," Jillian said. "That's when we were aiming for."

"Huh?" The dancer frowned at her friend. "Aimin' for what? I don't know what you're talkin' about."

The other three ignored Cheri and continued their conversation. "I'll say March 20th, just to be different," Helene said.

Alex closed his eyes and thought for a moment. "And I'll guess it's March 24th." He lifted the newspaper, checked the front page, looked up, and smiled. "Jillian wins. She's the closest. Happy Saint Patrick's Day—today's date is Thursday, March 17th."

"What the hell's goin' on here?" Rocco jumped off the bed and snatched the newspaper from the detective. "Gimme this. That date can't be right." He stared at the masthead. "This paper's gotta be more than two months old. But the lady at the desk said it was today's." He shook his head. "I don't understand..."

"How about this?" Alex asked, handing Cheri the sheet of paper the clerk had given him. "What's the date on this receipt?"

The bewildered couple examined the statement for several moments. Finally, the dancer shrugged. "I seen her give you this, but it says 'March 17th.'"

"Did you notice the time on the clock in the lobby?" the investigator asked Rocco.

"No." The big man continued to stare at the newspaper while Cheri still studied the receipt.

"What does your watch say?" Alex continued.

The bouncer stared at his wrist. "It still ain't working?"

"Mine neither," Cheri said, looking up. "I don't get it. Why'd they both stop?"

"Check the alarm clock," the detective said. "What's the time?"

"Quarter to two," the dancer said, frowning as she glanced at the investigator. "But that ain't right. It's gotta be around eleven. This trip didn't take that long."

"Okay, folks." Alex grabbed the newspaper and the receipt from the perplexed couple's hands. "Here's the deal. Our little 'trip' didn't take us to any faraway place, but it did take us somewhere very different. That little wind tunnel spun us into the past so right now we're in Thursday, March 17th. This is where Ryan is hiding and now we're going to start working on my plan to lure him out so we can bring him back with us to the present."

Cheri and Rocco stared at Alex, their faces registering expressions of total amazement. Then, speaking in a whisper, the bouncer asked, "Is this shit really true?"

"Yes," Jillian said. "Strange as it sounds, it's all true. We're over two months back in time."

"Wow!" Cheri sighed deeply. "I never would've believed this."

Helene patted the dancer's hand. "None of us believed this could happen at first. It takes a while to sink in."

"We're time travelers, just like in the movies," Cheri said. "Wow!" She sighed again, closing her eyes.

"That's why none of our electronic devices work here, like watches or hair dryers," the detective explained. "They don't belong."

"But we don't belong here neither," the dancer pointed out. "And we're workin' okay."

Alex nodded in agreement. "You're right, Cheri. We're not scientists so we don't understand everything about this time travel stuff. Somehow, we can co-exist while..."

"Hey, that's right—ain't we already livin' here in March?" Rocco interrupted, waving his beefy hand at the others. "I mean, I was here then and you guys was here too."

"Yes," Jillian agreed. "We all have ourselves walking around, doing whatever we were doing back in March. We're trying to avoid running into our other selves because we don't know what'll happen if we do meet."

"You mean we could like explode or somethin'?" Cheri asked, banging her fists together.

The investigator shrugged. "Who the hell knows? No one's ever proved any of this time travel shit has happened so we just don't want to take unnecessary chances." He turned to Cheri and Rocco. "Now that you two know what's happening here, we're all gonna take a short break to unpack and wash up and then we'll meet again in my room. Bring all the stuff I threw into your backpacks and be back here in fifteen minutes. Check your alarm clock for the time. It's nearly two o'clock here already—and we've still got lots more to do today."

# CHAPTER 23

Sara sat in her Volkswagen, across the street from Brad's garden apartment, at nine in the morning on a chilly Tuesday in early March, debating whether or not she should go ahead with her plan. It had been nearly two weeks since she had shown up at the artist's doorstep uninvited and he had driven her home. Yes, he had been mad at her, but he had promised to call with details about the upcoming gallery exhibit of his paintings.

She hadn't heard a word from the guy since then. And a search for a phone number for either "Brad Maxwell" or "Bradley Maxwell" at his home address had turned up nothing. She still didn't know his email address either.

Sara leaned her head back in the car seat and closed her eyes. Obviously, Brad didn't want to go out with her anymore. She was okay with that since the guy was more than a bit weird. But she couldn't stop thinking about what he was hiding. Why wouldn't he let her see his landscapes? What did they look like? Her curiosity was driving her crazy. She just had to find out.

Opening her eyes, she resumed watching his apartment. *So, if he goes out, what then?*

As Sara wondered what she should do when she confronted the artist, Brad's door opened and a stranger stepped outside. The gray-haired man, wearing a long tan overcoat, inserted a key into the lock.

*Who's that?* Brad had never mentioned living with his father or with anyone else. Maybe that was the secret—the reason he had never invited her inside. Moving silently, Sara slipped out of her car and crouched behind it, peering at the unfamiliar figure.

The gray-haired man strode from the apartment complex, walking at a brisk pace in the opposite direction and never glancing her way. When he was no longer in sight, the girl stood up, crossed the quiet street, and approached Brad's apartment.

Sara walked boldly to the door, and rang the bell. There was no answer. She wondered if maybe Brad had gone out earlier, before she arrived. She took a few steps backward and looked quickly to the left and then to the right. No one was nearby. Then, standing on her tiptoes, she tried to peek into the window, but the closed drapes prevented her from seeing inside.

She put her hands on her hips, trying to think of a way to get into the apartment.

Sara wandered to the rear of the complex and counted three units from the left, the location of Brad's apartment. Hoping no neighbors were watching, she began tugging on his window lids. They were all locked until she reached the unit's smallest glass, which had a slight opening on the bottom. After pushing that window open, she climbed into the bathroom, quickly closed the window, and walked through a short hallway into the living room.

"Nothing here," she muttered. The room contained just a couple of folding chairs and a small TV—no couch, table, or lamp. And where were all the paintings?

She turned around, heading into the bedroom, which was also

sparsely furnished with only one small bed, lamp, and night table. *That other man...?* It didn't seem like two people were living here. And, again, she saw no canvasses or art supplies.

She opened the bedroom closet and looked inside. *What the hell?* The closet was packed with clothes, scrunched tightly together. But this wasn't an ordinary collection of men's pants, shirts, suits, and coats. She tugged on one hanger and pulled out a cowboy outfit—shirt, neck scarf, and jeans. Then she grabbed another hanger, wrestling it free. That one was filled with New York Yankees gear.

Still holding the Yankees uniform, Sara glanced at the shelf above the clothes rack. A briefcase occupied the right corner and the rest of the space was filled with an assortment of different sized boxes. She removed one of the boxes, placed it on the bed, and opened it. Inside was a man's curly-haired brown wig. After putting that box back on the shelf, she removed another small box. When she opened it, she found a long-haired blond wig.

She stepped back from the bed, staring again at the contents of Brad's bedroom closet. "Too weird," she mumbled, rushing into the living room, toward the front door, her curiosity replaced by another emotion—fear. She could feel her heart pounding as her mind ordered her to get out of the apartment, ASAP.

Then Sara heard a key opening the lock.

# CHAPTER 24

The time travelers reassembled in Alex's motel room with the other four again sitting on his bed. "Does everyone have my packages from the backpacks?" the investigator asked.

Jillian, Helene, and Rocco all nodded.

"Good. Let me have them."

The three handed their batches of nearly identical plastic bags to Alex. "Thanks," the detective said. "It would've weighed me down carrying them."

"I don't get it," Rocco said. "Why do we need all these jellybeans?"

"You'll see." Alex opened the bags and began adding the colorful candies to a large glass jar on the bureau counter behind him.

"We're doing a contest," Jillian explained.

"Yup," Alex agreed as he continued pouring the jellybeans into the jar. "Our story is we're doing it to introduce a new brand of jellybeans, Jaybee's. And the person with the closest guess will win this." He raised a small sign that read "Guess the Number of Jellybeans and Win $1,000 in Cash!" and smiled. "That oughta get Ryan's interest."

The detective grabbed some small slips of paper and lifted

them. "These are the entry forms for our jellybean contest," he said, motioning towards a little cardboard box with a slit in the middle. "People'll put their entries in there."

"And our contest's free, right?" Helene asked.

Alex nodded.

Cheri, who had been quiet throughout Alex's presentation, now turned to him. "You payin' for all this and the thousand dollar prize too?" she asked.

"Just for now. But I'll be fully reimbursed later."

"From where?" the dancer asked.

"You'll see." He smiled at her and then addressed the others. "Okay, now that you all understand our contest, here's what I need everyone to do this afternoon." He pointed to Jillian. "You can finish the poster since we know today's date is March 17th. We'll end the contest in a week, on Thursday, March 24th, so go to the library and add that information."

"I'll do it real fast," the girl said, smiling at the detective.

Alex nodded at his audience. "Thursday's a good day, not a weekend, to have our results announcement party for everyone who entered the contest. We'll have free food there so they'll wanna come."

He turned to Helene. "I need you and Cheri to go to Village Terrace and see if you can book the place for next Thursday night. We'll only need a couple of hours—seven to nine—but it'll look suspicious if you ask for so little time. They may have something for today, Saint Patrick's Day, but even on short notice, I'm betting they won't have anything scheduled for Thursday night, March 24th."

"What if they do?" Helene asked.

"Then try the Elks Lodge and find a phone to call Jillian at the library to let her know what's going on. She's gotta finish the flyer this afternoon so we can hang it up everywhere."

"What about me?" Rocco asked, tapping his chest. "What do ya want me to do, Alex?"

"First go with Jillian to the library and wait for her to add the dates to the contest information sheet and print you out a copy. Then I've got a very important job for you."

Alex picked up the now filled jellybean jar and held it in front of Rocco. "I need you to take this to Town Hall with a letter I'll give you, addressed to the mayor's deputy, asking for permission to set up there. You'll be the one manning our contest desk most of the time. People will come up to you to guess the number of jellybeans in this jar and enter our little contest."

"Helene'll be your relief at Town Hall," he added. "But she'll be wearing a disguise."

The bouncer stared at Alex, totally perplexed. "How about me? Don't I need a disguise?"

"Nope. It doesn't matter at all if Ryan recognizes you."

"I don't understand. If I'm gonna be sittin' there waitin' for him, why can't I just grab the guy when he comes in? I won't make no noise."

The private eye shook his head. "First of all, you may not even recognize him. And, even if you do, he's carrying too much evidence from the future. We've got to make sure all that information's destroyed before we nail him." He leaned against the desk chair and chuckled at his small audience. "Be patient, folks. It'll happen."

They all sat quietly for several moments absorbing the investigator's words, the chatter of the television providing the only sound. Then Jillian quietly asked, "What about you, Alex? Where are you going this afternoon?"

The investigator took an envelope from his shirt pocket and waved it at the others. "I've gotta go to the newspaper office to make sure a certain article gets into next Friday's paper."

He pointed to the telephone on the night table. "Then, after that, I'm gonna pick up five prepaid cell phones for us so we can keep in touch. That reminds me..." He faced Helene. "After you book the place, I want you and Cheri to buy watches for everyone."

The lawyer nodded.

"I wanna get a hairdryer too," the dancer said. "This motel don't have one and I couldn't take mine. Remember?"

"Yeah," Alex said. "Go ahead." He looked at the alarm clock, which read 2:40. "Except for Rocco, we'll all meet at the library at five o'clock." Turning to Jillian, he asked, "You should have the flyers ready by then, right?"

"Yes."

"Okay, then." The detective clapped his hands together and stood. "Let me give everybody some cash for food, supplies, and cabs and we'll get this show on the road."

Alex stepped out of the taxi and entered the lobby of the *Daily Sentinel*, greeting the receptionist. "Hi, Yvonne," he said. "Is Fred around?"

"Sure, Alex." The attractive young African-American woman looked quizzically at the investigator.

"Something wrong?" he asked, noticing her expression.

"No." She shook her head, smiling at him. "Everything's fine. Let me get Fred for you." She lifted the phone, quickly punched in an extension, and whispered a few words before ending the conversation. "He'll be right out," she said to Alex, again smiling.

Seconds later, a short pudgy man with thinning gray hair, his sleeves unevenly rolled up, rushed towards the detective. "Alex!" He held out his hand, grinning widely. "Didn't expect to see you again so soon. Did you forget something?"

Alex grasped the man's outstretched hand without saying anything, hoping Fred would give him another clue about what he was talking about. *What the hell's happening March 17th?* He knew he hadn't been here celebrating Saint Patrick's Day.

Without waiting for a response, the newspaperman put his arm around the private eye's waist and prodded him gently. "C'mon. Let's talk about this in my office."

Since the mid-March weather was relatively mild and the Village Terrace was just a short distance from the Shady Elms Motel, Helene and Cheri decided to walk to the catering hall.

"So what do you think about all of this?" the lawyer asked.

Cheri took a deep breath and shook her head. "It still feels kinda weird, you know, us being here, but at another time. I don't really understand what happened."

Helene laughed. "Neither do I. But somehow we're here in the past and we can help Jillian by capturing Ryan and bringing him back with us."

"Yeah. That oughta be fun—the actin' part, I mean. I'm lookin' forward to that." Cheri smiled at the lawyer. "I always wanted to be an actress."

Helene returned the smile. "Well, you'll have your chance very soon. But you're really an exotic dancer in a club, right?"

Cheri nodded.

"I'm curious. How does someone become an exotic dancer? Did you study dancing as a child?"

"Nah! We didn't have no money for lessons. My dad left us when I was a little kid and my mom had to take care of me and my baby sister."

Helene stopped walking for a moment and studied the young woman's face. "Must have been tough," she finally said.

"Yeah. It was. In high school, Mom made me get an after-school job. I was a waitress in a diner. Hated it!"

"All the hard work? Carrying heavy trays of food?"

Cheri chuckled. "That part wasn't so bad. But I had to wear this dumb uniform—white shirt and baggy black pants. And the boss didn't like my purple hair and lipstick."

"So you quit?"

"Not at first. We needed the money at home. But then this customer asked me if I liked to dance. He told me about the Ooh-

La-La Club and said they was lookin' to hire pretty girls." She shrugged. "I went there and got the job."

"What did your mother think?"

"I didn't say nothin' about it at first. Told her my hours at the diner was changed and just gave her the same money as before." Cheri lowered her voice. "I kept the rest, and, you know, bought a couple of things."

Helene nodded. "So when your mother found out what you'd done, then what happened?"

"We had a big fight," Cheri whispered. "And I moved out."

They took several steps before Helene spoke again. "Is your mother okay with your job now?"

"Kind of," Cheri said. "Now that I'm the star."

Helene smiled at the dancer and pointed to a large sign on the next block. "We're here. Now let's see if Alex is right and we can book this place on short notice for next Thursday night."

Rocco, walking at a rapid clip, headed for Town Hall, which was less than a half-mile away. The bouncer carried a shopping bag containing all the contest essentials: jar filled with jellybeans, sign announcing the $1,000 prize, little cardboard box with a slit, entry forms, and information sheet—including the March 24th end date Jillian had just added and printed in the library.

For now, his flyer stated the results announcement party would be held at the Village Terrace. They would change that information, if necessary. The main thing, Alex had stressed, was to get the contest started. They needed to run it for a week to make it look legitimate.

As he reached the entrance to Town Hall, Rocco touched his shirt pocket. It was okay; Alex's letter was there. Then, opening the front door, he stepped inside. "I need to speak to Laurie Hunter," he said to the fifty-something brunette with bright red lipstick who occupied the reception desk.

"Can I tell her what this is in reference to?" the woman asked.

"I got an important letter for her." Rocco pointed to the envelope protruding from his shirt pocket. "Please call Ms. Hunter now."

The receptionist nodded and punched in an extension. "I have someone here who says he needs to talk to you," she said. After listening to a brief response, the woman replaced the receiver, looked up, and smiled at the bouncer. "She's on her way."

Alex took a seat in Fred Ludwig's messy office and waited for the newspaperman to speak.

"So what's this all about?" Fred asked, lowering himself heavily into the swivel chair behind his desk.

"What do you mean?" Alex saw his friend often on business and still didn't remember what had occurred during his original March 17th visit, more than two months ago.

"You know," Fred chuckled. "We just finished lunch not much more than an hour ago and I thought we'd straightened everything out with those blackmail pictures. Do you need something else? You coulda just called." The newspaperman stared at Alex's chest. "And why'd you change your shirt? Spill some ketchup on it at lunch?"

The investigator smiled, resting his hands on the man's cluttered desk. "Yeah," he said. "You know me, always makin' a mess...Listen Fred, I need a big favor. I couldn't ask you at lunch because I had to make sure we were alone." Alex rose and began talking rapidly. "This has nothing at all to do with the blackmail case. It's entirely different." He closed the office door before continuing. "And I had to do this in person because it's top secret stuff."

The editor leaned back in his chair, linking his hands behind his head. "Go ahead. I'm listening."

Alex took a sheet of paper from his shirt pocket and waved it at the man. "I need you to publish this little story—exactly as it's written—in next Friday's paper, March 25th. I can't tell you the details now, but it's gotta appear in the *Sentinel* on that date so I can catch a criminal." He handed the sheet to the editor.

After skimming the page, Fred glanced at the detective. "This is what's so important? You're running a jellybean contest?"

"Yeah, kind of." Alex shrugged. "Look, I can't explain what's going on, but I'm not doing anything illegal here. You gotta trust me, Fred, and just print this story. It can be anywhere in the paper, as long as it runs a week from tomorrow."

The editor grabbed a red pen, wrote something in large letters on the sheet, and placed it on the top of a large stack of papers. "Done," he said, smiling at his friend. "But, when this is over, you'll have to tell me what it's all about."

Alex shook his head and dashed to the door. "I'm not sure I'll be able to tell you, Fred. But thanks a lot for doing this. I really appreciate it." He grasped the doorknob, paused, and then turned around to again face the newspaperman. "Oh, and one more important thing. If you see me or even talk to me on the phone before next Friday, please don't mention this little meeting." He raised his forefinger to his lips. "This stuff is really hush-hush, so if you bring it up, I'll just pretend I don't know what the hell you're talking about."

Then, with a brief wave, he quickly walked out of his friend's office before the man could question him further.

Helene and Cheri entered Village Terrace and surveyed the catering hall. "This place is pretty borin'," the dancer said, pointing to the ceiling. "I thought it'd be, you know, more fancy, with like... chandeliers."

"I know what you mean," the lawyer agreed, glancing first at the institutional-looking overhead lighting fixtures and then at the unadorned almond-colored walls and white round tables, which were surrounded by plain cushioned chairs. "Maybe that's why Alex chose this place." When Helene noticed an attractive redhead wearing a brown business suit heading towards them, she stopped talking.

"Good afternoon, ladies," the woman said. "Can I help you with something?"

"Yes," Helene replied. "We'd like to book the Village Terrace for next Thursday night, March 24th. Is it available then?"

The woman stared at them.

"Is there a problem?" the lawyer asked.

"Of course not." The catering hall representative shook her head and smiled apologetically. "I'm sorry. I didn't mean to be rude, but we don't get many last-minute requests here."

"We had a problem with another hall and had to cancel," Helene said quickly. "I hope you're not booked for that March 24th date."

"Oh, I'm so sorry to hear that." The redhead turned and began walking away from them. "Let me get my list and I'll check."

"I didn't realize we'd sound suspicious," Helene whispered to Cheri as they waited for the woman to return.

"That sounded good, what you told her."

The redhead strode towards them, clutching a large padded book. "Please sit down," she said, gesturing towards the nearest round table. When they were all seated, she opened her book and began turning the pages. "Here we are. Next Thursday, March 24th, you wanted?"

"Yes," the dancer said.

Glancing up, the catering hall representative smiled at Helene and Cheri. "You're in luck, ladies. That date's still available."

The Town Hall receptionist with the red lipstick had barely finished hanging up the phone when a tall and slender African-American woman, her black hair in a prim bun, greeted Rocco. "Hi, I'm Laurie Hunter," the woman said crisply, extending her hand. Dressed in a conservative navy suit, she looked like a business executive and projected a distinct no-nonsense aura. "You need to speak to me?"

The bouncer grasped the deputy mayor's outstretched hand and smiled. "Thanks for comin' over so quickly." He reached into his shirt pocket, extracted Alex's letter, and gave it to her. "Here."

The woman opened the envelope and quickly read the contents. Then she dropped her all-business demeanor and, grinning at Rocco, said, "I'd do almost anything for Alex Drury." After tucking the letter in her suit-jacket pocket, she poked the bouncer's arm playfully. "Come with me."

Rocco picked up his shopping bag and followed the deputy mayor, who walked rapidly through the hall. When she reached an unoccupied office, the woman indicated he should enter and take a seat.

"Now tell me what this is all about," she said, scooting onto the top of the empty desk opposite him. She sat and crossed her long navy-suited legs.

"Um, like the letter says, we're runnin' a jellybean contest."

"Strange that Alex didn't mention it to me earlier so I could have prepared."

"It came up kinda sudden like," Rocco said, shifting his large body uncomfortably in the small chair. He hadn't expected to be cross-examined.

"And you need to set up here immediately?"

"Yes, please. We're only doin' the contest for a week."

Gracefully, the deputy mayor hopped off the desk. "Okay, I'll make it happen." Again she smiled at the bouncer. "Like I said before, I owe Alex. Thanks to him, I got a great divorce settlement from my slimeball ex. The creep was giving me a hard time until Alex found he was up to his eyeballs in a bunch of crooked business deals." She chuckled. "After that, the jerk was willing to pay me anything."

Laurie Hunter sauntered to the door of the office and nodded to Rocco. "Let's go back to the entrance and I'll set you up with a table there so everyone coming into the building will see your contest."

Alex was the last to reach the library. "How'd everything go?" he asked Jillian, Helene, and Cheri, who sat on a bench inside the front entrance.

"Posters are all done and printed," Jillian said, lifting a stack of flyers.

"Great!" The investigator pointed to several plastic bags on the floor next to Helene and Cheri. "Take all the shit and let's go outside to talk." They left the building and walked several feet from the door. "That's better," Alex said. "I know it's cold out here and getting dark so we'll do this real fast." He turned to the lawyer. "Any problem reserving Village Terrace for next Thursday?"

"No," Helene said. "And the woman liked being paid up front in cash. She reduced the price by five percent."

"Excellent!" He glanced at the bags Cheri was holding. "You have the watches in there?"

"Yeah." The dancer opened one of the plastic bags. "We got two men's and three for us girls."

"I'll take the watches for me and for Rocco."

After Cheri handed him the two men's watches, Alex immediately tore the wrapping off one and put the timepiece on his wrist. Then, reaching into the bag he was carrying, he removed three identical-looking cell phones. "Here," he said, handing a phone to each of the women. "I paid for a week's use and these come set with enough minutes included. I already put all of our numbers in each phone as 'Favorites.'"

"Did you have a problem buying five at one time?" Jillian asked.

"The salesguy gave me a funny look, but I told him my family was vacationing here for a week and we had decided before we left to buy cheap temporary phones instead of carrying our regular, expensive ones." He shrugged. "I think he believed it. I'm a pretty good liar."

"I can vouch for that," Helene said, grinning.

The detective took three folded sheets of paper from his jacket pocket and gave one to each of the women, along with a roll of cellophane tape and a pack of pushpins. "Okay, we're almost done here. We've all got a list of stores to go to." He nodded to Jillian. "Give each of us about twenty copies of the poster and let's get them hung up everywhere. We're ready to get Ryan to enter our little contest."

# CHAPTER 25

Ryan returned to his garden apartment Tuesday morning, opened the door, and stepped into the foyer. Then he quickly locked the entrance, even though he expected to be inside for just a minute or two. Still wearing his old man disguise, he headed straight for the bedroom.

His mind wasn't working properly today. Maybe it was the cold March weather? What else could explain the reason for forgetting to take the day's winning lottery numbers with him when he went to the store? He shook his head in disgust. That had never happened before.

As he entered the bedroom, he immediately saw an open box on the bed and his blond surfer-dude wig tossed carelessly next to it. Ryan hadn't lost his mind completely; he knew for sure he hadn't left that wig and box on his bed.

"What the f___!" he shouted, racing from the bedroom into the hallway, craning his head in every direction.

Ryan noticed the bathroom door was closed and flung it open just as a pair of jeans-clad legs were about to wriggle through the narrow window. Rushing to the window, he pulled up the legs, forcing the now screaming woman back into the room, face down.

"Shut up!" he ordered, holding the intruder's arms tightly as he closed the window. Then, turning the woman around, he looked into the terrified eyes of Sara.

"What the hell are you doing here?" Ryan asked angrily.

"I'm sorry," Sara whispered, staring at him in amazement. It was Brad, but he wore makeup that made his face look much older and a gray wig covered his dark brown hair. "I know I was wrong sneaking into your apartment, but I just wanted to see your paintings." She wriggled uncomfortably as he continued to pin both of her arms. "This hurts. Can you please let go of me?"

He shook his head. "I'm afraid that's not possible, Sara. You shouldn't have come here. Now you know too much."

"But I don't know anything," she said quickly. "Please Brad..."

"Don't lie to me." He spoke very softly, scowling at the girl. "You saw the surfer wig and I'm wearing this old man disguise. What else did you see in the closet?"

"Just another wig and a baseball uniform."

"What about the briefcase?"

"I didn't touch that."

"Good." He grinned at his prisoner, still gripping her tightly. "So what do you think about all of this?"

Sara forced herself to return his smile as she tried to choose an answer that would appeal to him. "You're very creative. You could've been an actor."

"Yeah." He chuckled. "I would've been famous."

"You can still be famous. You can get an agent and he'll..."

"Shut the f___ up!" Using his right hand, he punched the girl hard in the mouth. Blood trickled down her chin and she began whimpering.

After nearly a minute of silence, Ryan finally spoke. "So what am I going to do with you?" he asked, still holding Sara tightly and glaring at his terrified prisoner.

"Just let me go, Brad. I promise I won't say anything to anybody."

"You'll run straight to the police—and I can't let that happen. I've worked too hard to lose everything because of a stupid nosy bitch like you."

The girl didn't respond. The cut on her lip continued to bleed and the collar of the white top she wore underneath a navy sweatshirt was now stained with a crimson blotch.

"What? You're not gonna lie again and swear that you won't go to the police?"

"I don't think you'll believe anything I say," she said, speaking in a whisper.

"Well, you're right about that." He lifted Sara from the floor and, still grasping her arms, shoved her in front of him. "C'mon. We're going into the other room. Since you're so curious, you might as well hear everything."

"That's okay. You don't have to explain."

Laughing at her words, he pushed the girl into the living room and threw her onto one of the folding chairs. Then, holding her arms tightly with one hand, he tore off his belt and used it to tie her hands together behind her back.

"Please, Brad," she whimpered.

"And that's the first thing I want to tell you," he said, taking off his long tan coat and tossing it on the floor. "My name's not Brad; it's Ryan." He began slowly backing away from the girl. "Now I've got to get something from the bedroom." Glaring at her, he spoke slowly, emphasizing each word. "If you scream or move from this chair, I swear I'll hit you again—much harder."

She nodded and lowered her head.

Ryan returned to the living room holding a large red bandana that was part of the cowboy costume Sara had seen in the closet. He had taken off the gray wig, exposing his brown hair. But since he hadn't removed the makeup, he now looked like a vain old man who dyed his hair to make himself look younger. The girl stared at the incongruous sight.

"What're you looking at?" Ryan growled as he tied her legs to the chair with the bandana.

"Nothing. Sorry." Immediately, she glanced down again.

"Gotta get one more thing." He sprang up, dashing into the small kitchen.

She heard a drawer open and close and, soon after, Ryan returned to the living room carrying a roll of masking tape. He began taping her to the chair.

When he was finished, he stepped back, admired his work, and grinned. "Okay, you're not going anywhere. And now, just to make sure you keep your mouth shut..." He tore off a large piece of tape.

"Please don't," she whispered, unable to keep quiet any longer. "My lip hurts. I promise I won't scream."

He tossed the roll of tape on the floor. "Okay, but if you do, your lip won't be the only thing that hurts." After dragging the other folding chair across from the bound girl, he sat down and smiled. "I'm ready to talk now. And you, my captive audience, are ready to listen."

Ryan talked for a long time, telling Sara about his parents' deaths, his resulting hatred of Jillian Keating, and his elaborate plan to frame her for his murder. He told Sara everything— including details about the mini-whirlwind in Juniper Park that had transported him back in time. "So you understand that none of this shit with Jillian has even happened yet," he explained. "It'll first start in May."

The girl stared at him, nodding in agreement and feeling like a total idiot. How could she have gone out with this guy four times and not realize he was totally nuts—and scary dangerous? She had to be very careful not to say or do anything that would anger him.

"So what d'ya think?" he asked.

"You're very clever." She hoped her words sounded sincere and wouldn't disturb the lunatic.

"Yeah, I know," Ryan said, grinning. "It's a perfect setup. They can't find me because I'm not there now and, even though they won't find my body, all the evidence will point to Jillian. Having her take out that big life insurance policy on me was brilliant."

"Yes. It certainly was." She tried her best to sound enthusiastic.

"And I've camouflaged the area of the park trail leading to the wind tunnel that lets me time travel." He leaned back in the chair and chuckled. "No one else will ever find it."

She nodded again, not knowing what to say about all the time travel nonsense.

"You believe me. Right?"

"Of course. You came here from May in the future so you know everything that's going to happen. That's why you win the lottery."

Ryan jumped up quickly, glaring at the girl. "You're a f___in' liar," he said very softly. "You don't really believe any of it." Then, turning around, he marched into the bedroom.

Sara shifted in the folding chair, trying to wriggle her hands free of the belt. No luck. Her wrists were too tightly bound. Maybe she could maneuver her torso out of the chair? She tried to stand up, but the masking tape prevented her from moving. There was only one thing left to do. "Help!" she shouted as loudly as she could. "Someone, help...!"

Before she could say anything else, Ryan raced into the living room, holding a pillow in his right hand. He shoved the cushion against Sara's nose and mouth, knocking the girl and chair onto the floor, and effectively muffling her desperate cries. Her terrified blue eyes stared directly at Ryan as she tried to shake her head, imploring him to stop.

"Just what did you think you were doing?" he asked softly as he kept pressing the pillow firmly with both hands against her face. "I told you not to scream, but you didn't listen. You made a very bad choice."

Sara's head stopped moving, but her eyes continued staring at Ryan, still seeming to question his actions. He used his right hand to close the girl's eyes, keeping his left hand on the pillow. "Much better," he mumbled. She didn't open her eyes again.

He held the pillow over Sara's face for another minute before tossing the cushion aside. She now lay totally still, not moving at all. He held his hand in front of her mouth and felt nothing. She was no longer breathing. He checked her arm for a pulse and listened for a heartbeat. Nothing.

"It was your own fault, Sara," he whispered as he knelt on the floor and untied the belt and bandana. Then he got a knife from the kitchen and cut the tape that had bound the girl to the chair. "Too damn curious." He stared at the lifeless body, shaking his head in disgust.

After covering Sara's head with the bloodstained pillowcase so he wouldn't have to look at the dead girl's face, Ryan took the blanket from his bed and wrapped her body in it. He would buy some large, extra-strong trash bags, throw her in one, and dump his garbage into the river late tonight. There would be less chance of being seen then, he reasoned.

"Thanks to that nosy bitch, now I've got more work to do," he muttered, walking into the bathroom and thoroughly washing his hands to make sure he wasn't covered with any of Sara's blood. He returned to the bedroom, picked up the blond surfer wig and box the girl had left on the bed, and put the disguise back on the closet shelf. Then he pulled down his briefcase and punched in the correct code. After removing his list of winning lottery numbers for March 8th, Ryan carefully closed the case, making sure it was locked.

Once again he put on his gray wig, checking the bathroom

mirror to make sure the hairpiece was centered correctly. He slipped his arms into the tan overcoat he had tossed on the living room floor and stepped outside, ready to continue his day.

# CHAPTER 26

Alex walked into Town Hall just before six o'clock on Thursday, March 17 and immediately saw Rocco, seated behind a small table directly to the left of the receptionist. The investigator smiled, realizing everyone entering the building would notice the jellybean jar and the contest sign. "So my letter worked?" he asked the bouncer.

"Yeah." Rocco nodded. "Heard you did a big favor for the deputy mayor."

"Sure did. Knew she'd be glad to help us...How's business?"

"Pretty good. Ain't been here long and already lots of people have been takin' guesses." He shook the cardboard box. "Got about twenty so far."

"Great!" Alex reached into his pants pocket, took out a cell phone and a watch, and handed both to the bouncer. "Here. These are for you. The phone's already programmed with our numbers so we can keep in touch."

The detective pointed to the red-lipsticked receptionist, who was straightening the papers on her desk. "Town Hall's closing now and the gang's all meeting for dinner in a half hour. After you pack up the stuff and we get outta here, I'll bring you up to date on everything that's happened."

The time travelers met in a small diner near their motel. "You girls get your posters up?" Alex asked after the five of them were seated in a round booth in the corner.

"Mine are hanging in all the stores you gave me," Jillian said. "No problems."

"I had one guy that didn't wanna put the sign up," Cheri said. "But I told him the mayor'd okayed the contest and the jellybean jar was right in Town Hall. I figured Rocco'd work it out." She patted her boyfriend's hand and grinned at the others. "After that, the guy took the sign and taped it right in the front window."

"Good work," the detective said, nodding at her.

"Thanks." The dancer pointed to her nondescript jeans and makeup-free face. "This is real cool, dressin' in old clothes and lookin' so different. And I'm gettin' to practice my actin'."

Alex smiled at Cheri and turned to Helene. "How about you? Any trouble with the flyers?"

"No. I either put the posters on counters or in the windows, and a couple of stores even had corkboards for announcements, so I tacked the signs there."

"My signs are all up too," the private eye said, resting his elbows on the table. "Then we're all set. We've put out the bait. Now we need Ryan to see a flyer in one of the places and, when he does, I'm sure he'll want to enter and win our little contest." He picked up one of the menus, waving it at the others. "Nothing more we can do right now, so how about let's eat?"

After Alex paid the dinner check, he addressed the group. "We'll meet back at my room at ten to start practicing our parts for next Thursday night. Till then, you've got some free time. Go see a movie, buy something to read—do whatever you want to do." He shrugged. "You can also go back to the room and just relax. I know we gained a couple of hours here, but it's still been a very long day."

Helene grinned at Alex. "I know what I'm doing. I've got to research some upcoming cases. But then I'm buying a couple of mystery novels I've been wanting to read." She leaned back in her chair. "Relaxing sounds good and the next few days here shouldn't be very busy."

"No. They won't be," the investigator agreed. "We can't do much except prepare for our Thursday night production. I've gotta go see someone, but the rest of you may as well enjoy this spare time." He nodded at Cheri and Rocco. "Like I promised, you two get a nice little vacation."

The dancer frowned at him. "It's gonna be so-o-o borin'. There's nothin' to do here."

"Maybe you can go see a movie," Jillian suggested.

"I seen all the good movies from two months ago," Cheri said. "I don't wanna watch them again."

"How about a book or a magazine?" Jillian asked. "I'm going to look for something about astronomy and then pick up a few crossword puzzle books. What do you like to read?"

"I hate readin'," the dancer said, still scowling and folding her arms. "Guess I'll just go to a store and look around for clothes."

"Don't buy too much," Alex cautioned. "It's not the money 'cause we can afford it. But you can't take the stuff back unless it fits in your backpack."

"I know." Cheri made a pouty face at the private detective. "I can't even pick somethin' out that I like and come back for it next week."

Rocco put his arm around his girlfriend and hugged her. "Hey, hon, it'll be okay. How about we get a deck of cards and go back to the room and play some gin?"

She smiled at the bouncer. "I'll whip your ass, Dodo-Roc."

# CHAPTER 27

Dressed in his New York Yankees sports fan disguise, Ryan walked toward a local mini-market to play one of his daily lottery numbers. It had been over a week since the "incident"—the euphemistic term he favored when recalling his run-in with Sara— and, as the days passed, he thought less and less of the dead girl.

*Her own fault,* he reasoned, slipping his hands into the front opening of the team sweatshirt. *Too damn nosy.*

He had been very careful disposing of the girl's body. After wearing gloves to remove Sara's wallet and car keys from her jeans pocket and wiping away any traces of her fingerprints in his apartment, he had shoved her into one of the heavy-strength black plastic garbage bags he had bought, added a second bag, and then tossed in several rocks to weigh down the bundle.

That night, at two in the morning, dressed in his favorite walking clothes and wearing gloves, Ryan had driven Sara's Volkswagen to a scenic observation site overlooking the Hudson River and parked the car. After making sure no other vehicles were in sight, he had quickly opened her trunk and removed the bag, dragging it to the edge of the cliff. Finally, he had shoved the heavy load over the precipice. As he watched, the body-filled bag had splashed into the murky water and sunk to the bottom.

"Bye, Sara," he had whispered, smiling at the lingering ripples. "Enjoy your eternal swim." Then he had driven the car to a small shopping center, parked it—leaving the dead girl's identification and keys inside—and jogged nearly two miles to his apartment. Following all the late night exercise, he had enjoyed a wonderful, worry-free nine hours of sleep.

Ryan entered the small market, walked up to the young goateed man behind the counter, and handed him a lottery sheet. He was playing Pick 10 here and would hit eight of the ten numbers to win $300 tomorrow.

The kid smiled at him. "So these are the winners, huh?"

"I sure hope so," Ryan said, shrugging his shoulders as he handed the clerk a dollar.

"Here you go." The young man gave him the recorded ticket. "Good luck."

"Thanks." Ryan tucked the valuable lottery stub in his wallet, ready to leave the store. He still had work to do today: He had to go home, change his disguise, and visit a card shop at the other side of town to collect one of yesterday's payouts.

Before he turned to the exit, Ryan noticed a poster on the counter. "'Win $1,000'...What's this?" he asked, reading the headline.

"Oh, it's some kinda new contest in Town Hall," the young clerk said. "You gotta count jellybeans in a jar."

Ryan picked up the flyer and read all the details and rules, noting the results would be published in the local newspaper the day after the contest ended, before returning the sheet to the counter. "Sounds like fun," he said, smiling at the goateed man. "Maybe I'll enter."

"Yeah. But it's a real long shot, tryin' to pick the number of jellybeans. How can ya figure somethin' like that out?"

"Maybe I'll be lucky," Ryan said, walking slowly towards the door. "You just never know."

Still dressed in the geek outfit he had worn to the card shop in the afternoon to collect his winnings—wire glasses, long-haired greasy wig, and ill-fitting baggy jeans—Ryan entered Juniper Park. Since the sun was setting and the temperature was rapidly falling, he hoped few people would be lingering near the entrance to the hidden mountain trail.

He glanced in all directions, relieved he had judged correctly. No one was nearby. Far in the distance, he could barely see the outline of a solitary jogger. Quickly, he climbed into the woods and found his notched tree. Then after pushing aside the branches, he stepped into the tiny path, following it until he reached the clearing that housed the wind tunnel.

"Going for a quick spin," he mumbled as he hurled himself into the whirling eddy. First he had to return to the present. He landed on the other side next to the cave in total darkness and immediately dove into the little cyclone again.

Ryan concentrated as he spun, counting to 113 before throwing himself out of the twister. Then he rushed back into the swirling wind two more times, counting to 78 during the final rotation.

He had experimented with the small time travel portal—determining the count and number of spins necessary to reach a certain date—before catapulting himself into January for his disappearing act. His calculations had proven to be accurate within a couple of hours.

When he had finished spinning, Ryan waited for his dizziness to subside. Then he shook off the dirt and slowly continued down the small mountain. Upon reaching the end of the hidden path, he peeked through the trees and smiled. Again he was fortunate: No one was in the vicinity. After stepping out of the woods, he headed for the park exit.

Ryan walked into the same small nearby deli Jillian had discovered during her trip to the past, immediately dashing to the newspaper display on the lower right-hand shelf. He grabbed a copy of the *Daily Sentinel*, quickly checked the date on the front page, and grinned.

According to the newspaper, today was Friday, March 25. *Brilliant as usual.* After silently complimenting himself on his cleverness, he took the paper to the checkout counter and paid for it.

Before leaving the store, Ryan glanced at the wall clock. Seeing the time was 3:10, he frowned slightly. Since he had aimed to arrive at noon, his calculations had been off by more than three hours. "Not so good," he muttered, shaking his head, as he stepped outside. *Gotta be more accurate next time.*

He stood on the sidewalk near the deli and opened the newspaper, carefully scanning each page for the article he had traveled through time for. Finally, in one of the back pages, he saw a small story with the headline: "**Jellybean Contest Awards Sweet $1,000 Prize**." Reading further, he found the detail he needed— the correct number of jellybeans in the jar. There was no name or photo of the lucky winner because, according to the article, "the winner did not want to be identified."

"That would be me," he murmured as he tore the page out of the newspaper, tucking it neatly into his pants pocket. After throwing the rest of the paper into a trashcan, he turned and sprinted to Juniper Park.

When Ryan reached the mini-mountain area by the notched tree, he was annoyed to find three teenage boys tossing a Frisbee in the nearby grass. "Shit," he muttered, unwilling to risk entering the woods with the kids watching.

He returned to the park path and pretended to take a leisurely walk, frequently checking the Frisbee players to see if they had finished their game. Finally, about fifteen minutes later, he saw the teens leave.

Ryan jogged back to the little mountain, dashed into the clump of woods, and found his marked tree. He located the tiny trail, following it to the clearing containing the wind tunnel. Then, without any hesitation, he flung himself into the whirlwind and rolled out near the little cave.

He again launched his body into the swirling eddy, slightly modifying his count. Two spins later, he waited for his dizziness to subside, shook off the dust, and followed the tiny path until it ended. After peeking through the branches to make sure no people were in sight, Ryan stepped out of the mountain and left Juniper Park.

Since the deli was the nearest store that carried newspapers, he returned to the small shop and picked up a copy of the *Daily Sentinel*. The date read, "Friday, March 18." He dropped the newspaper and glanced at the clock. The time was now 3:50—just about perfect. *Good job!* he told himself. Then, feeling like he had already put in a hard day's work, Ryan slowly headed home.

# CHAPTER 28

Jillian and her companions ate dinner together Friday night, March 18, at a small café near their motel. She, Alex, and Cheri had spent much of the afternoon rehearsing for next Thursday's performance while Rocco had again manned the contest table at Town Hall with Helene—wearing a short brown wig and glasses—relieving him for a lunch break.

"So did you guys see anyone enter who looked like Ryan?" the investigator asked between bites of his burger.

"Nah." Rocco shook his head. "I didn't see no one like him."

"He could've been disguised as someone else," Jillian suggested. "Remember we told you what his sister said about how he loves to dress up and act out different parts."

"But no guy his size came by the table." The bouncer leaned back in his seat and chuckled. "Unless you think maybe he was in drag. I seen some tall ladies enterin' the contest today."

"I didn't see any man who looked even remotely like Ryan either," Helene said. "But lots of people entered when I was there so the posters must still be up and the word's getting around."

"Well, there's lots of time left," Alex said. "No reason to panic.

I'm sure he'll be coming in a day or so and he's got no reason to rush since winning our contest has nothing to do with how fast he enters. He's just gotta know the exact number of jellybeans."

Cheri sipped her white wine and glanced at the investigator. "Maybe he had trouble findin' out the answer. Maybe it's not in the paper."

Alex waved his hand in dismissal. "Fred's a real good guy and he always comes through for me," he said. "The article's there."

"You think Ryan could've had a problem going back?" Jillian asked. "Something with the wind tunnel?"

"Folks, don't worry." After lowering the remains of his burger onto the plate, the detective rested both hands on the table. "This plan is brilliant—and it will work. The only thing that's wrong right now is this crappy food. It really sucks. But every time I say we should go eat at Burger King, you guys all say 'no.'"

"And we still say 'no,'" Helene said, folding her arms and smiling.

"That's right." Jillian, attempting to look serious, nodded her head.

Cheri and Rocco glanced at each other and chuckled.

Jillian lay comfortably sprawled on her motel room bed after dinner, skimming through her new book, *Astronomy: A Self-Teaching Guide*, when she heard a knock on the door. She jumped up, peered through the peephole, and saw Cheri.

"Hi," Jillian said, opening the door. "Is everything okay?"

The dancer stepped inside, leaned against the door, and scanned the room. "Where's Helene?" she asked.

"She went to the supermarket to buy some fruit and snacks for us. Why?"

Cheri hopped onto her friend's bed, tossing the book aside, and lay on her back with her eyes closed. "I can't stand it no more," she said dramatically.

"What's wrong?"

"I'm so-o-o bored! There's nothin' to do here till next Thursday."

"That's not true," Jillian said, sitting next to Cheri. "We're busy practicing all the time so we can get Ryan."

"I know." Cheri flipped over, propped her body on her elbows, and held her head in her hands. "That actin' shit's okay. But I'm talkin' about at night. I'm used to workin' at the club, dancin'. Just lyin' around, playin' cards, watchin' old TV shows every night is drivin' me nuts!"

"But this is like a vacation for you, a time you don't have to work."

The dancer shook her head. "It's nothin' like a vacation. On my vacation, I'd be spendin' nights goin' to clubs, dancin', hangin' out, havin' fun..." She sat up quickly, stared at her friend, and smiled. "Wait a minute. I just got a great idea and I'm gonna need you to come with me."

"What's your idea?"

"Tonight I wanna go to the Ooh-La-La Club."

"Your club? The place where you dance?"

Cheri nodded. "Yeah. That'll be so cool."

"Why'd you want to do that now when you've got some time off?"

She poked Jillian gently in her side. "It'll give you a chance to see how good I dance."

"I can do that sometime when we get back. We'll pick a date and I'll come watch you. I promise."

Cheri chuckled softly, shaking her head. "You don't understand, honey. Yeah, it's true that you can watch me dance anytime. But this is the only chance *I* ever got to watch me." She tapped her chest with her thumb. "Dont'cha get it? Tonight, I can see me dance. How cool is that?"

Jillian stared at her grinning friend and spoke slowly. "I don't know, Cheri. It sounds very dangerous."

"What d'ya mean, 'dangerous'?"

"We'll, we don't know what'll happen if we get too close to our other selves in real time. Maybe we'll blow up or disappear or..."

"Then we won't get that close. We'll just sit in the audience real quiet like and watch. This way, nothin'll happen."

"I still don't like it." Jillian pursed her lips, again considering Cheri's words. "I can't go anyway. I don't have a fake ID to get into your club."

The dancer smiled again. "You don't need no ID. I got a key to the back door."

"What about Rocco? If you want to go to the club so badly, why don't you just ask him to take you? I'm sure he'll do it."

With a wave of her hand, Cheri dismissed the idea. "Nah. I already thought of that, but it ain't gonna work. Rocco's way too big. Even if he puts on a disguise, people at the club'll recognize him easy. He can't go back there. But I can make myself look real different, and goin' with you, we'll just be two girls havin' a fun night out."

"I still don't like it," Jillian repeated.

"Aw, c'mon." Cheri poked the girl's shoulder. "Pul-e-e-ze! I really wanna go and see how I look up on the stage. It'll be lots of fun."

"We can't get close to where you'll be dancing. You've got to promise me. Okay?"

"Sure, honey. I promise."

Jillian, wearing her blonde wig and Cheri's short, tight-fitting red dress the dancer had insisted she wear, cautiously stepped out of the cab. While Cheri paid the driver, Jillian stared across the street at the gaudy Ooh-La-La Club.

A large flashing neon sign dominated the white, windowless exterior. Three young men stood in front of the entrance, talking, holding beer bottles, and playfully shoving each other. Another man—middle-aged, with a huge stomach—leaned against the building puffing on a cigar and speaking on a cell phone. Loud pulsating music emanated from within the open door.

"Ain't the club great lookin'?" Cheri asked as she joined Jillian. The dancer had put her purple-free dyed brown hair into a prim ponytail and, without makeup and sporting Jillian's brown-rimmed glasses, looked nothing like an exotic entertainer. Even her clothes were conservative; under her sweater, she wore a simple long-sleeved black dress with a modest neckline.

"C'mon." The dancer took her friend's arm and began leading the girl across the street. "Let's get to the back door and go inside. I'm already up on stage."

Jillian moved as quickly as she could. "These shoes hurt," she complained. Since she only had sneakers, Cheri had loaned her a pair of red pumps for the evening. But the shoes were too small and pinched her toes.

The two young women walked up an incline to the rear of the club, reaching a closed door. "Do you see anybody?" Cheri whispered as she took a key from her bag.

"No. There's no one around."

"Great." After inserting the key into the lock, the dancer opened the door. "Quick. Get in." She practically shoved Jillian through the opening and followed her inside. "This way," Cheri continued. "Come with me."

As the dancer led her down a long hallway, Jillian noticed doors on each side featured hand-decorated signs with creative stage names. She glimpsed "Serena Sweet" in a pink heart surrounded by puckered lips and "Lola Lovely" in yellow and black stencil lettering.

Jillian felt a tap on her shoulder and watched the dancer nod towards a door that read "Cheri Orchid," with an enormous red star over the name. Cheri beamed proudly, pointing to her chest.

"Move it, Phil! Get your fat ass goin'!"

The sounds of men's voices and rapidly approaching footsteps broke the silence. Without saying a word, Cheri opened the door to her unlocked room, pushed Jillian inside, and closed it quietly, putting her finger to her lips. As the men reached Cheri's room, the sounds got louder and then the voices and footsteps began to fade as the pair continued down the hall. Finally, a door opened and quickly slammed shut.

"I think they're gone," the dancer whispered. "Wouldn't have been no good if Tony and Phil seen us here." She smiled at Jillian, who was studying her dressing room. "So what d'ya think?"

"It's very nice," Jillian said. But she was just being polite. In truth, she wasn't overly impressed with the tiny space. The room contained a large mirror surrounded by many overhead lights, a little bench seat, and a small dressing table completely covered with lipsticks, powder, mascara, and other cosmetics. A closet filled the entire left side and a folding chair leaned against the right wall. The two of them barely fit in the room.

Cheri opened the door slowly and peeked into the hallway. "Okay. It's all clear now. Let's get outta here before someone else comes."

The dancer led the way to the end of the hall and entered the stairwell underneath the "Exit" sign. As they walked down a half flight, the vibrating instrumental sounds became louder and louder. "Almost there," Cheri whispered. Then, cautiously opening the door, she waved the girl forward.

They entered the front left side of the club's showroom, very near the stage where colored spotlights beamed down on five curvaceous dancers. Four of the young women were topless, dressed only in shimmering silver tights as they sensually caressed long mirrored poles and gyrated to the sounds of pulsating dance music. The fifth showgirl, who had black purple-streaked hair and wore a form-fitting silver-sequined bodysuit, stood in the center of the stage and strutted back and forth, smiling at the nearly all-male audience as she executed her dance routine.

Jillian stood still, gaping at the performance. Cheri tapped the mesmerized girl's shoulder and, smiling proudly, pointed first to the main dancer and then to herself. Still smiling, she gestured towards a pair of empty seats at a rectangular table in the front.

Jillian shook her head. "That's too close," she whispered.

"Oh, come on," Cheri whined, pulling her friend's arm. "I wanna see me."

"Hi, sugar," a bearded middle-aged man cooed to Jillian as she and Cheri argued. "No date tonight? You and your girlfriend can come watch the show with me." He patted the empty chair next to him.

Jillian quickly continued to the vacant seats at the table beside the stage. After sitting, she immediately kicked off the uncomfortable shoes.

"That guy hit on you and not me," Cheri murmured. "That's a first."

"I'm a blonde and I'm wearing your flashy red dress," Jillian said, indicating the low neckline as she quickly buttoned her jacket. "And I'm taller than you so this dress is really short."

The dancer chuckled. "Yeah. That's right. I forgot." Then, staring at herself on the stage, she beamed. "I'm damn good, ain't I?"

At first, Jillian watched both Cheri's performance and the maneuvers of the half-nude backup dancers with great interest. Her friend really was good. It wasn't so much her dancing, which was only slightly above average; it was her stage presence that made Cheri special. The young woman projected a genuine enthusiasm and warmth, which the audience seemed to love. Every now and then, a man would shout, "Way to go, Cheri!" or, "Let it all out!" and the dancer would smile and either wave or blow kisses to the fan.

After a while, however, Jillian became uncomfortable. She reached over and whispered in her friend's ear. "I'm getting scared. There're hardly any women here. It's nearly all men."

"That's okay, hon." Cheri, continuing to stare at the stage, gently patted the girl's hand. "Nobody'll hurt you. Just keep watchin' me up there. Ain't I great?"

"Yes. You're wonderful, not nervous at all. I'd be a wreck, dancing like that in front of all those strange men."

"Hey, I worked hard to be the star at this club." She nodded her head. "I worked damn hard."

When the last dance number ended, the audience applauded and cheered—including Cheri who stood and clapped loudly for herself, even whistling through her teeth. The four topless dancers jumped off the stage after the ovation and began mingling with the customers. Men approached the semi-nude performers, some speaking to them, while others shoved bills into the girls' silver tights.

Then the star dancer walked off the stage and headed directly towards Cheri and Jillian.

"Get away from her," Jillian whispered. She grasped her friend's arm, trying to pull Cheri backwards. But the young woman didn't budge. She stared as if hypnotized as her other self approached.

"You look so familiar," performing Cheri said, pointing a finger at her disguised double. "Do I know you from somewhere?"

"No." Jillian spoke before her friend could respond. "We're just tourists, visiting from out of town. We came here because we wanted to see a dance club, and you were wonderful, but we've got to go now." Once again, she attempted to pull Cheri away from her performing self.

"There's somethin' about you though..." Still pointing her finger, performing Cheri reached out towards her counterpart and slightly touched the other Cheri's wrist.

As soon as she made contact with herself, a crackling noise erupted. The performing dancer's arm sizzled, radiating enormous heat, and a cascade of yellow sparks burst into the air. Although she immediately withdrew her arm, the white tablecloth was already engulfed in towering flames.

"What the hell?" Performing Cheri gazed in amazement at her fire-starting limb, which now seemed perfectly normal.

Men in the showroom began screaming and most rushed to the main exit, away from the raging fire. Someone grabbed a bottle of beer and emptied the contents on the burning table. Another man threw a chair at the flaming cloth.

"C'mon!" Jillian grabbed Cheri's arm and dragged her stunned friend to the side door they had used to enter the showroom.

In the hallway, away from her double, Cheri snapped out of her daze. "What happened back there?" she asked quietly as they rushed towards the rear exit.

"I don't really know. But whatever it was, it happened when your other self touched you." Jillian shook her head. "And she just tapped you very lightly. Who knows what would have happened if she had really grabbed hold of you. Maybe the whole place would have caught on fire. We could have all been killed."

After opening the door, the two young women stepped into the street. "Does your arm hurt where she touched you?" Jillian asked.

"A little," Cheri admitted. Glancing at her wrist, she noticed a small burn mark.

As they walked outside, Jillian peered at her bare feet. When the fire started, she hadn't had time to find Cheri's red pumps under the table. "I left your shoes back there at the club and my feet are freezing."

"Sorry," the dancer said, shaking her head. "This whole thing is all my fault. You warned me that somethin' bad could happen and I still made you come."

"Yeah. Well now we know how dangerous it is to get close to our other selves. We've got to warn Alex and the others."

Cheri looked at Jillian sheepishly. "Do we really gotta tell? He's gonna be so mad at me. And Rocco'll be mad too."

"We can't take a chance on any of them getting hurt," Jillian said, pointing to her friend's slightly wounded wrist. "You were lucky. You could have been very badly burned."

They walked back to the motel along a main road, hoping to flag down a cab. But since it was after midnight, traffic was minimal and few cars passed them. The streets were eerily quiet except for the approaching sounds of sirens.

# CHAPTER 29

On Monday morning, March 21, Ryan, dressed in jogging clothes and wearing his blond surfer-dude wig, entered Town Hall before making his usual lottery stops and immediately noticed the prominent jellybean jar display. He strode to the contest table, grabbed an entry form, and quickly filled it out.

"Think you got a good guess?" Rocco asked before Ryan dropped his entry into the box. "You hardly even looked at the jar."

"Don't need to," Ryan said, smiling at the bouncer. "I'm a quick study."

"Hey, I'm curious. Can I see what number you put down?"

"Yeah. When I win." Ryan shoved the slip of paper into the slot and then shook the box vigorously.

"So you'll be comin' to the party Thursday night?" Rocco asked.

"I'll be there."

"Okay. See you then."

After nodding his head, Ryan turned and dashed out of the building.

As soon as Ryan was out of sight, Rocco grabbed his cell phone and called Alex. "I think he was just here wearin' a blond wig," he whispered. "Can I go after him?"

"No. If he sees someone following him it'll ruin everything."

"I'll be real careful so he won't see me."

"Listen, Rocco, stop looking for shortcuts. I'm the detective and, I promise, it'll all play out on Thursday night. We'll get him then."

The bouncer hesitated before speaking again. "I tried to see what he wrote, but he wouldn't let me. Could've gotten his name..."

"He probably made up another name and address just to make sure no one'll know who he is when he wins. We'll check tonight when you bring back the entry box. If it was Ryan, we'll know his entry by the number he picked. Remember, it was in the newspaper."

"Oh, yeah. I forgot."

"If it's him, then tomorrow I'll have a friend of mine check out the name and address he put on his entry."

"Okay, I guess." Rocco made a face at the cell phone before ending the call.

"This must be it." Helene looked up from the desk chair in Alex's room and waved one of the entry forms above her head. "It's got the newspaper number." She handed the piece of paper to the investigator, who copied the name and address into his notebook.

"See—I was right," Rocco said, from his seat on Alex's bed. "That *was* Ryan who came in today." He turned to Cheri, who leaned on her elbows next to him. "I'd be a damn good investigator, don't ya think?"

The dancer nodded and caressed her boyfriend's broad shoulders.

"Good work," Alex said, smiling at the bouncer. "I'm gonna call Vince with this info right now and have him check it out." He took his cell phone and walked into the bathroom.

With the exception of Rocco, the time travelers had spent most of their days and nights—not counting meals—in the motel since Cheri and Jillian's near disastrous experience on Friday night.

"Now that you two proved touching our other selves here can kill us—and innocent people—we really can't risk a meeting," Alex had said.

"Can't I just go to stores and look at clothes?" Cheri had asked.

"No!" He had glared at the dancer. "You could be shopping in the same stores you went to back in March. What'll happen if you accidentally bump into yourself there? Another fire? An explosion? Something even worse?"

Then the investigator had addressed everyone. "I didn't tell you, but it almost happened to me too. Turns out I had eaten lunch with my newspaper buddy just an hour before I came to his office to give him the article about the contest. What if the other me had still been sitting there in his office?"

He had shaken his head. "It's just too damn dangerous. Go to the movies if you like or a quick trip to the supermarket's okay if you're real careful. But that's about it. Maybe catch up on some TV shows you missed. I'll go buy us some DVDs. Tell me what you want to see." They had been in their rooms since then, watching television or movies, reading, and playing cards.

Now, while Alex made his phone call, Jillian sat on a stool next to Helene, helping the lawyer put Monday's contest entries into a large envelope. "Do you think Ryan wrote down the name he's really using?" the girl asked.

Helene shrugged. "Probably not."

"Why? It's not his real name anyway."

"I'm figuring he's paranoid about keeping even his phony identity secret so the contest folks couldn't check him out."

"But he already knows the winner's not named in the newspaper."

"Even so, the ones running the contest—in this case, us—would have his name and address. Maybe he thinks we could be submitting his name to another media outlet—radio, TV, Internet. There are lots out there and he doesn't know the contest's fake." Helene shook her head. "I bet the information he gave us today is totally useless."

Tuesday morning, Cheri was resting in bed watching TV when she heard a knock on the motel room door. "One sec," she called, slipping into a tee shirt and jeans. Then she ran to the door and lifted the peephole.

Alex stood in the hallway. "What's up?" she asked, opening the door.

The detective stepped inside and scanned the room. "Where's Rocco?"

"In the shower. Why?"

"Vince just called me about the name and address that Ryan put down for the contest and I wanted to tell him first."

"Tell him what?"

Alex hopped onto the bed and shrugged. "The info was phony. There's no Ian Smart living at 324 Poplar Street. In fact, there's no number 324 on Poplar Street. He made the whole thing up."

The dancer sat down next to him. "Rocco'll be so pissed. He thought he really did good yesterday, you know, figurin' out it was Ryan."

The investigator nodded his head. "Tell him he still did good, Cheri. It's important for us to know what disguise Ryan was wearing, even if we don't know the name he's using here and, since Rocco talked to the creep, he'll probably be wearing the same blond wig and similar clothes on Thursday night." He patted her hand and smiled. "And this way you'll get a chance to do some acting. You've been rehearsing all week, working real hard."

"Yeah, I guess." She lowered her head and frowned.

Alex put his finger under the dancer's chin, lifting her head. "Hey, it'll all be okay. You'll see. You just have to wait till Thursday night."

# CHAPTER 30

"Did you check the drawers and the bathroom to make sure you have everything?" Helene asked Jillian late Thursday morning before closing their motel room door for the last time.

"Yes." The girl adjusted her backpack and shrugged. "I didn't take much stuff with me anyway. Where are we meeting everyone?"

"At the diner. The deadline for entries is noon today so Rocco'll join us there as soon as he packs up at Town Hall." The lawyer grinned at Jillian as they walked through the motel's hallway. "It's just hours till our prime-time performance. Are you getting nervous?"

"A little," the girl admitted. "Tonight is so important. I just hope we can pull it off. I know Alex seems so confident, but there's still so much that can go wrong."

Helene took her client's hand, squeezing it tightly. "I've worked with Alex many times and, believe me, if he feels good about this plan, then it'll work. The guy really knows how to get things done."

"I hope you're right."

They reached the motel lobby and approached the main desk. "Room 114, checking out," Helene said, placing two keys on the counter.

The same heavyset white-haired woman who had been on duty when the group had checked in the previous week, picked up the keys and glanced at her registration book. Then, raising her head, she smiled at the lawyer. "Mr. Ketcham already took care of the balance left on your room. Thanks for staying with us at the Shady Elms, Mrs. Moscow. I hope you and your daughter enjoy the rest of the day."

"We certainly will," Helene said, returning the woman's grin.

"Is everyone all set for tonight?" Alex asked as the time travelers finished eating lunch at the diner. "Everyone know your part? Got your costume?"

"I'm good," Cheri said, nodding as she took the last bite of her tuna salad.

"Glad to hear it 'cause you're the lead in this play," the investigator said.

"Yeah." The dancer smiled at him. "I know."

"What about me?" Rocco pointed to his broad chest. "I ain't got no part, no costume or nothin'."

"You know you've got a real important role in this plan, even though you're not in the play itself," Alex said.

"Yeah. But I don't get to see none of it."

"Oh stop whinin', Dodo-Roc!" Playfully, Cheri poked her boyfriend's ribs with her elbow. "We'll tell you what happens."

"When can we go to the place and set up?" Jillian asked.

Alex looked at his watch before answering. "At about five, so we've still got some free time. Any suggestions what you guys want to do?"

"Shopping," Cheri said quickly.

The detective made a mock-angry face at her.

The dancer giggled. "Just kiddin'."

"Maybe we should go hang out at the library for a while," Helene suggested. "You know, read a book or magazine—or just relax."

"Not much chance I'll run into myself there," Cheri mumbled.

"Me either," Rocco said.

"I think it's a good idea because then we can use the library to get changed for tonight." Jillian looked at Alex for approval. "Right?"

The investigator nodded and then rose. "Okay, gang. Let's go."

When the group walked into the Village Terrace at five o'clock, a stocky young man in a gray suit greeted them. After glancing at a sheet of paper, he smiled. "Jellybean contest?"

"That's us," Alex said, stepping forward. Although the investigator wasn't disguised, he had dressed for the occasion, sporting a navy blazer, geometric red tie, and black slacks. He reached into a shopping bag and pulled out the jar filled with jellybeans.

The heavyset young man, still grinning, again skimmed his paper. "I see you're having a party for your contest. Is there anything else you need?"

"I can use a small table next to the door," Alex said. "Otherwise we're fine."

"No problem. Is the setup here okay?" The catering hall representative waved at the round tables, which were covered in plain white cloths and arranged along the walls, leaving room for a center dance floor.

"Well, we're not going to be doing any dancing tonight so the tables can be moved closer together," the detective said. Then he pointed to two large rectangular tables in the rear of the room. "But leave those. They'll be good for our food and contest."

The gray-suited man nodded. "I'll get a couple of guys right now to bring in a small table and move the other ones for you."

"So far, so good," a petite woman whispered as soon as the young man left the room. Her white hair was pinned in a fake tight bun, she wore little wire-rim glasses, and was frumpily dressed in a cheap brown polyester pantsuit.

"You look so cute!" Cheri said, hugging Helene. During the short walk from the library to the catering hall, she had playfully referred to the disguised lawyer as "Granny."

"When's our food coming?" Jillian asked, nervously.

Alex checked his watch. "In about a half hour." Then he smiled at his client. "You look terrific."

"Thanks," the girl replied, her face reddening slightly. Although Jillian still wore her blonde wig and glasses disguise, the addition of tastefully applied mascara, eye shadow, and peach-tinted lipstick had a dual effect: The makeup highlighted her already attractive features and it made her look several years older. Her costume consisted of the conservative black dress Cheri had worn on Friday night and a pair of simple black heels. Since Jillian had purchased the shoes, this time they fit.

"I did a great job with the makeup, dont'cha think?" the dancer said, putting her arm around her friend and grinning. Tonight Cheri was dressed as herself. She had again dyed her hair black and wore the sexy red dress she had loaned Jillian for their visit to her club Friday night. Her face was heavily made up, complete with her trademark purple lipstick.

"I feel like I'm back to bein' me," she had told Alex.

"Not quite," he had reminded her. "You've still got an important part to play."

The food for the evening's party was delivered on time and the women arranged the platters on the rear rectangular tables. Alex had ordered cold cuts, cheese, vegetables, fruit, and cookies, plus several dips, assorted breads, rolls, and crackers. For beverages, they had only water and soda. Paper plates were stacked nearby, next to plastic silverware. "We're keeping it simple," he had explained. "For us, this party's not about the food."

The contest had netted a total of 172 entries and the detective told the group to expect at least 80 of the participants to attend the night's festivities. "Mostly 'cause it's free," he had said.

Now Alex looked at the wall clock and saw it was after six. "Better get going," he said to Rocco. "We'll catch up with you later."

The bouncer nodded, grabbed his backpack and jacket, wished the others good luck, and left the catering hall.

The remaining cast members finished arranging the food and drinks and filled the center of each round table with piles of little jellybean bags. Before traveling back in time, Jillian had designed a colorful logo for their phantom jellybean company. Then, during the week, Alex had bought additional jellybeans and Jillian had stuffed them into plastic bags, tied the packages with red ribbons, and placed stickers with her "Jaybee's" logo on all of them.

After making sure the contest jellybean jar was prominently displayed on one of the rear rectangular tables, Alex summoned the three women. "All right, girls. This is it. We're ready to start. Everyone take your positions."

Jillian bit her lower lip and looked at him questioningly.

"Don't worry," he said, grasping her hand and holding it for a moment. "It'll all be okay."

She smiled slightly and nodded. Cheri took her by the arm and the two of them walked to the back of the room together.

Alex headed to the front entrance to check off the names of their guests, Jillian moved past the dancer to the rear buffet area and sat behind the jellybean jar, while Cheri and Helene each grabbed paper plates. Act One was about to begin.

# CHAPTER 31

People began arriving for the contest party at the Village Terrace twenty minutes before seven o'clock. Each guest immediately grabbed a paper plate and loaded it with food from the rear table. Most of the men and women then poured drinks and found seats at one of the large round tables.

Helene and Cheri wandered independently around the room, holding food-filled plates, pretending to be members of the crowd. Jillian sat inconspicuously in the rear, behind the jellybean jar, watching carefully as new people entered and told Alex their names.

Jillian hadn't yet seen Ryan and was starting to have doubts. It was nearly seven-thirty. *What if he didn't come?* Maybe the thousand-dollar cash prize wasn't a big enough lure. Then all their work would have been for nothing.

As she continued to monitor the entrance, a young man with longish blond hair, dressed in a black sweatshirt and matching jeans, appeared at the doorway and spoke to Alex. He walked into the room, surveyed the scene, and smiled confidently. Jillian's heart started pounding as, even with his blond wig, she recognized Ryan.

Jillian leaned over the table and wrapped her hands around the jellybean jar as if to straighten it out. She repeated the action several times, hoping the others would notice their prearranged signal.

Ryan sauntered to the food table, grabbed a plate, and started piling cold cuts onto it.

"Good spread, huh? And just for countin' jellybeans."

Ryan, hearing the woman's comment, turned around and faced Cheri. "Yeah, it is," he said, smiling at the attractive girl as he continued to fill his plate with slices of ham and salami.

"I just came for the free food," Cheri continued, munching on a mini-carrot. "'Course I entered the dumb contest, but I never win those things."

Ryan snickered. "Well, I think I've got a good chance."

"Oh yeah?" She waved the carrot at his chest. "You a scientist or somethin', able to figure out the number of jellybeans that way?"

"Kind of." After pouring cola into a paper cup, he took plastic silverware and a napkin, and then grinned at the girl. "Want to sit down?"

"Sure." She pointed to her high heels with her free hand. "These shoes are startin' to hurt my feet."

Alex closed the entrance door and walked to the back of the room where Jillian continued to sit by herself. No one else was near her. He leaned his arms on the table and smiled. "How're you doing?"

"Okay." She took a deep breath. "They're still sitting together and talking."

"Yeah. Just like we planned."

Jillian shook her head and sighed. "I really wish I could hear what they're saying."

"Stay right where you are and keep watching. I'm pretty sure Ryan won't recognize you, but, just in case, I don't want you getting too close. You've gotta trust Cheri. She's worked hard and she's a damn good actress so I'm sure she can handle it."

"I know. I just wish I had a bigger part in all of this."

The detective grinned widely, showing off his dimple. "Does it really matter, as long as we nail the bastard?"

"I guess not." Jillian shrugged and slid lower in her chair.

After giving her a brief wave, Alex turned and quickly walked back to his post at the entrance.

Cheri speared a cube of Swiss cheese with her plastic fork and smiled at Ryan. "So you really think you coulda won this contest?" she asked.

Ryan nodded, taking a big bite of his cold-cut sandwich.

"You must be very smart."

With a shrug—but not denying the compliment—he took another bite.

"Me, I'm just such a dummy," the dancer said, staring at her plate. "I can never figure out stuff."

"Hey, don't talk like that. This is supposed to be a party so you gotta be happy here. What's your name?"

"Violet—Violet Begonia." She looked up at Ryan, smiling softly.

He stared at her in disbelief and chuckled. "C'mon. That can't be your real name."

"Nah. It's just the name I use on stage." Cheri arched her shoulders and theatrically tossed her mane of jet-black hair. "I'm an exotic dancer at a club around here."

Ryan grinned. "I can definitely see you as a club dancer. So what's your real name?"

"Anna Maria Buonoverduccio. See why I hadda change it?"

"Oh yeah."

"How about you? What's your name?"

"I'm Ian."

"Glad to meet ya, Ian. What's your last name?"

"Smart."

Cheri gave him an incredulous look. "You're kiddin' me, right?"

"Why do you say that?"

"A smart guy like you with the name 'Smart.' I don't buy it." She shook her head and pointed to her purple lips. "It's like me choosin' the name Violet 'cause I love the color."

Ryan chuckled. "You know something? You're not dumb at all, Violet. I see your point."

"So I told you my real name. Why'd you lie about yours?"

"It's not really a lie."

"Huh?" Cheri gave him a puzzled look.

"You know what aliases are, right?"

"Fake names like movie stars use?"

"Yeah. Movie stars and other people who don't want to be recognized."

"Why don't you wanna be recognized?" the dancer asked.

He leaned closer to Cheri and whispered, "Promise you won't tell anyone?"

"Sure." Under the table, she crossed her forefinger and middle finger.

"See, I'm gonna win this contest tonight, but I don't want a lot of publicity—newspaper stories, Facebook, Twitter—you know, all that kinda shit. That's why I put down this name, my alias."

"But why wouldn't you want people to know that you won? Sounds like fun to me. Maybe you'd be famous."

Ryan shook his head. "Nah. I'm a quiet type of guy. I don't need the fame. I just want the money."

"Okay, I guess." Cheri moved closer to him and ran her fingers along his cheek. "So what's your real name? I won't tell no one."

"Brad," he said, whispering into her ear.

She touched his lips softly. "Brad what?"

"Brad Maxwell."

For the next few minutes, Cheri steered the conversation towards small talk, not asking any other probing questions. "...'course I like watchin' movies too, 'specially love stories," she said and then abruptly stood up.

"'Scuse me for a sec, okay? Gotta run to the little girl's room." She waved her index finger in front of Ryan's face and grinned. "But don't you go anywhere, hon. I promise I'll be right back." She sashayed out of the party room and then rushed into the hall restroom.

Cheri strode to the massive mirror that spanned the length of the room above the counter, opened her purse, took out a small notepad and a pen, and quickly wrote the name Ryan had told her. Then, unzipping her makeup case, she began applying purple lipstick.

The door opened and, through the mirror, Cheri saw a brunette in a gold turtleneck and matching hoop earrings. After smiling at Cheri, the woman rushed into one of the stalls. The dancer took out her mascara brush, holding it near her eyelashes, and continued to stare at her reflection.

Again the bathroom door swung open and this time Jillian entered. Cheri nodded towards the stall section, placing her forefinger next to her lips. Then, tearing off a notebook page, she handed the paper to a beaming Jillian, blew her a kiss, and left the bathroom.

"She got it!" Jillian forced herself to whisper as she knelt next to Alex, reaching under the small table to hand him Cheri's notebook page so the small paper wouldn't be visible.

"Never doubted her for a second," the detective said, grabbing the paper and quickly stuffing it in his pants pocket. "You stay here while I go make my call." He took out his cell phone and rushed into the hallway.

Two minutes later, Alex returned. "We're good," he said,

grinning at Jillian. "Told you this would all work out. We're gonna pull this thing off."

The girl studied the large room, which was filled with adults of all shapes, sizes, and ages. A few stood at the back table poking at the remains of the various food platters, but most sat at the round tables happily eating and chatting with their neighbors. Some guests had sampled the jellybeans she and the others had piled on the tables. Empty plastic Jaybee's bags were scattered everywhere, several littering the parquet wood dance section of the floor.

"It really does look like a party," she said.

"That's because it is. We're having a real celebration here and everyone's having fun." He poked her in the side. "See, I'm a guy of many talents. I even know how to put together a great party. Should have been an event planner. It's probably a lot easier job than what I do now."

Jillian grinned at Alex and then began walking slowly to her post at the rear table behind the jellybean jar. She glanced surreptitiously at Cheri and Ryan, who sat closely together, still in deep conversation.

By eight-thirty, people had stopped coming to the contest party so Alex closed the door and pushed his little table against the front wall. He walked to the back of the room and whispered to Jillian, "We're almost ready."

"Have you heard from your friend yet?"

"No. But I told him to come straight here and not call so I'm sure he'll show up soon."

"What if it didn't work?"

"You still don't believe, do you?"

She glanced at her lap and spoke quietly. "I just want this whole thing with Ryan to be over."

"It will be—soon. You'll see."

The investigator leaned against the back wall behind Jillian, surveying the room. People still sat at the round tables, mostly talking. A bearded man with glasses stood at the food table nearby, piling cookies on a paper plate.

A few minutes later, the front door opened and a short pudgy man with curly black hair and a pencil-thin mustache appeared at the entrance.

"There's Vince," Alex whispered to Jillian as he waved both arms.

The man, carrying a canvas shopping bag, nodded at the signal and hurried to the rear table. "Looks like a good party...Hello." Vince smiled at Jillian, who returned his grin.

"Yeah," the detective agreed. "Party's good. So how'd it go with you?"

"No sweat. Took care of everything just like you wanted." He pushed the bag towards Alex. "Here's the stuff you asked for."

"Thanks." After taking the canvas bag and glancing inside, the investigator opened his wallet and counted half a dozen bills. "This oughta cover it," he said, handing the money to the man.

Vince, still holding the bills, looked at Alex quizzically. "That's more than we agreed."

"You did me a big favor—so just shut up and take it." The detective closed the man's hand into a fist around the money.

Vince smiled and shoved the cash into his pants pocket.

"Remember the other thing I told you," Alex continued. "Don't mention what you did tonight to anyone, even to me. If you say something to me about this job, I'm gonna have to pretend I don't know what the hell you're talking about. This is secret shit."

"Whatever you want, Alex. I'm good."

"Thanks again." The investigator shook the man's hand vigorously. Then Vince turned and walked out of the room.

"It's show time." Alex hoisted the canvas bag and smiled at Jillian. "We got what we need so there's no reason to wait any longer.

Here we go. Are you ready?"

After taking a deep breath, the girl nodded and moved to the wall along the right side of the room while the investigator took her place, standing behind the jellybean jar.

"Can I please have everyone's attention?" he yelled. "We're going to announce the contest winner." People tapped one another and stopped talking. Soon the room was completely quiet.

Alex smiled at his audience. "On behalf of Jaybee's, I want to thank all of you who entered our contest to introduce our great new brand of jellybeans. They should be on your supermarket's shelves in a few months.

"Now it's time to announce the winner of the thousand dollars, the name of the person whose entry was closest to the actual number of jellybeans in this jar." The detective picked up the large glass container, holding it in front of him before setting it carefully back on the table.

"Is everyone ready?" Alex asked.

Several people in the audience shouted, "Yeah!"

"Time to collect my money," Ryan whispered to Cheri.

The dancer smiled and nodded.

"C'mon!" a bald man yelled from one of the front tables. "That's enough talk! Just tell us who won!"

Alex reached into his shirt pocket and took out a small slip of paper. "All right. I won't keep you in suspense any longer. Here's the name." He looked at the entry blank. "The winner of the thousand-dollar cash prize is...Gladys Thompkins."

"That's me!" a petite white-haired woman shrieked. "I won!" She shook her head, grinning at the other people at her table in the middle of the room. "I can't believe it!" Helene, in her little old lady disguise, stood and rushed to the rear, still smiling happily.

Ryan slumped against his chair, a look of disbelief on his face as he watched a beaming Helene hug Alex. *What the hell...?*

"I thought you said you was gonna win," Cheri said, poking

him.

"Something's wrong with this contest. There's gotta be a mistake. I know my number was right."

"Yeah." The dancer nodded. "You figured it out with your smart brain."

"Hey!" the bald man in the audience shouted again. "You never told us—what's the number of jellybeans in there?" He pointed to the jar.

"Sorry." Alex picked up the entry blank again and glanced at it. "Mrs. Thompkins' guess was 4,148. She was the closest, only off by five. The total number of jellybeans in the jar was 4,143."

Ryan frowned. That wasn't the number in the newspaper article. That number—the number he had entered—the number that was supposed to win, was 4,134. *Shit! A typo!* The paper had transposed the last two numbers. As Alex counted ten $100 bills and placed them in Helene's outstretched hand, Ryan abruptly stood up, nearly knocking over his chair.

"What's wrong, Ryan?" Cheri asked. "Your plan didn't work so good, huh?"

He stared at the young woman. "What did you just call me?"

"Ryan." She smiled at him. "I know all about you, Mr. Slimeball Cornell. Check the back of the room, over by the right wall. Anyone there look kinda familiar?"

He turned and focused on Jillian, who had taken off her blonde wig and glasses and was shaking her dark brown hair. "That bitch," he muttered. "It's impossible. She can't be here."

"Why not? You're here."

Without saying another word, he raced for the door.

Jillian rushed to Alex as she watched Ryan run out of the room. "So we're just going to let him go?"

The investigator nodded and put his arm around the girl. "That was the plan. We don't want to have a confrontation or fight here and risk someone calling the police because there'd be a lot of questions we couldn't answer." He shrugged. "Besides, there's no reason for us to chase after him."

Jillian gazed up at Alex and smiled. "Did you see the expression on Ryan's face when he recognized me?"

"Yeah. He looked like he was gonna faint right there."

"And how he must've felt when Cheri said his real name."

"You'll have plenty of time to enjoy all this when we're finished." The detective released her and waved at the round tables where some people still sat. "Let's say goodbye to our guests, end this party, and get the hell outta here. We still have plenty of shit to do."

# CHAPTER 32

Ryan ran from the Village Terrace to his car and—ignoring the speed limit—sped to his Corview Street garden apartment. He checked the rearview mirror and saw no one was behind him. *Too fast for them,* he smirked. He'd be okay once he figured out what had gone wrong here and decided how best to fix it. But to do that, he'd have to get his money and leave—immediately.

After parking the Civic, he rushed to his front door and tried to slip his key into the lock. But the key no longer worked. He examined the lock and realized why: It had been broken.

"Shit!" he exclaimed, pushing the door wide open. He walked inside the apartment and checked the sparsely furnished living room. The folding chairs and TV seemed untouched and nothing looked damaged.

Ryan dashed into the bedroom, slid open the closet doors, and surveyed the top shelf. His boxes of wigs were still there, but no longer in neat piles. It looked like they had been opened and then thrown back. In fact, a couple of open wig boxes were on his bed. Quickly, he thumbed through the hanging clothes, which were still tightly bunched together. All his costumes seemed to be in order.

Just one thing was missing—his briefcase.

Although Ryan would have liked to change his disguise, he realized he didn't have time. Without taking further inventory, he ran out of the apartment and got into his car.

Ryan parked one block from Juniper Park, thinking it was a shame he had to leave without destroying the license plate. "Won't matter though," he murmured. The police might trace the Civic to Brad Maxwell, but, in a few minutes, that person would cease to exist. He hopped out of the car, opened the trunk, and grabbed his flashlight.

*Need to make new plans*, he thought as he rushed into the dark deserted park. For now, he'd just quickly spin himself back to the recent past, hang out there for a short while, and gather newspapers. Then he'd get a new identity and pick another time, much further back—*maybe as much as a year*—and choose a new location to hide in.

"Gotta be more careful," he muttered, shaking his head disgustedly. *Dumb bitch. How the hell'd she ever find me?* At least they hadn't followed him here. There were no cars in the park's lot.

He reached the area near the hidden trail and turned and glanced in every direction. Except for a few rustling noises he attributed to nocturnal animals, the park was silent and seemed totally empty. Ryan climbed into the woods, aimed his flashlight, and soon found the notched tree. Then, after shifting the beam to the ground until he recognized the little path, he separated the branches and followed the tiny trail towards the wind portal.

In the darkness, Ryan heard the welcome whooshing sound of the little cyclone and prepared to step into the clearing.

"Going somewhere?" a deep voice directly in front of him asked. "I think not."

"Whaa?" Ryan pointed the flashlight upward, revealing a huge bald man, arms folded together, who blocked the path. He recognized the big guy from the jellybean contest table in Town Hall. *Shit!* He'd forgotten about him.

Rocco reached out to grab Ryan, who darted away, trying to retrace his steps down the trail. But the path was narrow and difficult to follow at night, even with the flashlight beam.

The husky bouncer soon caught up to his quarry, grabbing Ryan's leg, and knocking the smaller man to the ground. As Ryan squirmed in frustration, he hit Rocco several times on the arm with his flashlight, but the jabs seemed to have no effect on the big man. Then Ryan bashed Rocco's forehead with the flashlight and the bouncer fell to the ground, stunned by the blow.

Ryan stood and rushed to the whirlwind as Rocco got to his feet. Shaking his head in anger, the bouncer dove at Ryan, tackling the smaller man just as he was about to step into the twister.

"Uh, uh, uh," the big man chided, pushing Ryan roughly to the ground.

The flashlight fell out of Ryan's hand and rolled a few feet away, illuminating the trees behind the two men.

"Help me!" Ryan screamed. "I'm being attacked by a homicidal maniac! Please someone..."

"Shut up!" Rocco ordered, punching him heavily in the mouth. "I already got a headache from you. Yell again and I'll knock you unconscious. Understand?"

Ryan nodded, but said nothing. Blood flowed from a cut in his lip.

Holding the smaller man tightly with his left hand, the bouncer took a coil of twine from his pocket, rolled Ryan onto his stomach, and tied Ryan's hands firmly behind his back. Then, ignoring the prisoner's continuous kicks, Rocco grasped the man's legs and tied them together.

When he was finished, Rocco turned Ryan on his back, stood

up and retrieved the flashlight, directing the beam at the trussed man. He admired his handiwork and smiled. "That oughta do it, dont'cha think?"

Ryan, his face smeared with blood and dirt and the long-haired blond wig half off his head, glared at the bouncer. "You and your friends—you'll never get away with this."

"We'll see about that." The burly man positioned the flashlight on the ground and sat in front of the clearing, next to his disheveled prisoner. "Make yourself comfy. Now we just gotta wait for the others." Then, again grinning at Ryan, he took his cell phone from his pants pocket and made a call.

Alex closed the phone and turned to his three female companions, who were putting on their backpacks. "That was Rocco. He got him, just like I said he would."

Cheri let out a "Yay!" and gave Helene a high-five.

Jillian stood motionless, staring wide-eyed at the detective. "Really?"

"Yes, really," he said, feigning anger. "I told you my plan would work, but you—you didn't believe."

"Sorry, Mr. Detective, sir." Jillian, no longer wearing her blonde wig and glasses and now dressed in jeans, smiled at him. "I promise I'll never doubt your genius again."

With her backpack in place, Helene approached the two of them. "I think we're all done here so let's get going." The lawyer had removed her little old lady disguise and wore traveling clothes—jeans, sneakers, and a sweatshirt.

"Yeah," Cheri said, still fidgeting with her heavy backpack as she joined the others. "I wanna see that piece of scum again and spit right in his face." She had also changed into her hiking clothes and sneakers. "C'mon." Playfully, the dancer shoved Alex in the back.

"Okay, everybody," the investigator said. He walked to the entrance of the Village Terrace, wearing his backpack over his suit and clutching the canvas bag Vince had given him. "Heigh ho! It's back to the woods we go."

The four time travelers, looking like they were embarking on a late-night hike, entered Juniper Park and reached the trail area. After sprinting into the woods, Jillian quickly found the notched tree and motioned the others to follow. Then, shining her flashlight at the ground, she recognized the trail and again signaled her companions.

They walked single-file with Jillian leading the way. "We're almost there," she said, pointing straight ahead. "See the light over there? That's got to be Rocco and Ryan!" She ran the final few steps until she reached the smiling bald giant, sitting next to his snarling, bloody-mouthed prisoner.

"Well, it's about time!" the bouncer said, waving in mock anger at the tethered Ryan. "Us two have been hangin' around here with nothin' to do, just waitin' for you guys."

"Rocco!" Jillian gasped, trying to regain her breath. "You got him! Thanks so much!" She dropped the flashlight, bent down, and hugged the big man.

"Yeah." The bouncer nodded at Ryan who glared at them, but said nothing. "He hit me in the head with the flashlight, but the guy ain't much of a fighter."

"He's not much of anything," Alex added, stepping next to Jillian and putting his arm around her.

Cheri pushed in front of the others and ran to the bouncer. "You okay, Dodo-Roc?" she asked.

"Yeah. I'm good, hon. Lucky I got a hard head."

"And a soft heart," Cheri said, hugging him. Then turning towards the dirty-faced prisoner, she giggled and pointed to his head. "Check out the wig. Like an ugly yellow mop. You're gonna get yours, Mr. Ryan lyin' Cornell." She stuck out her tongue at him.

Jillian leaned down and gazed sadly at her former boyfriend.

"How could you do this?" she asked quietly. "I trusted you. I thought you loved me."

"Go to hell," Ryan growled, spitting at the girl's face.

Alex aimed his fist at the prisoner's cheek. "Why you..."

"No," Jillian interrupted, pulling the detective's arm away. "Let me handle this." She wiped the spittle from her chin and again spoke to Ryan. "You're all mixed up about this. You blamed me for the accident because it was my father's fault and I've always felt guilty about it too. But I'm finally starting to understand that you're all wrong." She shook her head. "The accident had nothing to do with me. I know your parents died, but you seem to forget that mine did too. And since my father's dead, there's no one left to blame. Carrying all that hate around will only end up destroying you. You've got to let it go."

"F___ you," Ryan snarled.

"That's enough, all of you," Helene said, stepping in front of the prisoner before Alex could react to the man's hateful words. "We'll have plenty of time for discussion later. I want to remind you that, right now, we're still in the past. We have to go through the wind tunnel, get back to the right time, and finish this."

"Okay," Alex said. "Just one more thing before we head back." He reached into the canvas bag he carried and pulled out a black briefcase. "This look familiar, Cornell?"

"That's mine! You can't..."

"Oh yes, we can." The detective dropped the briefcase back into the bag. "It's filled with money, right?"

Ryan continued to scowl at Alex, but said nothing.

"None of it really belongs to you. It's all stolen money—money you got only because you knew the future."

"You can never prove that."

"Don't have to...All right then, I've heard enough." Alex dug inside his suit pocket, found his discarded red tie, and wrapped it around the prisoner's bloodied mouth. "Just in case you decide you want to say something, we're not listening—and neither is anyone else."

Ryan glared at the detective, moving his bruised lips, but no sounds emerged.

Ignoring the gagged man, Alex called to Rocco. "Let's get him up and untie his legs. We're ready to go back now, and just in case there's a problem, we're all gonna go into the time tunnel together."

With Rocco firmly grasping Ryan, the group entered the clearing. Alex shined the flashlight at the mini-whirlwind, which continued to spin in place opposite the dead tree trunk. "Okay!" he shouted. "Everyone in together at the count of three."

Holding hands, the six time travelers—Rocco still clutching his tethered prisoner—jumped into the wind portal and rolled onto the ground on the other side of the clearing next to the little cave.

"Are we back?" Jillian asked as she stood up and shook herself.

"I wore one of my regular watches so I could check," Helene said. After glancing at her wrist, she smiled at the girl. "I've got no idea what the time really is, but the watch is ticking."

Alex pointed to a small patch of sky visible through the dense woods. "Look up there. It's not nighttime here yet, so it's definitely not March 24th anymore. Hold on and let me make a quick call." He moved into the nearby trees.

"We're good," the investigator announced when he returned a minute later, closing his regular cell phone and holding the black plastic bag he had stashed in the woods before their last trip. "We're back in the present."

"That spinnin' thing's so cool," Cheri said, brushing dirt off her clothes and staring at the mini-tornado. "I really like the fun wind ride."

"That's too bad 'cause this carnival ride's gotta end right now." Alex reached into the plastic bag and removed a large chainsaw.

"You're going to try to destroy the wind?" Jillian asked.

"Yup—too dangerous," the detective replied.

"But what if someone else used the time tunnel and still's in the past?" Jillian continued. "They'll be trapped there forever."

"Tough shit. Hey, listen: Anyone traveling back in time this way is probably like your former boyfriend here." Alex poked Ryan with his foot. "Up to no good. And I don't think anyone's found this place anyway. We didn't see other signs—marks on trees—and hardly any hikers even use the trail."

He nodded towards the roped man and addressed the three women. "So here's what we're gonna do now. Rocco'll move the creep up against the cave and I want you girls to sit on him. The two of us are gonna do the rest."

"Big strong guy stuff, huh?" Cheri asked, smirking.

"You wanna do it, tough girl?" Rocco grabbed the chainsaw from Alex's hand and thrust it towards her. "Here."

"Just kiddin.'" Still grinning, she motioned the tool away. "I'm gonna go sit."

After the bouncer dragged Ryan next to the cave and retied the prisoner's legs, he began sawing the trunk of one of the largest live trees. "We want it to fall right over there," Alex said, pointing in the direction of the wind tunnel. The two men took turns using the chainsaw and, several minutes later, the huge pine groaned and began tilting. Rocco quickly removed the blade.

"Now—push!" Alex called. He and the bouncer jumped on the tree and the massive pine crashed heavily onto the little wind swirl.

"I don't see the thing spinnin' no more!" Cheri shouted from her seat on Ryan's stomach.

"Me neither," Jillian, sitting on his chest, agreed.

"And it's quiet all of a sudden," Helene said, her rear end planted firmly on the prisoner's knees. "We don't have to shout anymore." The loud whooshing noise was gone.

"So far, so good," the investigator said, looking at Rocco. "Let's chop another big one, just to be sure." He and the bouncer sawed a tall maple, which landed on top of the other downed tree, forming a large tangled cross.

The two men stepped on the toppled branches, needles, and leaves, making crunching sounds as they moved towards the center. "What d'ya think?" Alex asked.

Rocco bent down and pulled apart pieces of tree debris. "Nothin' here no more," he said, turning to the private eye. "I don't see no wind and I don't feel it or hear it neither."

"Then we're done." Alex approached the women, who still sat on the prisoner, and crouched so he could stare into the eyes of the scowling man. "No more time traveling for you anymore, Mr. Cornell."

They entered the cave and, one by one, each person crawled into the hollow log and exited on the other side. Rocco was the last to go, giving Alex his backpack and forcing Ryan's partially tethered body into the opening and roughly shoving him up the wooden passageway before taking his turn.

After tossing away the leaves, sticks, and rocks that hid the nearby clearing, the travelers entered the open area of the designated park trail. Cheri sat on the broken log, took off her heavy backpack, wiped the dirt off her body, and massaged her aching shoulders.

Jillian moved next to the dancer, staring at the exposed view of the massive hollow trunk. "There's no reason to hide this anymore," she said, shrugging. "Nothing here has to be kept secret."

"Yup." The investigator nodded in agreement, then motioned with his hand. "Everybody up 'cause, even if you're tired, we gotta keep moving. From what I remember, it was nearly three hours earlier here last week when we left. If that's still the case, then it's almost seven now so it'll be getting dark and we've still gotta finish our hike."

The weary hikers trudged down the path, Rocco still pushing Ryan, until they reached the end. When they entered the park, the sky had shifted into twilight. The fading day was clear and the temperature seemed to be in the mid sixties. Two joggers were running in the distance, but no one was near them.

Alex stopped the group just before they reached the exit. "Okay," he said, turning to Cheri and Rocco. "Thanks for your help. We couldn't have pulled this operation off without either one of you guys." After hugging the dancer, he shook the big man's hand. "I know I could use you for some of my other jobs. Interested in doing any freelance work? The pay's pretty good."

"Sure," Rocco said, smiling. "I could always use the money. Just give me a call." He told Alex his number and the private eye punched it into his phone.

"Go on home now," the detective continued. "I can handle the slug from here."

"Okay," the bouncer said. "Here you go." He pushed Ryan towards Alex, who grabbed the man forcefully by the back of his sweatshirt.

"What're you gonna do with him?" Cheri asked.

"We're turning him over to the cops," Alex said.

"Cool!" The dancer grasped Jillian's arms, holding her friend tightly. "Let me know everythin' that happens with the scumbag."

"I will."

Cheri kissed both women on their cheeks and Rocco hugged each of them. Then, after waving to everyone, the couple walked out of the park.

# CHAPTER 33

The four remaining time travelers stood just outside the Juniper Park entrance, partially hidden from the road. "So are we going to take Ryan to the police now?" Jillian asked Alex.

"Not immediately," the detective said. "Gonna make another stop first."

Helene pointed to their filthy prisoner, shaking her head. "We can't take a cab with him looking like that." Although Alex had adjusted Ryan's blond wig, the man's arms were still tied, his mouth was gagged, and blood trickled down his neck from the cut on his lip.

"That's why I made a call," the detective said. With one arm still grasping the back of Ryan's sweatshirt, he surveyed the street. "Our ride'll be here soon."

Five minutes later, a large black sedan pulled up to the curb next to the group. "Here we are," Alex said, opening the door and shoving the prisoner into the backseat. "You girls get in the front."

Jillian stepped into the car first and the driver smiled at her.

"Hi, Miss," the man said. "Nice seein' you again. We met a coupla months ago at that party. But you looked kinda different. You were a blonde, wearin' glasses."

"Yes. I've changed my hair since then." She smiled at the driver, a short overweight man with a thin black mustache. "And, of course, I remember you—but it doesn't really seem so long ago."

Helene stared into her lap, muffling her laughter.

"Thanks for coming on such short notice, Vince," Alex said. "I owe you one."

"Nah." The man shook his head of curly black hair. "You overpaid me for that hush-hush contest job so now we're even." He gazed at the dirty prisoner through his rearview mirror. "I guess you can talk about it now. That the guy you was after?"

"Yep."

"Took you a while to get him, huh?"

"You can say that again. But I'm gonna give him to the cops tonight. Couldn't have done it without your help."

"Easy work, like I said. Just glad you got what you needed." Vince slowed the sedan and parked in the driveway of a small Cape Cod-styled house. "Home sweet home."

"Whose home is it?" Jillian asked.

"Mine," Alex answered. "Everyone out. We're making a quick stop here."

After tying Ryan to one of his wooden dining room chairs, Alex removed his suit jacket and tossed his backpack and the canvas bag on the living room floor. "We're gonna ditch all our hiking shit. If we walk into the police station looking like we've just come from a camping trip, the cops'll have a lot more questions."

He nodded to the two women. "You girls go use the hall bathroom to wash up. If you want to shower, there are extra towels in the closet. I'm gonna go change into jeans. We all wanna look like we've been to the same place."

Jillian gazed at Ryan, who squirmed uncomfortably in the chair. "Can we just leave him there alone?"

The investigator chuckled. "Trust me. He's not going anywhere."

Jillian and Helene each took a quick shower and changed into cleaner clothes from their backpacks before returning to the detective's living room and adjacent dining area. Alex was sitting on his cream-colored couch, waiting for them.

"You girls finally ready?"

"Come on, Alex," the lawyer said. "That's not fair. You're the one who suggested we take showers."

"Yeah. But I forgot how long women need for a 'quick' shower. It takes me two minutes."

"Well good for you!" Helene said, easing onto the couch next to the detective. "You get the 'Quick Shower Award.' Now that we've settled that issue, what's next?"

Alex took Ryan's briefcase from the canvas shopping bag, placed it on his glass cocktail table, and tapped on the smooth black leather. "It's time to check out the contents of this. Let's take a look at exactly what's in Mr. Cornell's fancy case."

"The briefcase's locked, isn't it?" Jillian asked.

"Yeah," Alex said, picking up the satchel and fingering the combination dial. "So unless our pal here gives us the numbers, I'm gonna have to bust this beautiful piece of leather wide open."

He stared at the tethered and gagged man who glowered back at him. "So you wanna tell me the combination?"

Ryan continued to glare at the detective, but didn't move his head at all.

"Okay. I'll take that as a 'no.'"

The investigator placed the briefcase on the table again and stood up. "Be right back." He dashed into the kitchen and returned with a sharp carving knife. "This oughta do it."

With Helene holding the case, he made several deep gashes and then ripped the material apart. "Hope I'm not cutting up the cash," he said, sticking his fingers through the torn leather. "Here we go."

He dug inside and began pulling out the contents, removing wads of bills, most of them hundreds. While Helene tried to uncrumple the money and arrange the bills in neat piles, Jillian sat in the director's chair opposite the couch, gaping at the growing mountain of cash.

"Wanna do some digging for dough?" Alex asked her as he scooped out the money. "This is a fun game."

The girl shook her head. "That's okay. You can do it."

The detective continued to extract bills from the broken briefcase until he removed his hand. "There's some other stuff in here too," he said, and, using the knife, made several new slices to widen the opening. Then, thrusting his hand back inside, he pulled out a batch of papers.

After quickly scanning the sheets, Alex smiled and waved the pages at Ryan, who still scowled. "The genius's inspiration! Winning lottery numbers and horse racing results."

"What are we going to do with all this money?" Jillian asked, leaning forward.

"We're not giving it to the cops, that's for sure," Alex said. "We could never explain how we got it."

"But we can't keep the money," the girl continued. "It's not ours."

Alex pointed to their prisoner. "Well, it's not his either."

Jillian, Helene, and Alex sat quietly, staring at the enormous pile of cash. They had counted to $50,000 and then stopped—and there was lots of money left.

"Here's what we're gonna do," the detective finally said. "First, I'm gonna repay myself for the expenses for our little trip."

"That's fair," Jillian said. "You used your own money."

"And then I'm gonna take some of it to pay Helene and myself for our services."

"Also fair," the girl said, shrugging. "I don't have the money to pay both of you for all your hard work."

Helene chuckled and pointed to the mountain of hundred dollar bills on the table. "I know I'm supposed to be a hot-shot lawyer, but even I don't charge my clients that much—and Jillian's a co-worker." She grinned at the young woman. "That's a discounted rate. So what should we do with all the leftover money?"

"Can we give some of it to Cheri and Rocco?" Jillian asked. "They worked so hard to help me without ever asking for anything."

"Good idea," Alex said, nodding. "How much do you want to give them?"

Jillian thought for a moment. "Is five thousand okay?"

"Sounds fine to me," Alex said, turning to the girl. "How about you? Do you want to take some of the cash?"

Jillian shook her head and glanced at the prisoner. "I don't want anything of Ryan's—including the money."

"I understand," Alex said. "But we've gotta do something with the rest of this cash. What?" He rested his chin in his hands. "I've been thinking about that question for a while now. How about we give it to a charity?"

"That's a great idea!" Helene exclaimed and then looked at Jillian. "Why don't you choose the organization?"

The girl smiled at her two companions. "I've got one. If it's okay with both of you, I'd like the money to go to Mothers Against Drunk Driving." She glanced at Ryan who continued to scowl. "Even you should be all right with donating it to MADD."

"Doesn't matter what he thinks or wants," Alex said, patting Jillian's hand. "But I think you made a good choice." He stood up, motioning towards the prisoner. "I'm gonna put the cash away in a safe place for now and then I'm gonna search the creep. Let's see what he's carrying."

Five minutes later, Alex returned to the living room and dug his hands roughly into Ryan's pants pockets. "Here it is," he said, removing a black leather wallet. After quickly thumbing through the money, he addressed the tethered man. "Chump change. We'll do you a favor and let you keep this. We already have the big bucks."

"Does he have anything on him that could look suspicious?" Helene asked.

"I don't know. Let me check in here first." Alex opened one of the wallet compartments and withdrew two small slips of paper. "Aha! Pay dirt." He thrust the papers in the faces of Helene and Jillian. "See!"

The two women stared at lottery tickets for Sweet Million and Pick 10, dated Thursday, March 24.

"A couple of winners, huh Cornell?" the investigator said to the glowering prisoner. "But you won't need these where you're going... Here ladies." He handed one slip to Jillian and the other to Helene. "Consider this a going-away present from our silent friend here."

Alex continued to inspect Ryan's wallet, but found nothing else that had to be discarded. "The Bradley Maxwell shit will just prove to the police that he's been hiding all this time under an assumed name."

The detective frisked the man and discovered a set of keys, which he returned to Ryan's pocket along with the wallet, minus the two lottery tickets. "Okay," he said, yanking the prisoner to his feet. "It's about time we got this scumbag out of my house and into the place where he belongs."

Alex dragged Ryan to his Corolla and again threw him into the back seat. With Helene sitting in the rear—"just in case"—he drove the four of them to the police station.

"Time to get you to your new home," the investigator said, pushing the prisoner out of the car, untying his legs, and propelling him towards the entrance. It was nearly ten o'clock and the station was empty with just one officer behind the counter.

"We've got someone for you," Alex said, removing the tie from around Ryan's mouth and shoving him forward.

The stocky policeman stared at the bloody-lipped, dirty prisoner. "Who the hell's this guy?" he asked.

"Maybe he'll look more familiar without his wig," Alex said, lifting the blond hairpiece and revealing Ryan's dark brown hair. "This any better? Look like someone you've been searching for?"

The officer behind the desk continued to study Ryan. "Yeah." He nodded his head several times. "That's the missing guy..." Suddenly, he seemed to notice Jillian. "Wait a minute. You're the girl who was supposed to have killed him."

"Well, he looks pretty alive to me," Helene said, interrupting the policeman's recollections. "His name's Ryan Cornell and we'll leave him with you tonight and I'll be in touch tomorrow morn..."

"I want to call my lawyer," Ryan muttered. "These people kidnapped me and stole my money."

"He's a little nuts," Alex said. "Don't forget this guy staged his own murder and disappearance. He'll probably tell you lots of strange shit."

The policeman shook his head. "Sorry, but I'm not really too familiar with the case."

"Call Officer Forsythe," Helene suggested. "I'm sure he'll be very happy to fill you in." She took a business card from her pocket and placed it on the counter. "I'm Miss Keating's lawyer and I'll be contacting the district attorney's office too. But now it's late and we're very tired. Have a good night."

"It's been a really long day," Alex said as he slid into the driver's seat of the Corolla. "It's time you two ladies went home and I'm pleased to be your chauffeur service tonight." He pretended to doff an imaginary cap.

"What'll happen now?" Jillian asked from the front passenger seat.

"Like I told the policeman, I'll call the DA's office tomorrow morning and explain that Ryan's been found alive," Helene said, leaning forward. "Obviously, all the charges against you will be immediately dropped."

"What about Ryan?" Jillian continued.

The detective chuckled. "Now that should be very interesting. I can't wait to hear his version about how all this happened."

"Will he go to jail?" the girl asked.

"It depends," Helene said. "We'll have to see how it plays out." She placed her hands on Jillian's shoulders and gently massaged them. "But now you can relax, sweetie, and get on with your life. One thing's for sure: You're going to be a free woman."

Jillian leaned back in her seat and grinned.

# EPILOGUE

*Four months later*

Jillian, wearing a prim white blouse and black slacks, sat in the front row of the courtroom gallery. Next to her, a long-haired teenage boy held the hand of a bleary-eyed older man. Across the aisle, Ryan, dressed neatly in a gray suit and tie, slumped in his chair and scowled as he listened to the expert witness his attorney, Kate Wilcher, was standing next to and questioning. Ryan's sister, Danielle, and his Aunt Marie sat directly behind Ryan.

"So, Dr. Kramer, based on the evidence you've reviewed and your sessions with Mr. Cornell, what conclusion have you reached about my client's sanity?" the slender blonde lawyer asked.

The distinguished-looking bald man scratched his shiny head before answering. "He's completely insane," the psychiatrist finally said. "And therefore he's mentally unfit to stand trial."

Ryan jumped up quickly. "I'm mentally fine!" he shouted at Dr. Kramer. Then pointing at Jillian, he shook his forefinger. "All this happened because of her! She's a liar! She and her goddamn friends stole my money and..."

"That's enough." The ruddy-faced judge thumped his gavel on the counter, his face becoming even redder as he stared angrily at the defendant.

Ryan's lawyer turned away from the witness and glared at her client, mouthing the words, "Be quiet." Ryan had first asked Steven Placado to defend him, but the attorney had refused, claiming he couldn't work for a man who had lied to him by planting the letter in his safe that accused Jillian Keating of murder.

"As you can see from the man's behavior, he has no concept of reality, Your Honor," Dr. Kramer said, turning towards the judge. "All that talk about his missing money and those crazy claims about traveling back into time from a wind tunnel in Juniper..."

"It was there!" Ryan yelled, springing up again. "I swear I'm telling you the truth. They destroyed it!" He snarled in the direction of Jillian, who sat quietly, not showing any emotion.

"Stop the outbursts, Mr. Cornell, or we'll hold the rest of this hearing without you!" the judge warned, again rapping his gavel on the counter and then pointing it at Ryan. "Let's take a fifteen-minute recess and, during that time, I expect you to calm down. Then, hopefully, we can get this hearing over with."

Jillian rushed out of the courthouse, found a quiet spot under a tree, and took her cell phone out of her bag. She hadn't thought she would ever want—or need—a portable phone, but she had discovered she liked it. Since Ryan's capture, people had been calling and texting her and she had also initiated calls and text messages. After clicking a saved name and number, the phone was answered on the second ring.

"How's the competency hearing going, Jillian?"

"Great, Helene. I'm trying my best not to show any emotion, but I feel like sticking my tongue out at Ryan and cheering every time somebody calls him 'crazy.'"

"I bet—what's going on right now?"

"Ryan's lawyer just finished questioning another psychiatrist so, when we go back inside, she'll still be up."

"I've heard Ryan's sister and aunt instructed her to go the insanity route, no matter what her client wants."

Jillian chuckled. "Ryan still wants to blame everything on me. But, this time, it's not working."

"His lawyer probably doesn't have to do very much to convince the judge that he's insane. Thanks to the newspapers, everyone already thinks Ryan's crazy and there's no proof for any of his ridiculous claims."

"That's for sure."

After the time travelers had left their prisoner in police custody in early June, the investigation of Ryan's plot to frame Jillian for his murder had quickly become a front-page story. Alex had informed the police that one of Ryan's keys would open a room in Secure Self-Storage on Wildwood Road and the room had contained a treasure trove of incriminating material, including Ryan's laptop. The police determined that all the newspaper articles about Jillian and web searches for her name proved the man had been stalking her. The tabloids loved the story of Ryan's twisted obsession and, for several weeks, Jillian had become a minor celebrity.

Ryan had continued to fan the tabloid flames by accusing Jillian and her friends of stealing his money, nearly $100,000. But since he didn't have a job—and couldn't prove anything—the newspapers scoffed at the allegation. When Ryan insisted his income came from lottery winnings and bets on horse races resulting from his time travel sojourns, the papers again had a field day. "Wouldn't we all like to be able to know the future and make easy money like that?" one article had asked. Even now, the name "Ryan Cornell" evoked snickers and chuckles.

"Too bad framing you for his murder wasn't enough of a crime to prosecute Ryan for," Helene said.

"That's okay. What he did to me was bad, but he only hurt

my feelings, not my body." Jillian hesitated for a moment before continuing in a whisper. "I was really lucky. Ryan actually killed that poor girl, Sara. It's a shame that he probably seems too crazy to go to jail."

"I know. But even if he doesn't, he'll still be put away for a very long time."

"I hope so," Jillian said, checking her watch. "I've got to get back inside now, Helene, but I'll keep you up-to-date."

As she neared the courtroom, Jillian thought about the girl whom Ryan had murdered in early March when he traveled back in time.

The police had been working on Sara Langsten's disappearance without any new clues until late May when a badly decomposed body had washed up on the banks of the Hudson River. Forensics had determined the remains belonged to the missing girl.

Then, with all the publicity surrounding Ryan after his arrest, Sara's teenage brother, Michael, had recognized Ryan's photo and told police his sister had dated that man, who had called himself "Brad." Of course, the police already knew about Ryan's alias since the wallet and driver's license he possessed when she, Alex, and Helene had dragged him into the police station identified him as "Bradley Maxwell."

In addition, Ryan's landlord had reported a different-looking Brad Maxwell's sudden disappearance at the end of March. The police surmised Ryan had been living a double life, using the Corvair Street residence under his false name and wearing a multitude of disguises, which they found in the abandoned apartment. They concluded that, after staging his own murder and fleeing the home he shared with Jillian, he had again disguised himself and hidden somewhere else until Alex and the others had found him, as they claimed, in Juniper Park.

Following Michael Langsten's tip, the police had shown Sara's picture to Ryan's neighbors in the garden apartment complex and one woman had reported watching a female, who resembled the girl in the photo, crawl through a bathroom window on the last day Sara had been seen. The woman had told police she assumed the girl lived there and had simply been locked out of her apartment. After dusting the sills and window, the police had found traces of Sara's fingerprints.

Even when confronted with the evidence, Ryan at first had denied any connection in Sara's disappearance. Although he had admitted knowing the girl and going out on a couple of short dates, he had insisted he'd never taken her to the garden apartment. "I've already admitted that I was hiding there," he had told his police questioners. "If I was hiding, then why would I let her visit me?"

"It looks more like she snuck in," a police officer had pointed out.

"Well, if she did, then she was a thief, trying to steal something of mine, and she must have snuck back out again. I never saw her."

But the police had repeatedly questioned Ryan, each time more forcefully, and he had finally broken down and admitted the crime.

"Why did you kill her?" the police officer had asked.

"I was honest with Sara. I told her everything and she didn't believe me. She thought I was crazy." Ryan had shaken his head. "Then she started screaming. She promised to keep her mouth shut, but she lied. First she breaks into my apartment. Then I tell her the truth and she thinks I'm nuts and, when I tell her to keep quiet, she doesn't listen to me..." He had stared beseechingly at the policeman. "You can see why I had to do it."

Jillian took her seat next to Sara's brother, Michael, and his father, and smiled at the Langstens. Then, as the defense attorney rose, Jillian turned to face the front of courtroom.

"I know it seems strange, Your Honor, but Mr. Cornell insists that somehow he was able to go back in time," Ryan's thin blonde lawyer said to the rosy-complexioned judge. "He says a wind tunnel in Juniper Park..."

"Miss Wilcher, we've been over all this territory before," the judge interrupted, slowly enunciating each word. "There's absolutely no proof that a wind time tunnel exists." He shook his head. "I can't believe we're even wasting time discussing this nonsense. Please move on."

The lawyer glanced at her notes. "My client swears he never meant to hurt Sara Langsten, but she broke into his apartment and saw his disguises, which really upset him. Still, he only lost control when she didn't believe that he had traveled there from months in the future and then started to scream. I know this sounds farfetched, Your Honor," the woman said, shrugging her shoulders. "But my client insists that's what really happened."

The judge turned to the sullen defendant, who slouched in his chair with his arms folded. "Mr. Cornell, I can't listen to any more of this time travel drivel so I'll just talk about the facts. You're accused of a horrendous crime—the murder of a young woman. Although you've admitted to killing Sara Langsten, your explanation is that you were outraged when the girl didn't believe your story and started screaming. Then you explain your version of the truth— time travel, whirlwind, horse races, lottery winners—and none of it makes any sense.

"Everything goes back to your hatred of Jillian Keating. It's very clear to me that you've spent your life blaming Miss Keating for the death of your parents. While her father was indeed responsible for that horrible car accident nearly twenty years ago, Jillian Keating had absolutely nothing to do with it." The judge shook his head. "She was just a baby—and you refuse to acknowledge that she lost both of her parents too. You've wasted your entire life because of your misplaced hatred and now it's even ruined your ability to function rationally.

"I wish you could be tried for second degree murder for the death of Sara Langsten—the Prosecution has presented enough evidence for a case to be made against you—but, unfortunately, since you're completely delusional..."

"No!" Ryan shouted, jumping from his chair. "You're all wrong!"

His attorney pushed him down into the seat.

"...I hereby order you to be placed in maximum security in the State Hospital for the Criminally Insane."

"No! I'm not crazy!" Ryan pointed at Jillian, who stood up, preparing to leave the courtroom. "It's all her fault! You can't let her get away with this! The bitch set me up, she and her..."

Jillian, walking out the door, didn't hear the rest of Ryan's rant.

After calling Helene with the result of the hearing, Jillian stepped into her blue Accent and drove home. She had moved out of the apartment she had shared with Ryan—expensive and too many bad memories—and found a small place, at a much lower rent, in a nearby private house.

She was still working for Helene's law firm, but only part-time. This semester, she was taking three graphic arts courses, which she hoped would improve her chances of securing a steady job in her chosen field. School was more fun now. She had made several good friends, whom she sometimes hung out with before or after classes.

She and Cheri still kept in touch too, each enjoying the other's company despite their many differences. Jillian had also gone out socially with Cheri and Rocco as part of a foursome. She had a new boyfriend.

Jillian smiled. Now that she was no longer Alex's client, she and the investigator had begun dating. Their relationship was honest—without secrets—and totally different from her disastrous experience with Ryan. It had only been a few months, but so far, the Jillian/Alex pairing was working.

After parking the car, Jillian walked to the entrance of her home. She leaned her back against the door and glanced up at the clear blue sky. The world was wonderful—full of endless possibilities.